Praise for Garry Disher and th

AUSTRALIAN CRIME WRITERS
LIFETIME ACHIEVEMENT /

The Heat

'Beautifully crafted. Like its hero, it's lean,
spare and trenchant.' *Sydney Morning Herald*

'Once again, Garry Disher has turned out a winner.'
AustCrimeFiction

'Sparely written, with an entertaining set of villains,
an unfathomable antihero and dry humour, reading this
book is like riding a thrilling switchback.' *West Australian*

'Garry Disher deserves his reputation as one of
Australia's finest crime writers.' *Stuff NZ*

'I read the book in a day, which shows what
a page-turner it is.' *Otago Daily Times*

'Fast-paced and action-packed…A brilliant read!' *BookMooch*

Wyatt

WINNER, NED KELLY AWARD FOR
BEST CRIME FICTION 2010

'Intensely exciting…one of the standout Australian
crime novels of 2010.' *Canberra Times*

'Distinctly Australian noir writ large across Melbourne suburbia.' *GQ*

'A cleansing breath in contemporary crime
fiction…It's fascinating how so few words can
draw a man so completely.' *Courier-Mail*

'Everything about him is hard boiled and Disher's writing
is short, dry and fast-paced to match.' *West Australian*

'Gritty…uncompromising.' *Otago Daily Times*

'The story starts flat-out and never lets up…
Verdict: hard and fast.' *Herald Sun*

Garry Disher titles available from Text Publishing

THE WYATT THRILLERS:

The Wyatt Butterfly
comprising *Port Vila Blues* and *Fallout*
Wyatt
The Heat

THE PENINSULA MYSTERIES:

The Dragon Man
Kittyhawk Down
Snapshot
Chain of Evidence
Blood Moon
Whispering Death
Signal Loss

Bitter Wash Road
Under the Cold Bright Lights

GARRY DISHER has written more than fifty novels and won numerous awards, including the German Crime Prize (twice) and two Ned Kelly Best Crime Novel awards, for *Chain of Evidence* (2007) and *Wyatt* (2010). In 2018 he received the Australian Crime Writers Association Lifetime Achievement Award. Garry lives on Victoria's Mornington Peninsula.

garrydisher.com

KILL SHOT

GARRY DISHER

TEXT PUBLISHING MELBOURNE AUSTRALIA

textpublishing.com.au

The Text Publishing Company
Swann House
22 William Street
Melbourne Victoria 3000
Australia

First published in 2018 by The Text Publishing Company

Cover design by Text
Cover image by Aaron Foster/Getty
Page design by Susan Miller
Typeset in Baskerville by J&M Typesetting

Printed and bound in Australia by Griffin Press, an accredited ISO/NZS 1401:2004 Environmental Management System printer

ISBN: 9781925773224 (paperback)
ISBN: 9781925774115 (ebook)

A catalogue record for this book is available from the National Library of Australia

This book is printed on paper certified against the Forest Stewardship Council® Standards. Griffin Press holds FSC chain-of-custody certification SGS-COC-005088. FSC promotes environmentally responsible, socially beneficial and economically viable management of the world's forests.

for Chris and Pippa

1

WYATT WAS BASED IN Sydney this year. All the documents to prove he was a citizen of New South Wales. On a grubby night in late March—humid, toxins in the air—he stood watching a two-storey house in Rushcutters Bay. Light from the cloud-streaked moon threw busy shapes over the street and flared briefly on the face of Wyatt's old Longines. He unstrapped it from his bony wrist, shoved it into a pocket. Now he was ready, a shadow among other shadows. A shadow you'd take for a bush, not a thief.

He had no need of a wristwatch anyway; his sense of time passing was acute. He waited now for thirty minutes. He didn't think the law was interested in Alan Hagger, even though the guy was bent. But still, he watched for a surveillance team—a van, a powerful sedan that hadn't been on this street on any of the other nights Wyatt had been here. Or a movement, a twitched curtain, a dim light in a window overlooking Hagger's house.

Nothing. And no sign of another man like Wyatt, either, with the same job in mind. But Wyatt always planned for the unexpected variable—a rain storm; Hagger receiving a late-evening visitor; a junkie burglar setting off an alarm. Other things he couldn't plan for he hoped to absorb, accommodate or outrun.

About ten-thirty now and Hagger would be going to bed at eleven. The usual routine: take his elderly cat into the backyard and wait while it did its business. Lock up, set the alarm, teeth, bed. Wyatt moved. He knew how to wait, but in motion was calm and focused—with an edge that was not pleasure, exactly, but a cool, clear absorption. He wanted the money, of course. But he also wanted the thinking and the action.

He drew closer to Hagger's house, melting from shadow to shadow, his movements unhurried, unremarkable to a neighbour drawing curtains for the night. Then he was on Hagger's side path, slipping into the backyard and crouching beside the patio deck as he drew on a silk ski mask. He gazed the length of the garden, eyes unfocused but ready for movements he might need to face or ignore. He was familiar with the property. He'd been watching for several days, knowing that something trivial might prove to be crucial. He watched in layers, too—the broad picture, then the details. This job, like all the others he'd ever pulled, boiled down to ordinary tactics, not an overthought master plan. He waited. He felt compact.

He was merely a moon shadow to Hagger when the man emerged in summer pyjamas and a loose robe and placed the old cat on a garden bed. Hagger liked to relieve himself, too, and was watering the lemon tree when Wyatt slipped into the house.

Wyatt moved unobtrusively, knees bent slightly, breathing deep and even. To the staircase first, creeping, placing the flat of his hand against a plasterboard wall. Then another wall, a third wall, feeling for the transmissions that might indicate movement elsewhere in the house. There was nothing. Hagger lived alone. No one was visiting.

Plan for the best, expect the worst, note the exit points.

Then swiftly up the stairs, keeping to the edges where the treads were less likely to creak, until he was in Hagger's bedroom. Vast, lit softly by a bedside lamp. A king-size bed, a walk-in wardrobe, heavy curtains, a plain thick carpet, an ensuite bathroom. Of interest to Wyatt: several cabinets and chests of drawers. Some would contain Hagger's clothing, others his 'famed collection of Kellyana'—as the *Sydney Morning Herald* put it. A story that had been passed to Wyatt by a day-release prisoner named Sam Kramer. Most of Wyatt's recent jobs had been brokered by Kramer.

A quick check under the pillow and mattress and inside the bedside cupboards. No gun, knife, taser or alarm. Then he made sure the bathroom was empty and slipped into the walk-in robe. He waited. Hagger came up the stairs shortly after that, washed his hands, threw his gown on the chair beside the bed, climbed in and got settled, turned out the light.

Fifteen minutes later the man's breathing settled to a slow, laboured rhythm. Wyatt edged into the room and waited, assessing the dark void between himself and the bed. Ready to slip into and become absorbed by it. The handcuffs would stay in his pocket for now, the metal cushioned against any stray sound.

He reached the bed and paused to let his eyes adjust. Hagger was faintly illuminated by the bedside clock. Supine; bulbous nose aimed at the ceiling, arms outflung above the bedcovers. Wyatt had already noted the bedhead, a plain but usefully laddered arrangement of wooden slats and uprights. Now he clasped Hagger's right wrist gently, drew it across the soft, respiring chest, and manacled it to the bedpost behind the man's left shoulder. Hagger stirred. Went very still. Tried to rear up when Wyatt turned on the bedside light and the shadows fled, but was thwarted by his own arm. Discomfort, a twinge of pain that might be eased if he flipped onto his stomach—but then he'd have his back to whatever trouble he was in. He subsided. Wyatt watched him work it out.

'Who are you? What do you want?'

That was expected, too. Wyatt knew there'd be more rage, fear and embarrassment. He was prepared to wait until it had all drained away and he could get on with the job.

'What do you want?' Hagger said. 'Money?'

Then, as if rethinking that: 'My son's due home any minute.'

Wyatt waited.

'There's an alarm sounding at the nearest police station this very second, so why don't you run off back to whatever hole you crawled out of.'

A blusterer. You didn't engage with them. It only worsened until they felt ridiculous. Then they'd go to some other extreme to counter that impression, and it would go on until someone got hurt. Wyatt waited.

Hagger's heavy chest expanded for another outburst, and then it all went out of him. 'Are you going to hurt me?'

Wyatt shook his head. No point in giving the man a voice to remember.

Hagger said, 'The newspaper story?'

Wyatt nodded. It was a common mistake of collectors, the newly rich: boasting in the lifestyle sections. Wyatt crossed to the first cabinet in the room. Underwear, socks. Fresh and folded and, Wyatt was certain, ironed.

'There's nothing here,' Hagger said. 'It's all in a safe deposit box in the bank.'

No. An obsessive collector of anything related to the Kelly Gang would keep it all close by. If it wasn't in the room—and why else were there so many cabinets?—it would be downstairs somewhere. But this was where Hagger could grab the most valuable items if the place ever caught fire.

'I mean it about the alarm.'

Wyatt shrugged. He'd entered the house before it was set. It would go off when he left, but that was okay. This was the only way Wyatt had to get past a modern alarm, though. In the past he'd been able to disable most alarm systems, but technological advances had left him behind. These days he adapted to circumstances. Use a crowbar if he had to. Let a careless householder do the work for him.

A glass-fronted bookcase caught his eye and he pulled experimentally on one of the doors. A magnetised latch—it popped open. He reached in.

Hagger, straining to see, sagged again. 'Please don't take that. It's very rare. I'd never be able to replace it.'

Wyatt checked: first edition. Original—if slightly scuffed—dust jacket. Worth a quarter of a million. He thought about it for a very long moment. But a *Gatsby* coming onto the market any time soon would attract attention. He put it back.

Reached in again and pulled out J. J. Keneally's *The Inner History of the Kelly Gang* and G. Wilson Hall's *The History of the Notorious Kelly Gang*. The latter was as priceless as the *Gatsby*, only four copies known to exist, but the next person to own it wasn't likely to boast about it.

Hagger tried to prop himself on an elbow. 'Not the Hall. Please, mate, not the Hall. I can tell you're a reasonable man.'

Wyatt had never thought about it one way or the other. He ignored Hagger and crouched. Two plain wooden doors in the bottom half of the bookcase. He tugged. Locked. He took a slim pry bar from an inner pocket of his thin jacket and Hagger shrieked, 'No! Please, that bookcase is worth seven and a half grand!'

A man who knows the cost of a beautiful item of furniture. But does he know its value? Wyatt stood, turned to Hagger with raised eyebrows.

'Please. The key's here in the bedside cupboard.'

Wyatt nodded, found the key, returned to the bookcase.

Behind the doors he found crammed shelves. Grunted in satisfaction to see, on the top shelf, a legal brief titled *The Queen v Edward Kelly*. He removed it, verified the number of pages—fifty-five—and that it related to the murder of Constable Thomas Lonigan at Stringybark Creek on 26 October 1878.

Worth up to fifty grand at auction.

On the bottom shelf, certain objects. A Bowie knife, an East India Company cavalry pistol and a .32 calibre pocket revolver. Sam Kramer had been clear: not the knife. The name carved into the handle was 'S. Harte', who was not Steve Hart. And notwithstanding the poor education of a backblocks kid in the 1870s, there was no proof the bushranger had ever owned it.

And not the revolver. Reputed to have been Joe Byrne's—JB scratched along the barrel—and purportedly found under the floorboards of a house where Byrne grew up. But the pistol had been manufactured in 1884, four years after Byrne was shot dead.

The cavalry pistol was the real thing, according to Kramer. *1876/Dan Kelly* carved in the walnut handle.

Wyatt took a nylon drawstring bag from his pocket, unfolded it, carefully packed it with the legal brief, the two books and the pistol.

'You prick,' Hagger said. Resigned, sullen—but with enough greed and panic to hope Wyatt might relent.

Wyatt regarded him with cold interest. It was often like this, the layers of self-regard and caution peeling away until the true man or woman peeked out. He slipped back into the slumbering streets, which stirred as Hagger's alarm began to wail. Wyatt had barely thought about Hagger while he'd been robbing him. Now his detachment was complete.

2

THE WAY IT WORKED was, Sam Kramer used information from his network of informants, lawyers, police and hard men, or just from newspapers and magazines, to identify an object worth stealing. He passed that information on to Wyatt. Wyatt pulled the job then used a fence to find a buyer. Sometimes a buyer started the process, but mostly the thieving came first, and a fence would have a buyer in mind. One fence might specialise in art, another in stamps or coins. The best man to move the Kellyana was Axel Blackstock. He'd take his cut and pay Wyatt the balance. Wyatt would pay Sam Kramer a brokerage fee. Twenty per cent.

Or rather, Sam would get his twenty per cent at the end of the year, when he was due for release from prison. His cut amounted to about ninety thousand dollars now, stowed in a safe deposit box. Wyatt dipped into it every now and then. A thousand here, three thousand there, to help Kramer's wife, daughter and son cover the mortgage or fix the roof or replace a gearbox. Never enough to pique the interest of state or federal police, who, lacking the evidence to charge Sam with a host of outstanding crimes, continued to monitor his family. The daughter, Wyatt's age, looked after the wife, who was crippled with rheumatoid arthritis. There was a son, but he was a waster. Slow horses, cocaine and punishing franchise agreements on half-a-dozen takeaway pizza outlets.

'Deal only with Phoebe,' Sam told Wyatt. 'I love Josh, but money slips through his hands like grease.'

WYATT DROVE STRAIGHT TO Blackstock's rambling Bondi guest house on a steep side street. Vines, broad verandas, sea salt in the air. Blackstock owned the building and rented rooms to a mix of backpackers and other transients, and a few permanents. Cheap rent for rooms that were unadorned sweatboxes in summer and chilly holes in winter. Nothing was ever done out of the goodness of the heart in that building, but Axel was a fair and tolerant landlord and had no interest in selling to a developer.

Wyatt stood at the top of the street for half an hour. Watching, as usual, for watchers. When he was satisfied, he sent a text from a burner phone to Blackstock's burner. They'd meet in the cramped carpark under the building, accessed from the rear. He waited; Blackstock's text arrived.

He walked along the side of the building and down the slope into a region of stale air, oil-stained floor and scraped walls. Blackstock, a skinny guy with a grey ponytail, dressed in his standard outfit of shorts, T-shirt and paint-speckled Crocs, stepped out from behind a Kombi van. The handover was mostly wordless, the fence as dour and silent as ever—which was a sign to Wyatt that he hadn't had unwelcome visitors since the last time.

'Forty-five grand,' Blackstock said, proffering a bulky envelope.

Wyatt nodded and left. This was the dangerous time. Rather than re-enter the main street he took back alleyways and slipped over fences, quick and silent but with no time to melt from one natural pool of darkness to the next. Dogs barked. A woman yelled at him. There might be sirens if she acted on it.

Reaching the side street where he'd left his car he waited, yawning once to clear his ears. The night was still and he wanted to distinguish the sounds of ordinary life from those that meant injury or death. Tunnels, stairways and basements always demanded extra caution, and this steep, narrow street was like a tunnel draining down to the beach.

He could do something about his appearance. He shed the jacket after removing the envelope from the inside pocket. Untucked his shirt, turned up the collar, rolled the sleeves. Donned a pair of heavy-rimmed glasses with plain lenses. Altered his stride, too, hunching his shoulders, dragging one heel a little on the footpath. Past his car; left turn at the first side street. The sounds of the night were vivid to him: TV sets, a grumbling drunk outside a corner pub, distant traffic. But no sudden disturbances of the air—no hurrying footsteps or anticipatory intakes of breath, no cigarette flaring in a patch of darkness.

A man appeared from around the next corner. Young, slim, a strut full of teenage potency. But Wyatt was looking at how he moved, how he wore his jeans and hoodie. No pistol or blade weighing down his pants, pressing against his spine, affecting his gait.

'Evening,' the kid said, and then he was past, and then he was gone.

WYATT PARKED HALF A kilometre from his apartment on Coogee Bay Road and walked the rest of the way. He felt as calm and concentrated as he'd been earlier, in Hagger's house, but a part of him was permanently alert for signs that his current life was over. That he was on the edge of a situation better left alone. He knew not to ignore the feeling; it had always served him well.

He came to his street, a tide of seawater odours and the semi-tropics in his nose, and watched for thirty minutes. His apartment was on the ground floor of a building that looked like a stack of CDs but less beautiful. A higher floor might have given him a glimpse of the sea and a better one of the traffic, but he wanted access to the exits if trouble came knocking.

Nothing seemed wrong. The rubbish bin he'd carelessly placed half across the little crazy-stone path to his front door hadn't been moved onto the patchy lawn. It was an old apartment, venetian blinds on the front windows, and the slats were still partially open. Someone poking around inside with a torch would have closed them.

Still he waited, the night swollen with the sounds he was accustomed to. Another half-hour passed before he crossed the street and let himself in. He sat in an armchair for some time, thinking about the evening. He'd made no errors. There was nothing to improve on.

3

In a Surry Hills wine bar, Joshua Kramer was saying, 'Laz, mate. Great night.'

Nick Lazar gave a noncommittal grunt. *Laz.* Fucking liberty. But he let it slide. Still gleaning information from the little prick.

'Good acoustics,' Kramer was saying.

Pizza shop franchisee by day, rock star by night. He still lived with his mother and sister, but right now Josh Kramer was flushed, sweaty and elated. On stage he'd thrown himself around as if he didn't know he was playing to half-a-dozen punters in a fucking church hall. More scrawny than wiry, more bum-fluff than designer stubble—and the band was crap: Springsteen covers and turgid originals. Lazar suspected the kid paid venues to book him and put the hard word on his pizza cooks, counter staff and delivery boys to front up.

Lazar scratched the NightWatch Security logo on his T-shirt. Half an hour past midnight, the two men at the afterparty two blocks from the church hall. Piss-poor afterparty. The bassist and drummer had gone home, along with most of Kramer's employees. Lazar's security guys had also left—all two of them. The wine bar was too dark and too full of desperate singles to host a celebration, and the music, some kind of dire percussive techno, reached Lazar's ears—blunted by years of front-line action in Afghanistan—like distant mortar fire.

Suddenly the kid was standing, fishing an envelope from his back pocket. 'Before I forget.'

Lazar nodded his thanks and counted the money. Counted it again: a hundred dollars short.

'Joshua,' he said sadly.

Kramer raised a pacifying hand. 'I know, I know, but I'm good for it.'

'You were short last time,' Lazar said, angry with himself for taking tonight's job. As if he'd had a choice. Between escorting second-tier celebrities to and from opening nights and standing on street corners while some shopkeeper took the day's takings to a night-deposit slot, running 'crowd control' for Josh Kramer was as good as it got.

He sipped his beer—you wouldn't want to drink the wine in this wine bar—and kept all inflection out of his voice: 'Why don't you get this Wyatt character to shell out some coin.'

He wanted a repeat of that evening a month earlier when young Joshua had suddenly begun boasting how his father was a mover and shaker in the Sydney underworld. How back in the day he'd put together hold-up crews: banks and payroll vans. How insiders had provided him with police radio frequencies, security-van routes, and locations of roadblocks, major operations and surveillance teams. And how, even now, behind bars, he was still putting jobs together. 'Twenty per cent finder's fee. Must add up to a quarter of a million by now.'

Well, Lazar had taken notice of that. Careful not to let his interest show, he'd shrugged. 'I guess he doesn't get to spend it where he is.'

Whereupon the kid told him that Kramer senior's quarter million was being held in trust by a hard man name of Wyatt.

Tonight, Lazar intended to find out more about this Wyatt. 'I mean,' he continued, 'it's no skin off your father's nose if you get slipped a few hundred now and then.'

'Yeah, well, easier said than done,' the kid said, staring into his bloody mary.

Lazar let it pass. There was a woman eyeing him from a stool at the bar. Seeing him return her gaze, she took a slow, red-lipstick sip from something foul-looking in a martini glass.

Clearly the kid was in a funk. Time to get him talking. Lazar said, 'You can always ask him. No harm done.'

Josh Kramer seemed to flinch. 'Actually, me and Dad don't get on that well.'

And here we have the crux of the matter, thought Lazar. 'Too bad.'

The kid smiled weakly. 'Hard to please, my old man.'

Lazar could see the inner struggle. Kramer wanted to earn his father's approval in the long term—but in the short term he wanted to get back at him. By stealing his quarter million, for example. Not yet prepared to be upfront with Lazar, put himself in a position he couldn't retreat from. Happy just to circle the matter, drop the odd hint.

Meanwhile the woman at the bar was lifting a shoe to the rung of her stool, skirt hem artfully riding her thigh. The stiletto caught, and she lurched, sloshing her drink. She flushed. Turned her back in a lonely hunch over the bar. Lazar shook his head, completely and utterly weary. 'What about your mother and your sister?'

Kramer shifted to get comfortable on his squeaky, overinflated leather booth seat and shrugged. 'They're not on my back twenty-four seven, if that's what you mean.'

'Can *they* lend you money till you get established?'

Kramer shot Lazar a look, as if Lazar hadn't been paying attention this evening. 'Like I said, we're broke. Dad doesn't want the cops sniffing around, which is what they'd do if we suddenly came into a quarter of a mill.' His manner saying, *I told you all this.*

'Right, right,' said Lazar slowly.

'So, we make do with Wyatt doling out a grand here, a grand there.'

And the kid was bitter about it. Lazar let silence settle around them, wondering if in fact there *was* a quarter of a million dollars, or considerably less, or none at all. The bar-stool woman was climbing down from her perch, casting him a hurt look, teetering off with her head high. He said casually, 'Let's hope your bloke doesn't get arrested or decide to piss off with the lot.'

Kramer gave him a look. 'The thought's crossed my mind.'

As if I might offer to do something about it, Lazar thought. Like steal it for him. Lazar had every intention of stealing it, but not in partnership with the little prick. 'How do you all get in touch?'

Kramer shrugged, sour again. 'I'm out of the loop.'

'Joshua,' Lazar said patiently, 'this guy pulls robberies put together by your father, right? So how does he get the information required?'

'He's not stupid enough to visit Dad in jail, if that's what you mean.'

Lazar wanted to smack him about the chops. 'No, I guess that would be asking for trouble. But how do you *think* they communicate?'

'I *know* how they communicate,' Joshua Kramer said. 'When Dad's on day release.'

14

Lazar tingled. 'Day release.'

Kramer said, as if Lazar was slow, 'He's *low* security, not high security. They let him out to pull up weeds, clean graffiti, that kind of thing.'

Okay. This was hopeful. There would be a problem, though, with finding out how, when and where Sam Kramer was allowed out on day-release work details. It might be easier to locate Wyatt through the women.

'Perhaps get your mother and sister to give you a few hundred bucks next time Wyatt forks out.'

Kramer snorted. 'Like I said, I'm out of the loop.'

This was useless. Lazar waggled his empty glass. 'Mine's a Coopers.'

As Kramer tottered off to the bar, Lazar brooded. The kid knew bugger all. Sounding me out, hoping I'll take the bait, no actual information about the main players.

He was aware of a groin at his shoulder: the woman from the bar stool. 'I noticed you before. Buy a girl a drink?'

What a fucking cliché, thought Lazar. He stared up at her. Seeing the void, she swallowed, said, 'Suit yourself,' and disappeared.

The waste-of-time Kramer kid was returning from the bar, baby face expectant, drinks riding high in his hands. Lazar would sit and listen and maybe he'd learn some tidbit that would help him find the moneyman. He wouldn't be holding his breath.

4

First thing the next morning Wyatt logged into a shared email account. Phoebe Kramer was the other user: the conduit between Wyatt and her father, currently residing in Watervale, a medium security facility west of Sydney. She'd contact Wyatt via emails that she would not send but save into the drafts folder of the account. Never the details of the job, only the day and place of her father's next day-release outing. With a C3 security rating, Sam was allowed out once or twice a fortnight to tend flowerbeds, lawns and parkway shrubbery with other trusted prisoners.

Wyatt would log on, read, delete. Likewise, his messages to her were always stored in the drafts folder and deleted when read. No one else had access to the account; messages that were never sent or received couldn't be intercepted.

Phoebe had lodged a message overnight: *$2000.*

It was immaterial to Wyatt why the family needed two thousand dollars. It was Sam's money. He replied: *art gallery at noon.*

He showered, dressed, deposited the forty-five grand from Blackstock in his safe deposit box, then walked along the nearby beach, stopping for a coffee on Arden Street. He liked the rock pools along the Coogee-Bondi coastal walk. He wasn't interested in swimming; he just liked to look. The tossing seawater was a wild comfort, somehow.

LATE MORNING NOW. A sky lidded with gunmetal clouds driven by a wind that carried the scent of distant rain. Wyatt walked uphill from the Circular Quay ferry station and across parkland to the Art Gallery of New South Wales. He'd spent an hour shaking off a possible tail—doubling back, short taxi and train rides, entering buildings by one door and leaving by another. He was confident he hadn't been followed. As the ragged cadence of the streets receded, he could hear birdsong in the trees, briefly silenced when thunder rolled across the harbour behind him. He glanced upwards. No downfall yet, but the air was electric. Rain might absolve this thieving old city.

He had no umbrella, but he did have a five-dollar canvas backpack containing two grand in cash. He thought of Sam Kramer's wife in her wheelchair, Phoebe steering it through puddles. He looked about but didn't see them.

Joining other gallery patrons at the coat-check, he pocketed the claim token and began to roam. The main exhibit was named *Fake or Copy* and contained a number of big Sydney Harbour views attributed to Brett Whiteley and subject to court actions regarding provenance, materials and technique. Wyatt got a kick out of that. He'd stolen paintings that proved to be fakes, in his long career, and he'd replaced real ones with fakes.

But he was also taking in the men and women around him. In particular, recurrent but unfamiliar faces. People catching his gaze and looking away too quickly or casually or at a companion.

A flicker of recognition, a hand jerking to a pocket or inside a jacket flap.

Still no sign of the Kramer women. It had been a year since his last visit to the gallery and he found Tom Roberts' Coogee painting and tried to match it to the Coogee he knew. Then he paused a while at Elioth Gruner's *Frosty Sunrise* and tried to understand where his mind was taking him, as he took in the hillside, the fences, the grass striped by the rising sun shadows of a farmer and his animals. Nothing from his Struggletown childhood, anyway. But back when the jobs were easier and he'd amassed a lot of money, he'd lived in a sometimes-misty landscape south-east of Melbourne. A place of hill folds down to the distant sea, and grasses and fences hung with webs jewelled by the sun as it rose. That old life was gone. He could not match it earning twenty thousand here, fifteen or thirty there, with long, unoccupied periods in between.

Then Phoebe Kramer was standing at his shoulder, ignoring him and fussing over Cindy in her wheelchair. 'Comfortable, Mum?'

'Yes, thank you, dear.'

Phoebe was half a head shorter than Wyatt, with dark cropped hair framing a wryly magnetic, faintly off-centre face. The only time Wyatt had been alone in her company she'd bestowed on him an almost-smile full of a certain guarded appeal. She wouldn't be taken in by the legend any time soon, but she might give the actual man the benefit of the doubt. Now he was aware that the attraction still existed, and he didn't know what to do about it. She was Sam's daughter. Cindy's carer. And it was likely the police had a watching brief on her.

But his task here was to act as if he didn't know her, had never met her. He viewed the painting. A metre to his right, Phoebe and Cindy Kramer viewed it. He moved on two metres to the next painting, just as Phoebe bent to her mother to straighten the rug and accidently tipped her open handbag onto the floor.

Wyatt said, 'Let me.'

He squatted, harvested and tumbled everything onto Cindy's lap, and now they had exchanged bag-claim tokens. Next time it might be a left-luggage locker key inside the spine of a hardcover in the State Library. Some ruse or other to fool a watching gaze.

Wyatt nodded, smiled, moved on to the next painting. He happened to catch Cindy Kramer's expression in the corner of his gaze, a look full of humour and appreciation, with a sideways eye flick to her daughter. Almost as if she were gathering him in from the cold.

5

WYATT STROLLED ACROSS the park, scanning everyone without appearing to. Japanese tourists, a Chinese wedding party, lovers on the grass, noisy schoolkids, office workers on early lunch. These were his general impressions. He homed in on specifics: a woman wearing an earpiece—she was on her phone. A brawny tattooed guy—but there was a second one just like him, and a third. Two police constables ambling along, but with restless eyes. A man wearing a winter coat in the mild sunshine. If he heard a sound he didn't like—footsteps, a ticking bicycle—he'd turn his whole body, not just his head, because the half-second delay in turning head, then body, and bringing his fist, foot or gun into play might cost him his life.

Doing this was as automatic to Wyatt as breathing.

He did it twice on the way out. A squeaky wheel turned out to be a child's stroller; running footsteps a jogger. The jogger gasped and veered away when she saw a flicker in Wyatt, a tall, solid man but light and fluid, too. His face as he assessed her would have been frighteningly direct, his hands corded with veins.

A short ferry ride and then into his car, parked at a supermarket—the edge, not the middle where he could be trapped. There had been street parking, but all they'd need was one vehicle to hem him against the kerb, whoever they were. He always avoided multi-storey carparks with their stairwells, ramps and ambush points.

He climbed behind the wheel, locked his doors and rolled through the carpark and out onto the street. Heading back to Coogee, he used his mirrors constantly. There was a red Mazda two cars behind him for some time, then a silver Camry three cars behind him. A guy on a scooter, a ponytailed woman in a Suzuki. Bike messengers, van drivers, commuters. They all peeled away eventually, and he arrived at his street unattended.

He pulled over and watched. No service vans sporting dishes or discs; no crews working on a water main; no gardeners, couples wheeling prams, powerful sedan cars of a uniform type.

EARLY AFTERNOON NOW.

Hungry, Wyatt changed his clothes and left the flat. Twenty minutes later he was in the shade of a bistro table umbrella, forking calamari and salad leaves into his mouth. The wind came in cold from the sea. He rolled down his sleeves and shrugged into the jacket he'd hung on the back of his chair.

He finished eating and looked out over the whitecaps. Now that his body was at rest his mind would not let go of the gallery and Phoebe Kramer. Thoughts he couldn't name.

Back before the Kramer family's realignments and reversals, Phoebe had simply been the daughter, a hard-to-read presence in a corner of the room whenever Wyatt visited to confer with Sam. But eventually it became clear that she was responsible for some of her father's intel, and one day Wyatt found himself working

21

alongside her, gun for hire on a job that she'd planned and her father had bankrolled.

An IT specialist at the University of New South Wales, she spent her spare time tweaking software weaknesses in the university's relationships with donors and business partners to siphon off funds for 'scholarships' and 'goods and services', and pass on insider corporate information to her father.

One day she hacked into the Exclusive Assembly Church, which had donated fifty thousand dollars to a right-wing thinktank associated with a professor in the Business School. She hadn't been able to sideline any of that money but did learn from the church's email accounts that the Australian offshoot relied on twice-yearly cash infusions from HQ in Alabama. Literal cash: stuffed into envelopes folded into handbags and flown in, eight at a time, by elderly women posing as a tour party of widows. On arrival at Sydney Airport, the women would rent a Hertz minibus and drive to the church's rural enclave an hour south-east of Sydney.

As Wyatt eyed the tossing sea, he recalled the hold-up. A Sunday in October, a quiet side road, the sun warming the front seats of the stolen Chrysler 300. Phoebe Kramer calm and focused beside him, a laptop resting on her thighs. A quiet, unscented, barely stirring presence in hiking pants and black running shoes. Strong bare arms, faintly tanned. She was watching the screen, fingers poised over the keyboard. The only things she'd need to hack into the bus's onboard computer, she'd told Wyatt at the planning session, was a laptop, a mobile phone, the bus's IP address and software she'd already devised.

He'd glanced at her once or twice as they waited; she'd glanced back, expressionless but for lazy-lidded eyes and the hint of a smile. He had a job to do, she had a job to do; but there was an undercurrent. Wyatt didn't know how to read it. He knew how to read the nuances that forewarned him of treachery or attack. He was less certain about desire.

Nothing was said or done and then Phoebe's fingers flew over the keys. The bus was behind them, then alongside, already slowing. The horn sounded. The wipers swept the windscreen madly, the emergency lights flashed. Wyatt saw the driver lift her hands from the wheel, then clutch it again as the bus ran out of steam, and steer into the kerb a few metres ahead of the Chrysler.

Wyatt pulled on a ski mask and got out. A lonely back road, spring grass choking the fence wires, a bird like a paper scrap above, the cloudless sun laying a scattered brightness over the dusty vehicles. He stepped onto the bus, stood with a small pistol resting against his breastbone, and said two words: 'The envelopes.'

He waited. The women were more indignant than afraid— they're used to guns, he thought—as they debated the issue. *Not worth getting shot over...Different method next time...*

An hour later, he was in a motel room with Phoebe Kramer. She was still sleepy-eyed and withholding, but not in the ways that mattered.

Only that once. She continued to resurface in his thoughts from time to time.

Now, as his fingers toyed with a paper napkin, the wind picked up, the chill factor high, and he zipped the jacket to his neck. Little wonder that he registered a man who didn't seem affected by the conditions. A man who'd evidently strolled onto the sand from the carpark, neat in trousers, a plain shirt, sunglasses. Looking one way along the beach, then the other, all the time in the world, and he'd been at the art gallery.

This was unfinished business and Wyatt got up to leave, looking to end it. But he'd had to compromise when choosing his table. It had given him a view of the water and any possible tail, but it was far from the entrance and overlooked a steep drop. By the time he'd ducked and weaved his way out onto the side path to the sand, the man was gone.

Wyatt returned to his flat. The venetians were open, as if someone inside needed advance warning of his return, and the recycle bin he'd left half over the path had been moved aside.

He didn't bother to go in. He didn't want to kill. Killing was usually not the answer to anything, and there was the risk of attracting the law. About the only thing he could do was walk away from it all, as he'd done many times before.

6

THESE DAYS, MOST OF Nick Lazar's friends were ex-2nd Commando Regiment men he'd served with in Uruzgan and other areas of Afghanistan. Every one of them damaged in some way. They'd seen mates killed when a helicopter came down or shredded by a roadside device. Told to write a 'dead letter' to family before every mission, to ease the burden for some lilywhite officer—never held a gun, let alone got shot at—charged with knocking on the family's door. Told to face skirmishes and battles with controlled aggression, when, in Lazar's experience, all the aggression in that shitty place had been *un*controlled. Ask for help, say your nerves were shot, Command would tell you, 'Be part of the next mission, as ordered, or go home for good.'

A strange, rootless existence. You'd yearn for home—Sydney Harbour, Bondi, your mother's cooking, a girl's bed—but after about a day you'd yearn to be back in the stony desert with your mates.

Then the special hell that was post-army life. Most guys came home with nothing to show for their years of service but hearing loss and slipped discs. Disastrous personal lives; couldn't hold down a job; depression; addiction; suicide. AVOs. Jail. Veterans Affairs either useless or openly antagonistic.

Help, if there was any, came from your buddies. Lazar had met Marty Welsh at the Parramatta Recruiting Centre and served with him in Helmand Province and the Shah Wali Kot Offensive. Since leaving the army in 2013, the two of them would meet for a drink every now and then. Welsh worked as a private investigator these days, mostly tracking people: an accountant who'd skipped with clients' money held in trust, a millionaire's daughter missing from her boarding school, an estranged father whisking the kids away from their mother. He had contacts in the Tax Office, the Department of Motor Vehicles, Centrelink, in the state and federal police and among security firms like Lazar's. A lot of his work was reading files, peering at a screen and making phone calls. Otherwise, he knocked on doors. Flashed his ID and said, 'I'm licensed by the State of New South Wales as an investigator...'

Given that Josh Kramer had been no help, Marty was the logical guy to find Sam Kramer's moneyman. And now, over lunch at an outside table between the bridge and the ferry terminal, Lazar was hearing that hadn't panned out, either.

'Tried everything, mate. It's like he doesn't exist. You're sure of the name?'

'Wyatt, that's all I know.'

They kept their voices low, even though the tables were far apart and the air full of distorting harbour sounds. Cool sunshine, gulls wheeling, a scrappy breeze tossing cellophane and newspaper about.

'No social network that I can find,' Welsh said. He was lanky: all sharp angles, prominent bones and gloom. 'Most people have friends or family, some kind of tribe. Not this guy. Don't know where he was born, where he's lived, or where he is now.'

'He has friends,' Lazar protested. 'Sam Kramer for one.'

'Who's in jail,' Welsh pointed out.

Lazar dipped a chip in tartare sauce, a tendon flexing in his tattooed forearm. 'Go back in time. He's solo now, but he used to hit banks and payroll vans. There must be drivers he used, safe crackers, armourers.'

Welsh shook his head. 'Normally a guy like that gets noticed, but this one evaporates after he pulls a job. All I can get from my contacts are vague impressions. "I knew a guy who knew a guy who worked with him on a jewellery raid," kind of thing. Nothing concrete. However, and it's worth bearing in mind, I get the feeling no one wants to cross him. So watch yourself.'

'He must have rubbed *someone* up the wrong way, enough to talk.'

'Not that I've heard.'

Lazar dipped another chip. They were cold now, his hunger sated, but his hands and mouth ruled him somehow. 'Habits? Interests?'

Scorn on Welsh's skeletal features. 'You mean like he collects stamps and goes to folk music gigs?'

Lazar shrugged, feeling foolish. 'Current or ex-wife? Disgruntled kid? Elderly mother in a nursing home?'

'Nothing.'

Lazar nodded. He felt a deep tiredness, the earth pulling at him. 'Kramer's wife and daughter?'

'Got nowhere there. They're hard, reclusive, distrustful. I went in as a journalist writing a family-left-behind-when-the-man-of-the-house-goes-to-jail story and was told to fuck off.'

'Our guy communicates with them somehow.'

'Look,' said Welsh, 'I could keep poking into paper and digital trails and people's lies and evasions until the cows come home and still not find him. He doesn't have a past I can excavate. Most people say, "Here I am" or "Look at me" to some degree, but he doesn't. No ego. No hunger.'

'Oh, he's hungry,' Lazar said.

'Then work out what he wants.'

'Money.'

'Sure, but how does that make him any different from the rest of us?'

'The challenge.'

'That's no good to me,' Welsh said. He shifted to get comfortable, threw his napkin down. 'Mate, whatever's going on, I want in. I'm going out of my brain with boredom.'

Lazar nodded slowly. 'I'll take it under consideration.'

'Fuck you. I want in,' Welsh said. He paused. 'There is one thing you could try.'

'Hit me.'

'You told me he probably makes contact when Sam Kramer's out on day release.'

'According to the son, yeah. But finding out where and when is another matter.'

'I did some digging,' Welsh said. 'There is someone…'

Anticipation crept through Lazar. 'Okay?'

'Brad Salter.'

'Oh, Jesus Christ,' groaned Lazar.

Salter had been under his command in Afghanistan. Discharged for habitually taking pot shots at village dogs. And villagers. And he'd probably killed a kid, but the details were murky. Even so, Lazar hadn't been covered in glory, being Salter's commanding officer, and he'd been edged out of the army eighteen months later.

'What about him?'

'He's in Watervale with Kramer.'

7

THREE YEARS FOR AGGRAVATED burglary, divorced by his wife in the meantime, and long forgotten by his family and friends, Bradley Salter was pleased, if wary, to hear he had a visitor. Surprised to find it was Nick Lazar, looking cleaner and more collected than he had in their army days.

He shook hands. 'To what do I owe the pleasure?' Determined to control this situation, Salter sat relaxed in the plastic visiting-room chair. Arms folded, face unreadable, in case the Laz tried to pull some officer bullshit on him. 'Didn't bring a hacksaw with you?'

Lazar laughed unconvincingly. 'I need a favour.'

Salter glanced around the room at the wives, girlfriends and kids visiting their fuckup menfolk. 'What kind of favour?'

'Information,' Lazar said, and waited.

'Spit it out, Laz.'

A brief flare in Lazar's eyes at the diminutive. 'Sam Kramer.'

Salter kept his expression neutral but leaned over their nasty little table. 'Keep your voice down. The guy's a big wheel in here.'

And Lazar leaned forward, until their heads were half a metre apart. 'Who visits him, who his friends are and, more specifically, what he does and who he sees on day release.'

'Not my scene, man. No way they're letting me out to pick up rubbish or whatever.'

'I understand. But maybe you can get close to a guy who works alongside Kramer? Offer him money or smokes or something, and get him to report back?'

'What guy?'

'Any guy,' Lazar said, a touch of irritation.

'Big ask.'

'Brad, he doesn't have to take photos or ask questions or talk to Kramer or do anything that'll attract attention. All he has to do is tell you the where and when of each time he goes out on day release, and whether or not Kramer is handed anything, or talks to anyone, and what this person looks like.'

Salter watched Lazar, trying to work out the angles. What hadn't been said?

'Plus,' Lazar went on, 'who visits him here in Watervale. Who he hangs out with, so on and so forth.'

Salter tried to think of Kramer as a man with friends. A couple of minders followed him around…'There's one guy, Kyle Roden.' He pursed his mouth. 'White collar. Ripped off investors or some shit.'

'He's a visitor?'

'No, no. He's in here.'

Lazar gestured irritably. '*Visitors*, Brad.'

Salter couldn't shake off his unease. He checked the room again. No Kramer. No Kramer minders. 'I've seen this one chick wheeling an older one in a wheelchair.'

'Wife and daughter,' Lazar said. 'Anyone else?'

30

'A suit. Lawyer?'

'Any of his old crowd?'

'How would I know who his old crowd is?'

'Guys with a certain look, Brad,' Lazar said heavily. 'Toe cutters.'

Salter sank his solid head into his pneumatic shoulders. Walls have ears, Laz. And although Sam Kramer looked like a retired accountant, he had clout. Everyone wary of him, inmates and prison staff alike. 'Not exactly fighting off the hordes on visiting day myself, Laz. I wouldn't know who else comes to see him. Anyway…' He sat back again, folded his arms. 'Aren't you forgetting something?'

'There's five in it for you,' Lazar said immediately, his voice very low.

'Half up front.'

'Done. Where and how?'

That was easy. Salter, starting to think he should have asked for more, rattled off a BSB and account number, an account no one and certainly not his ex-wife knew about. 'As soon as it hits the account, I'll go to work.'

'Deal.'

'Plus,' he said, 'I want a job when I get out.'

Lazar stiffened and ducked minutely, as if he'd been shot at. 'Mate, I don't know, security staff need to be clean as a whistle this day and age.'

'Off the books, all right? Put me in one of your stretch limos.'

Lazar's eyes were evasive. 'Ah…business is actually a bit slow at the moment.'

'So, no stretch limo?' Salter said, enjoying himself.

He kept up with the news. Every muscle-bound Pacific Islander and steroid-abusing ex-con in Sydney wanted to work security, and Nick's firm had taken too many assurances at face

31

value. Last December one of his guys had king hit and hospitalised a drunk on the steps of a Darlinghurst nightclub. Which might have been swept under the rug except that the bouncer had a criminal history, the cops got interested, and Nick had been sued by the drunk.

'I can type a bit. Answer the phone?'

'I'll see what I can do, okay?'

'Okay,' Salter said. He cocked his head. 'I can't see myself ringing you every day with updates. Or you dropping by every visiting day.'

'All taken care of.'

TWO DAYS LATER SALTER got word to help a civilian volunteer catalogue and shelve new books in the prison library, a poky room along a dead-end corridor leading from the rec hall. Expecting an earnest mouse of a librarian, he was met by a cute, rounded, sleepy-eyed brunette who startled him by placing a fat doorstopper titled *Theories of Communicative Action* in his hands. 'Our friend thought you might like a read of this.'

He shelved it. When she'd gone and the library was deserted, he sat on a stool between the stacks and the far wall where he couldn't be seen. He opened the book. An iPhone nestled in a hollow between pages 100 and 300. One number had been programmed into the phone, and there was a note telling him to keep the sim card separate and always clear the call and text history.

FINDING A SNITCH WAS easy in the end. Using cash, cigarettes and intimidation, he obtained a list of men with day-release privileges and shadowed each one for an hour or so. Carl Ayliffe was a stupid, sweet-faced, permanently scared kid who'd been passed around a few times. Liked to hide in the library, in fact. Thought

Salter was there to rape him and was wary, then relieved and wary, when told he had nothing to worry about.

'What do I have to do?'

'That's the spirit. First, keep your mouth shut.'

'And?'

'Sam Kramer.'

Ayliffe shrank. 'You know who he is, right?'

'Has he had a go at you?'

'Wouldn't even know I exist.'

'Let's keep it that way. All I want you to do is keep your eyes and ears open. I need you to let me know in advance when you're leaving these fine premises to pick weeds or whatever, and whether or not Kramer's on the roster that day, and what he does when the rest of you are standing around scratching your balls.'

'Like what?'

'Anything. Does he talk to anyone? Use a phone? Disappear for ten minutes? Anything at all.'

Two weeks later there was something.

The library was generally quiet before dinner, but Salter cleared it anyway, shooing out the senile wreck who shelved and reshelved books all day long and a guy trying to crack the computer for porn, leaving only Ayliffe and himself. He listened to the kid's report, clapped him on the back and sent him off to the rec room.

It was 6.08 now. Salter opened *Theories of Communicative Action*, removed the iPhone from its hollow and turned it on. Still plenty of charge. Using a paperclip, he removed the sim tray and inserted the sim card, which he'd hidden inside his shirt collar.

Texted Nick Lazar: *Call.*

Lazar would be waiting. The arrangement was, if Salter had any news he'd text in the lead-up to six-thirty chow time. Any later and Lazar would be at work, running crowd control at some club or other.

The phone vibrated. Salter stood where he could see along the corridor and not be seen by the cameras and said, 'Yep.'

Lazar's voice crackled in Salter's ear. 'Something?'

'They were in The Rocks today, stripping old posters or some shit off walls, and Kramer chatted to a guy wheeling a bike. My guy said there was a feeling to it, you know, like it was staged.'

'Ah. Good, good.'

'Who is this guy?'

'Later,' Lazar said. 'What did he look like?'

'Like a ponce in lycra and a helmet, messing with the chain on a mountain bike.'

'That it?'

Salter thought back. 'Strong, fit. That's about all.'

'Let me know when they're going out again and I'll see if I can spot him.'

'Bit of a long shot, isn't it, mate? What if it's just some random—'

Lazar said, 'That's my problem. Your job's to keep me informed, that's all,' and ended the call.

Salter switched off the phone, tucked it away and returned the sim card to his collar. He was being sidelined, that's what it boiled down to. He thought he'd play hard to get next time, give a little, take a little, until he had answers. Five thousand bucks was not to be sneezed at, but Nick had come up with it pretty easily. It might turn out to be a drop in the bucket.

8

MEANWHILE, WYATT HAD FOUND a new home. He had the paper for half-a-dozen new identities, built up over the years. It was easy for him to move on and settle in a new place under a new name; jettison both and move on again if they were compromised. Walking away from his car and the Coogee flat, as he'd walked away from many possessions in his life, he'd bought a Holden ute, headed south and rented a farmhouse on a hectare of grass and old fruit trees inland of Batemans Bay. He spent a little time shopping at the general store, sinking an afternoon beer at the pub, filling his tank at the Caltex until he was on nodding terms with some of the locals. He added a library card to his wallet, a car wash loyalty card, a 'fifth pair free' coupon from the shoe shop. Careful to seem busy in a vague kind of way, but always prepared to smile and lift an eyebrow hello, even stop for a pointless chat. And careful not to attract the wrong kind of attention—he didn't splash his money around, drive fast, drink too much, allow bills and rent to go unpaid, or encourage anyone who was drunk or lonely. His landlady, an elderly widow, warned him that thieves were known to target properties in the district, but Wyatt had nothing much worth stealing. If he were burgled he'd not report it anyway—he didn't want elimination prints or DNA to tie him to an old crime. He'd been careful, but you couldn't be sure there wasn't a trace of him on some database.

And if anyone came for him here, he'd simply walk away again. Unless they came in hard and fast enough to leave him no choice.

Wyatt was a chameleon, socially. In dress, manner, lifestyle and apparent beliefs he appeared amiable, tolerant, low-key. Unremarkable. But in two important respects, he stood out. One, he was tall, lithe, alert, in a land of slow, soft, flabby people. He had a story to explain that. He'd been a military fitness instructor in a previous life; now he was seeing a bit of Australia with a view to settling down, maybe starting a gym. He knew enough about people to know they were obsessed with health and fitness, even as they did nothing about it. His apparent interest in these things didn't mark him out, it made him as boring as the next guy.

Two, his face gave people pause. Dark, narrow, slightly hooked and hooded, the olive skin tight over the bones, it was more prohibitive than approachable. When not expressionless, it was unimpressed. Once or twice in his past a woman had slipped under his guard long enough to tell him he ought to lighten up, so he knew he had to work on his face when he was in public. People expected—needed—warmth, acknowledgment, respect: reassurance. If all they got was a pleasantly neutral face, that was okay, too. But they remembered being made to feel unimportant.

And so Wyatt worked on his facial muscles, and he worked on his looks. Short, neat hair. A tight shave. Plain glasses with heavy rims; a permanent half-smile.

36

He supposed he could be found again by the wrong people, but it would be through bad luck, not family or friends or lovers or habits or interests. These didn't define him. If Wyatt were found, it would be through something he couldn't plan for—his face among bystanders in a newspaper photo; an old acquaintance happening to spot him on the street.

He mused on events in Sydney. It was possible someone who knew his face had spotted him leaving or entering the Coogee apartment one day, and sent word along a chain. But it was more likely he'd been found through the connection with the Kramer women. He'd have to find another way to pass them their dribs and drabs of Sam's money.

HE'D HEARD NOTHING FROM Phoebe Kramer until a day in late April, when the coastal towns were trying to decide that cooler weather was coming. Sam had another job for him. *The Rocks*, the email drop said. It gave a day and a time, and Wyatt had got himself a mountain bike and some cycling gear and walked through the area until he'd found Sam and other day-release prisoners scraping poster scraps from a wall. He fussed with the chain until Sam drew near. Listened; asked a couple of questions when Sam told him where he could find a pair of uncirculated 1967 five-dollar notes. Normally such a banknote was not worth much, but the final zero on the serial number of these notes had been hand-numbered, ensuring their combined worth was about a hundred thousand. He'd stolen them that night.

Handy for him, the best fence for the notes was a man named Barry Hartzer, in Wollongong, which was on his way home. Hartzer, thinning hair, jockey-sized, was as taciturn as Axel Blackstock, except for a remark he made as Wyatt was leaving: 'Until next time, Mr Warner.'

Normally Wyatt didn't know when he'd next see any of the

men and women who fenced the items he stole. It depended on Kramer having a job for him, it depended on the type of haul. But he'd known at once there would not be a next time with Barry Hartzer. 'Warner' was one of Wyatt's old names, last used fifteen years ago. It was Barry's way of sending a warning. Maybe their encounter was being recorded, video and audio, or the police or someone from his past had been by: questions, pressure, too much curiosity. Wyatt was uneasy. People were looking for him. After checking for a tracking device, he'd taken two days to get home, detouring into the middle of the state, doubling back, then down into Victoria and up the coast road. It was enough to shake a tail loose, but if they were shadowing him from *in front*, they'd be harder to spot.

AND TODAY, ANOTHER EMAIL: *Centennial Park*, time and date.

To the casual observer Wyatt was a public servant. Paperwork secured to a clipboard, Sun Safe hat, high-vis jacket with *Sydney City Council* on the breast pocket. A man like that, like a man driving a taxi or walking along a street in a grey suit and swinging a briefcase, is largely invisible. And for the duration of this visit to the park, Wyatt *was* a council worker with a clipboard: he wasn't playacting. He eyed the paths and garden beds in Centennial Park, crouched to take sightlines, made notations, so full of purpose that no one questioned or interrupted him.

Presently he drew closer to three gardeners wearing jeans, cotton jackets, boots and work gloves, and two bored-looking guards on a nearby bench. There was nothing to mark the former out as day-release prisoners. One man was in his twenties, shy, intent, sweet-faced, forking in the rich loam around clumps of flowering kangaroo paw. The second man was in his mid-thirties, stocky, with a shaved head, stubbled cheeks and a small barcode tattooed beneath one ear. His hands moved busily, expertly, so no

38

one could complain about his work ethic, but his expression was snide. Gardening, clearly, was beneath him.

They were some distance away. The closest man to Wyatt was Sam Kramer: sixty-something, with glasses slipping down his nose, clean, neat, fastidious. A man who might conceivably have spent his life marking university essays instead of swindling investors or passing heist information on to men like Wyatt.

Time passed. After a while Kramer came closer to where Wyatt crouched, looking along a garden border. He leaned in to pluck at some weeds. 'Mate,' he murmured. 'Appreciate your help with the family.'

Wyatt's face showed nothing, but he was surprised. He'd given his word. Why wouldn't he do what he'd said he'd do? Anyway, that wasn't why he was here. 'What's the job?' he said, his mouth barely moving.

'Jack Tremayne,' Kramer said, knowing Wyatt would remember the name and do his research.

Wyatt got to his feet. Flicked through his clipboard sheets, a busy man. Kramer continued to pluck weeds. Apart from the guards and other day-release prisoners, there were occasional tourists in this area of the park, office workers enjoying the sun. Coins of sunlight speckling the ground; damp earthen odours and the snicker of lawn sprinklers.

'Tremayne's facing jail time for a Ponzi scheme,' said Kramer softly. 'His partner is already inside. Kyle Roden.'

Wyatt understood at once. 'Roden told you something.'

'Got it,' Kramer said. He might not have been conversing with anyone. He brushed the soil from his gloves and fished in a pocket for a handkerchief. A man with a mild sniffle.

Wyatt waited. Kramer would tell him without prompting anything he needed to know. He moved a metre to his left. His eyes were restless without appearing so, his face immobile, a man alone with his thoughts. But he'd already isolated the main exit points and was preternaturally aware of the guards and any other men or women in uniform, or with the covert bulge of a weapon under their clothing. The morning was crisp and peaceful. The other day-release men continued to dig and fork and scrape.

'When things went pear-shaped for Tremayne and Roden, they started stashing money away. Roden's went on fines and legal costs, but he reckons Tremayne's salted away close to a million in liquid assets. He intends to skip the country when things get too hot.'

That was the job. Relieve Tremayne of his million. Wyatt said nothing, his broad hands and sinewy forearms holding the clipboard as he walked a short distance, crouched to sight along a path between garden beds, got to his feet again and contrived to come closer to Sam Kramer.

Then he murmured, 'A million. Bulky.'

'A mix of cash and jewellery or bearer bonds, probably. He can't risk paper or electronic records. The police are looking at him; failed investors, the SIPC.'

The Securities and Investments Probity Commission. Pretty much a toothless tiger, but sometimes it chased blatant Ponzi-scheme chancers like Tremayne and Roden through the courts. Wyatt said, 'Does Roden know where Tremayne's got the money?'

'No. Tremayne's been raided a couple of times, files seized, that kind of thing, no mention of money, so I'd say it's with a friend or in a lockup somewhere. He's smart, mate. Slippery. So far, he's run rings around anyone who's tried to bring him down.'

'Married?'

Kramer nodded. 'They would have looked at her with a fine-tooth comb, too.'

'Friends? Family?'

'Same treatment, what's left of them. He's a bit on the nose.'

Wyatt began a familiar process, imagining himself inside the skin of someone else. Tremayne would have known he'd be raided, that he was vulnerable to search warrants, that his phone calls were monitored, his movements shadowed, his receipts double-checked.

Was there someone he trusted?

One aspect of the story Wyatt didn't like: that Sam's source was Tremayne's business partner. He'd gone to jail; Tremayne hadn't. He'd be resentful. He'd want to fuck up Tremayne's plans. So who else had he told?

'Roden,' Wyatt said.

'I know what you're thinking,' Kramer said. 'I think he's reliable. I've been protecting him, mate. Taken him under my wing. He's a sad fuck, doesn't mix with anyone else.'

Wyatt glanced covertly at the other day-release prisoners. The young guy was still beavering away with a trowel. The stocky man stretched the kinks in his spine. 'Why do you think he told you about Tremayne's money?'

'Good question. Idle chat, partly. But I think he kind of hopes I'll act on the information. He's convinced Tremayne's slippery enough to get off scot free.'

It was then that the guards cast Wyatt more than the occasional look. He said nothing more but, giving the appearance of finishing with the current aspect of his clipboard job, moved away. Behind him, Sam Kramer muttered, 'Tight window, mate. Tremayne's likely to face a committal hearing sometime soon.'

AGAIN CHECKING FOR GLANCES that seemed to avoid him, or lingered too long, Wyatt headed along a side path to a toilet block. No one in the men's stalls or at the urinals. He stripped off the jacket and shoved it and the clipboard into a trash bin; dampened half-a-dozen paper handtowels and stuffed them on top. Then, pulling a khaki towelling hat over his skull, he slipped on a pair of sunnies and headed for the exit.

A prison guard and the sweet-faced day-release prisoner were in his way. There was a little dance of precedence before Wyatt stepped aside to let them in. As he walked away one man was saying, 'Make it snappy.'

The other replied, 'Prison food, mate. Fucks up your guts.'

9

CARL AYLIFFE—SIX MONTHS FOR minor but repeat possession and distribution offences—kept his eyes closed, head resting on the window. The Correctional Services people-mover crawling back through the western suburbs' peak-hour traffic. His limbs ached. He was deeply fatigued: the tiredness of physical labour and watching Sam Kramer constantly without attracting attention to himself. What Kramer said and did. His interactions with clipboard guy. A close shave, encountering clipboard guy in the toilet block. Curious, too: he'd completely changed his appearance. Something to tell Brad when he got back.

The people-mover hit a speed bump hard, the driver getting his kicks. Ayliffe's head thumped the glass. Kramer, seated one row ahead, turned around and locked eyes with him. Ayliffe shrugged, a way of saying, 'Yeah, the guy's a prick but what can you do?' He closed his eyes again, heart beating a little faster. He didn't want Kramer to give him another thought, didn't want Kramer thinking back on his day of weed pulling and deciding his tete-a-tete with clipboard guy had been noticed.

A guy with a clipboard; a cyclist adjusting his bike chain in The Rocks earlier in the month. Ayliffe was pretty sure it was the same man: tall, contained, but a sense of coiled energy under the stillness. And the same choreography of approach, retreat, approach, retreat, as if he and Kramer merely happened to share the same general space for a short while and otherwise had no connection with each other. Ayliffe was certain they'd talked today—not that he'd heard voices, only noticed an ear inclined here, a jaw working there. Kramer the soft, greying, white-collar crim, clipboard guy a slab of lean muscle; the eyes, what could be seen of them, fathomless.

As soon as he got off the bus, Ayliffe showered, changed into grub-time jeans and a T-shirt, and headed for the library.

Brad Salter was there. He'd cleared the room and fronted up to Ayliffe with his bulky chest and jaw wanting answers.

'Well?'

Ayliffe described the day.

'What did they talk about?'

'I couldn't hear. And they might not've talked.'

'Describe him.'

Ayliffe described the man, the clipboard outfit, the costume change, and saw Brad chew his bottom lip, an oddly defenceless tic on a guy you'd want on your side if you were a soft kid incarcerated with hard men.

AFTER TELLING AYLIFFE TO get lost, Bradley Salter took out the iPhone and installed the sim card, checked that the phone was on silent, and texted Nick Lazar: *call*.

Did some thinking as he waited. To his knowledge, no man fitting the description given by Carl had ever visited Kramer in jail. Probably wary of appearing on CCTV or showing ID. But

Kramer was a crook. He was up to something. Not a prison break—he was low security, due for release at the end of the year. Planning a job? Which Nick's going to hijack?

The phone vibrated. 'Yo,' Salter said.

'What's up?' Lazar sounded put out.

'What do you mean, what's up? Obviously I want to know if you managed to tail the guy today.'

A long silence, then Lazar said, 'Look, you did what I asked, time and date and place. The rest needn't concern you.'

Salter ground his teeth. But that was a *tone* he'd read in Lazar's voice. He relaxed his jaw. 'Didn't pan out, did it? What, you slept in? Got a puncture?'

Another silence.

Salter said, 'He gave you the slip.'

Silence. Then: 'Something like that.'

'Did he spot you there? When he was leaving?'

'Don't think so. He just seemed to disappear.'

This was good—keep him talking, learn something. 'I'd say he's a pro. Evasion tactics.'

Lazar grunted.

'Who is he? Who is he to Kramer?'

'Look, just keep me informed, okay?'

'There might not be any more information, Laz.'

Lazar spat back: 'And there might not be the balance of your five grand.'

For the next couple of minutes, they went back and forth like a baseline rally in a game of tennis, until Salter knew a little more—a name, Wyatt, and what Wyatt was doing for Kramer—and he'd extracted promise of more dough. Just as he was concealing the phone again, the six-thirty bell sounded. He sauntered through to the dining room. Almost sat with Sam Kramer. Told himself not to be a dickhead.

45

Carl Ayliffe wandered through to the rec room after dinner, watched the news, took a chess lesson from an old guy in for embezzlement. Now that Brad Salter had his back, he could do what he liked.

Then there was a shift in the atmosphere, the hubbub fading into expectant silence. He looked up. A cockatoo near the rec room entrance was waving his arm and hissing a warning: screws on way. A moment later they were there, zeroing in on Ayliffe.

He stared down at the chessboard like a kid trying to be invisible. It didn't work: the screws loomed, and one of them said, 'Visitor, Carl. *Important* visitor.'

That's right, shout it out to the world. He looked up. 'Me, boss?'

'On your feet.'

One on each side of him, escorting him across the rec room and into the corridor that led to the admin block. The word 'dog' floated in the air behind him.

He was shown into an interview room, empty but for a chair on either side of a small table and a man, middle-aged, wearing a creased Peter Jackson suit over a wrinkled shirt. The man stood, stuck out his hand, said his name was Detective Sergeant Greg Muecke. Polite, grave. Not respectful, of course; but not aggressive or contemptuous, either, which was how Ayliffe was normally treated by the cops.

'Water? Juice?'

'I'm good.'

'Please sit.'

And when they were looking at each other across the table, Muecke said with an empty smile, 'You're a freshie here, right, Carl?'

Where was this going? 'Yes, boss.'

Muecke glanced at a file. 'Due for release by the end of the year?'

'Yes, boss.'

'They treating you all right?'

Was this about Brad Salter taking him under his wing? 'Yes, boss.'

'Comfortable? Your slot okay?'

Ayliffe shrugged. 'A cell's a cell, boss.' At least he wasn't sharing. 'No offence, boss, but am I in trouble?'

Muecke shook his head. 'Perish the thought.'

That did nothing to ease Ayliffe's mind. 'I never did nothing.'

Muecke kept his neutral face on. 'Sam Kramer.'

Now Ayliffe was frightened. 'Who?'

Muecke's fingers clamped around Ayliffe's forearm. 'Carl, do us both a favour. I don't want "no comment", I don't want "don't know the name", I don't want "can't remember what happened today".'

'Today...?'

'Today.' Muecke remained composed but for a faint tightening of his face. 'Today you were in Centennial Park, pulling up weeds. I need you to tell me everything that happened. Who was there, what was said, what was done. In particular, I want to know about the man Mr Kramer was talking to.'

Ayliffe went colder still. 'You were there?'

Muecke ignored that. 'What do you remember? Anything at all. Anything that was said to, or by, Mr Kramer.'

'I wasn't the only one pulling weeds. And there were like these screws there, I mean, correctional officers.'

'I'll speak to them in due course. It's your input I want at the moment.'

So Ayliffe told Muecke about the man with the clipboard, the impression that he'd listened to Sam Kramer and maybe asked a couple of questions, and how he'd altered his appearance afterwards.

47

Muecke asked questions, casting them in different ways, for another thirty minutes before Ayliffe was escorted back to the rec room. The atmosphere was hushed, prickly and dangerous, no one meeting his gaze. He hurried to his slot to read a book and go back to being invisible.

Just before lights out, Sam Kramer filled his doorway, a couple of hard men behind him. The corridor silent, no sign of any screws. Kramer saying expansively, 'Mate!' Not meaning it.

10

After the prison interview, Muecke returned to the Property Crimes squad room at police HQ in Parramatta. Sam Henderson, from Robbery, was waiting for him. He wasn't surprised. Property detectives often liaised with Robbery and Serious Crime, both squads coming under the umbrella of Serious Crime Command.

Henderson barely gave Muecke time to enter the room. 'Kid give you anything?'

'Not to speak of,' Muecke said. He draped his jacket over the back of his chair.

Henderson shook his head. 'Balls-up from beginning to end.'

He was a fast-track hotshot, a science graduate in a flash suit with expensively clipped blond hair and a sense of entitlement. Along with that went impatience and barely veiled contempt for old-schoolers like Muecke, his senior in rank.

'You win some, you lose some,' Muecke said.

Henderson curled his lip. 'Well, what *did* you learn?'

Using his flattest voice, Muecke relayed Carl Ayliffe's

impressions of the man who'd apparently conversed with Sam Kramer.

'So, nothing new then.'

Nothing new? A guy who was super careful talking to another just like him, thought Muecke.

'For all we know, he *was* a council worker,' said Henderson, disdainful, 'and they were discussing hardy perennials.'

Muecke shook his head. 'I checked.'

'If you hadn't lost him…'

If I'd had more officers to shadow him, Muecke thought. If I'd had more cooperation from the Robbers, rather than this ongoing fucking pissing contest.

'Twice you've lost him now,' Henderson said, satisfied with himself but not the world at large.

Not true. The Art Gallery of New South Wales operation had been a success in that Muecke's overstretched team had tracked the man to an address in Coogee, and from there to a seafront bistro. Except that something or someone had spooked him and he'd vanished. Walked away from his car and his flat.

Nothing had spooked him today, however. Muecke had been extremely cautious about that.

'What now?' Henderson said, his tone freighted with meaning: *Any plan of yours is unlikely to cover us in glory.*

'Lend me a few more bodies and we'll saturate the area next time.'

Henderson tipped back his head and looked down his nose: a first-rate-mind-at-work pose. 'That's all you've got?' Then he was gone.

Muecke collapsed into his swivel chair and fired up his computer, anxious to do some work. In part, it was a waiting game now. Wait for Kramer and Warner—if that was his name—to make contact again. Wait for rumours to trickle upwards in the

Watervale prison population—which could be sooner rather than later. Prison rumours spread like small-town gossip.

The other part was footwork, phone calls and emails. Operation Cirrus had been formed a year ago, after Muecke had spotted similarities in a string of high-end domestic break-ins. On two occasions the thief had bailed up the occupants, who described him as tall, athletic, quiet, composed, efficient, gravely menacing. If the same man was behind the other robberies, his haul included coin and stamp collections, rare watches, one guy's collection of Kellyana, and, most recently, a pair of rare five-dollar banknotes.

Muecke had been tapping into his network of contacts for some time. Patrol cops, security guards, pawnshop owners, bouncers, taxi drivers, small-time break-and-enter merchants, fences. As usual, the rumours trickling in were contradictory. The robberies were the work of one thief; they were the work of two or three, depending on their particular skills. The thief was local; the thief flew in from another state, pulled the robbery, flew out again. The thefts were solo; they were the work of small teams; they were random; they were brokered and bankrolled.

But it all added up to something, and two names cropped up more than once: Warner and Kramer. Those names were also disputed. There *used* to be a thief named Warner. And Kramer wasn't known for arranging the theft of rare coins and stamps. He'd gone to jail for receiving and distributing nearly two million bucks' worth of cigarettes stolen from a Smithfield warehouse.

An enigma, Kramer. Well spoken, university educated, grandfatherly. North Shore upbringing, but rumoured to have taken part in, or at least organised, a number of armed hold-ups of banks and security vans in the late 1990s. Genial most of the time, with a volcanic temper a bit of the time.

If he had a man on the outside pulling robberies for him, how did they communicate? And so Muecke and his team had checked the prison's visiting-day logs and calls in and out. Nothing. Then they'd watched Kramer's family—the loser son, the crippled wife, the carer daughter. Where they went, who visited them, phone calls, bank transactions.

And that had given them the Art Gallery of New South Wales encounter, an almost-conversation involving wife and daughter and a stranger in front of a landscape painting. A stranger who seemed to take evasive tactics on his way home. And who then disappeared. From the city, for all Muecke knew.

It hadn't been until he'd gone back over the surveillance photos and gallery CCTV footage that he'd understood one aspect of the communication process: Phoebe Kramer and the man from Coogee had been carrying similar daypacks.

Muecke had sent Centennial Park surveillance photos to all of his contacts before interviewing Ayliffe in Watervale. Now, he saw, he had a result: an email from a Wollongong fence named Hartzer. *He calls himself Warner.*

That name again. Muecke swivelled in his chair. He'd shared some information with Sam Henderson and his team of Robbers, and might share more as it came in. Or not.

MEANWHILE A HEAP OF other cases needed his attention. The next day found him at a boatshed in Sans Souci for a routine follow-up on behalf of South Australia Police, who were seeking a yacht stolen from the Eyre Peninsula town of Tumby Bay. A messy case; just as well he wasn't required to do more than poke around. The yacht, named *Sandman*, had been owned jointly by a builder named Dirk van Horen and his brother, Albert, who ran a string of motels. Dirk, short of cash after his business went down the tubes, sold his half share to Albert for $45,000. Albert immediately put *Sandman* on the market with an asking price of $250,000, whereupon Dirk and his wife Missy sailed off in it. *Sandman* had been spotted twice since then. First near Lakes Entrance in Victoria and later, displaying storm damage, in the waters off Byron Bay. Now an anonymous call had come in placing the yacht, renamed *Santa Ana*, at Rowntree Marine in Sans Souci. The caller wouldn't give her name.

Muecke parked. Rowntree Marine was a wreck of a place: rusted fuel drums, mildewed coils of rope, the listing ribcages of rotting watercraft. A miasma of bilge water hanging over everything. The only shiny thing here was a glossy black Audi SUV, indicating to Muecke that most of Rowntree Marine's business was transacted under the counter. He felt tired. He didn't care. He did care that the tipoff had been anonymous—more valid, somehow, than simple misidentification by some harbourmaster.

Missy, the thief's wife? In over her head?

He entered the office, a fake log cabin that creaked under his weight. A chipped counter with a young woman behind it, pecking at a keyboard and peering short-sightedly at a dusty screen. A shore-to-ship radio on a bench behind her, nautical charts and an ancient nudie calendar on the walls.

The woman looked up, blinked Muecke into focus. 'Can I help you?'

Muecke showed her his ID. 'If I could have a word with the boss?'

She looked at him helplessly. 'The boss…?'

Muecke jerked his head. 'The black Audi—is it yours?'

Her hand flew to a silver talisman on a leather strap around her neck. Silver everywhere, Muecke realised: earrings, finger rings, nose and eyebrow studs, bangles. 'Oh. That's Mr Rowntree's.'

Muecke said patiently, 'May I have a word with him?'

'He went sailing.'

Muecke nodded. 'You do repairs and refits here?'

53

She nodded, on surer ground now. 'We do.'

'A yacht came in, called *Santa Ana*.'

Silence. Something in her body language.

'You called the police?'

She nodded again, wouldn't look at him.

'Why?'

'It doesn't feel right.'

'You're not in any trouble, and I won't reveal your identity to anyone,' Muecke said gently, 'but could you give me some indication…?'

'*You* go and see,' the young woman said, pointing to the shipyard clutter beyond the window. 'Berth two.'

Berth two was a short distance along a pier of crumbling planks. Here Muecke found a careworn yacht sitting free of the water in a hydraulic cradle, two lithe young men scraping the hull, a tubby older man on the cabin roof fiddling with what might have been antennas or windspeed indicators. To Muecke's eye, the trio had barely begun work. Torn sail rigging, the tip of one mast broken away, one porthole missing, a small hole above the waterline.

A woman was watching from a deckchair on the pier— watching the young men, Muecke thought. Wearing a bikini despite the chill in the air. Cigarette in one hand, wine glass in the other. Maybe she thinks she's on the Riviera, thought Muecke. It was a ghastly tableau.

But he went to her first. The men were busy. 'Mrs van Horen?'

She looked at him over dark glasses, all ageing cleavage and scraps of fabric. 'Sorry, who?'

'Is your name Missy van Horen?'

She was astonished. 'Not me. Who're you?'

The pudgy man clambered down to join them, making a meal of it, as if the stationary yacht might pitch him into the sea. Thrust his drinker's nose at Muecke and insisted he wasn't Dirk van

Horen. What gave Muecke that impression? Ownership papers? ID? No problem, back in a tick.

While the man climbed aboard again and ducked below decks, Muecke eyed the young shipyard hands, if that's what they were. Slender, shirtless gods. They continued to scrape barnacles but seemed, from the tension in their rippling torsos, very aware of Muecke. Interesting.

He turned to the woman again. She also seemed tense. 'Storm damage?'

'What? Oh, no, just a refit. We're off to sail around the world.'

'Just the two of you?'

She shook her head. 'Bit beyond us. No, the boys are coming too.'

'They're your sons?'

She wouldn't look at him. 'That's right.'

Muecke glanced at the yacht. 'Much more to do?'

She hesitated. Muecke thought she couldn't very well deny that more work was needed, but she didn't want to nominate a time frame in case the police took the opportunity to do some digging before the *Santa Ana* set sail again. She was saved by her husband, who returned with a crisp set of papers that seemed to confirm the yacht was named *Santa Ana*, owned by Bryce and Felicity Reschke.

'May I see some personal ID?' said Muecke.

The man frowned. 'Not on us, no. It's all at home.'

'Where do you live?'

The man named Reschke gestured. 'Over in Sylvania.'

'You're originally from South Australia?'

'What? No. Is something going on? Should we be worried?'

Muecke left it at that. Things to do, crooks to catch. He'd ask SA Police to send him photographs of Dirk and Missy von Horen—should have asked for that in the first place, on reflection.

11

J ACK T REMAYNE. W YATT DIDN'T want to use a library computer or
link a broadband account to the farmhouse so he bought an iPad
and used the various free Wi-Fi spots in town. He'd park outside
the shire offices with the tablet in his lap, or prop it on one of the
little tables in the café attached to the bookshop.

There was plenty of public-domain material, and it proved to
be a local story, a regional story, like so many other bogus
investment schemes in Australia. Type *Ponzi scheme Geelong* into
Google, and you found out about the sixty-eight million lost by
ordinary investors there. Typing in *Ponzi scheme Newcastle* gave you
Jack Tremayne and Kyle Roden.

Two entries told Wyatt almost all he needed to know about
Tremayne as a person. Twenty years earlier he'd listed himself as
Sir James Tremayne in the Brisbane White Pages, and his third
(current) wife was a hot young blonde named Lynx.

Tremayne the businessman was an accountant who'd been
convicted of fraud in 1998 and declared bankrupt in 2005. Banned

for five years, he seemed to drop out of sight before resurfacing in Newcastle as plain Jack Tremayne in 2013. He quickly made a splash in the old industrial city on the coast north of Sydney. He seemed to arrive out of nowhere and created a front-page buzz: he owned a Bentley, ran a Darby Street eatery and a Honeysuckle Drive club, lived in a sprawling house with harbour views on The Hill, and hosted extravagant cocktail parties with his less flamboyant partner, Kyle Roden. Soon he'd donated a hundred thousand dollars to the children's wing of the hospital, and another fifty thousand to various sporting clubs. Breathless articles referred to him as a man of drive and vision, a financial planner, an investment analyst, a real-estate developer, who saw 'great things' for Newcastle. He was 'getting in on the ground floor'.

Tremayne and Roden began to attract investors, many of them first paying $33,000 for a seven-day seminar on stock market investing and property development. The pair promised returns of up to thirty per cent, and the early investors did achieve high fortnightly earnings. They spread the word among friends, neighbours and work colleagues, who also made money, thus sealing Tremayne's reputation for knowing how to exploit investment loopholes and pick profitable trades using computer analysis. His 'patented' trading software was 'guaranteed' to analyse currencies, securities, options and indices in the local and international markets, and he liked to whisk potential investors through a trading room fitted with a wall of widescreen monitors flickering with marketplace graphs.

No one—not the investors, the bankers, the business and lifestyle reporters—looked beyond the dollar signs to dig into his history. No one discovered that he didn't, as claimed, have an Australian Financial Services licence.

Although Tremayne and Roden attracted a handful of wealthy investors, most were average people who wanted to build on their superannuation or life savings. They were lured by the success stories of those who'd gone before them, and by Tremayne's evident wealth and glib charm.

Not just charm, though. Contempt seemed to work, too. He'd known when to tip his nose in the air and say, 'I can't waste my time if you don't have a quarter mill to invest.' He'd known how to shut down anyone who requested documentation or wanted to see an investment property. 'It's a privilege, investing with me. You don't get to question my acumen.'

Lynx Tremayne was an asset in the image-building side of things. Wyatt googled her: straight-backed, icy cool. She'd have got the meeker clients over the line.

In late 2017, the first cracks appeared. The Tremayne-Roden businesses were rumoured to be in strife. A punter who asked to see her investment property was given a false address. Fortnightly returns stopped landing in bank accounts. When worried investors contacted Tremayne, he talked them down. Mostly, and for a time, it worked. People left their money with him. New investors took the risk.

But then TR Investment Corporation, TR Futures and Tremayne-Roden Capital were wound up. Many investors lost their homes and savings and a retired schoolteacher who'd sunk $850,000 in TR Futures committed suicide. The *Newcastle Herald* ran an investigative piece on Tremayne and Roden, claiming they'd been running a Ponzi scheme, using the investments of new punters to cover the fortnightly returns of original investors until the whole edifice collapsed. Even then they'd continued spending on salaries, office rents, company limousines, car, house, boat and plane loans, credit card debt and cocktail parties.

Oh, and Kyle Roden had paid $480,000 to Madam Carla, an ex-circus acrobat from Byron Bay, for astrological trading tips, aura analysis and general office feng shui advice.

It didn't do him any good. The Securities and Investments Probity Commission recognised him as the weak link. In return for a reduced fine and jail sentence, he'd pleaded guilty to fraud charges and agreed to testify against Tremayne.

Tremayne was made of sterner stuff. He lawyered up and employed delaying and withholding tactics. Said he had no knowledge of various transactions, meetings and paperwork. Held press conferences to express his dismay at his old partner's dishonesty. Claimed, hand over heart, that he, too, was a victim; that meanwhile investors needn't worry: he'd make things right for everybody. Lynx Tremayne got busy on social media, hitting back at her husband's critics.

All the while, the two of them were selling off assets—the Bentley, the yacht, the holiday house. They settled a few small debts and partially settled larger ones, keeping the loudest creditors at bay.

Wyatt thought: what happened to the rest? His exit stash.

He sat back and closed his eyes to rest them. Did the wife know Tremayne was planning to run? Was she going too? Did she know where the money was?

And was it a million? There was plenty of out-of-pocket—plenty of palm-greasing—involved in going into hiding. Twenty bucks wasn't going to do it. A million at least, Wyatt thought. Of course, that was just getting there: Tremayne would doubtless have access to hidden accounts overseas.

Another day passed. Wyatt read on. Investigations into Tremayne and Roden had started at a local level, and Wyatt was betting progress had been slow and piecemeal. Delays, mislaid documents, lack of staff. Not many people were trained in the sophisticated forensic techniques needed to investigate complex financial arrangements. Witnesses and other victims were spread far and wide. Any who'd made a profit early and cashed in would have disputed the claims of those who'd lost everything.

Even when major fraud investigators from Sydney took over they made little headway. A *Sydney Morning Herald* reporter accused the Fraud Squad and the Probity Commission of poor case management and lack of sympathy for the victims: 'By and large they are not greedy silvertails who can afford to lose a few hundred grand but ordinary mums and dads whose modest retirement nest eggs have been lost forever.'

The investigation into Tremayne limped along, which further incensed the reporter:

> The liquidator of TR Wealth Management and TR Blue Chips has demonstrated conclusively that both firms failed to maintain accounts, employ staff, hold assets or conduct business of any kind. The public is entitled to know if the Fraud Squad and the Probity Commission do in fact have a threshold for taking action. It appears to be so high as to be undetectable.

The Probity Commission stirred. It charged Tremayne with operating without a Financial Services licence ('Like hitting him across the face with a damp tissue,' the reporter said) and seized his passport.

Tremayne continued to duck and weave. With what Wyatt considered to be a fair amount of chutzpah, he told his investors their money was held in a blind trust in Panama that only he could access. First, though, he needed them to help him get his passport back, pay his legal bills, withdraw all allegations against him and agree to a settlement of sixty-five cents in the dollar.

When that was leaked, Tremayne's health took a downturn. He confessed that he was suffering from depression and anxiety, and said he was under the care of a psychiatrist who considered him unfit to be interviewed, let alone stand trial.

That was two weeks ago. Since then a TV game-show host had been accused of sexual assault by several women, a One Nation party member had defected to the Nationals and two ferries had collided near the Sydney Harbour Bridge. Tremayne faded from public consciousness.

A good time for him to run, Wyatt thought. On a Sunday in May, he packed a bag and headed north to Newcastle.

12

THERE WAS A TIME when Wyatt had used hotels and motels for work. But with CCTV cameras proliferating in carparks, doorways, lobbies, lifts and hallways, there was a growing risk that his face would be linked to a major robbery or a death one day. That doormen and receptionists would remember him if the police came around asking questions.

Not that he could ever pass entirely unnoticed, but there were ways to reduce the possibility. He often used caravan parks. A cabin or onsite van a safe distance from a job. Places full of grey nomads touring the country, holidaying families, the temporary homeless, seasonal and short-term contract workers and men or women, like Wyatt, with no apparent ties, history or future. People who might appear one day, bother no one, and move on again sometime later, the barest physical or memory trace left behind.

Other times Wyatt used an Airbnb account in the name of Wreidt. He'd had to supply a photograph, but he ensured his online photo was fuzzy and unmemorable: neatly combed hair, heavy-rimmed glasses. Often there was no one to see his real face anyway. He tended to book self-contained places not attached to the owner's house and arrive late, so that a key or a keypad code would be left out for him. Establishing an Airbnb history had been easy—he rented several places for two-, three- and five-day stays, left them clean and tidy, and wrote glowing reviews. Soon Mr Wreidt was glowingly reviewed in turn.

It shouldn't take more than a week to locate and steal Jack Tremayne's running-away money. Wyatt booked a seven-day stay in a cottage behind an old house in Anna Bay, north-east of Newcastle. The owner was expecting a birdwatcher with a special interest in marine birdlife. Wyatt arrived with his neat hair, glasses and disarming smile, together with a long-peaked cap, clip-on sunglasses, a camera case and a jacket and trousers stitched about with useful flaps and pockets. He was an everyday enthusiast, with nothing interesting to say about the world or the weather: that was all that registered with the owner. Wyatt was driving a white Toyota Corolla with a fake Hertz rental sticker on the rear window for this job, and there was no reason to suppose his camera case contained tracking devices rather than lenses.

On Monday morning he drove the fifty kilometres down to Newcastle, removed his hat, swapped his outdoorsy jacket for a cotton pullover and poked about by car and on foot. As much as he ever liked a place, Wyatt found himself drawn to the region close to the harbour and the old mercantile hub. Palm trees, Norfolk Island pines, small warehouses transformed into galleries, very little in the way of billboard advertising. He walked along the harbour promenade, ferries, ships, silos and Stockton on one side, stretches of open areas, hotels and eateries on the other. People strolled, jogged, sat in the sun. The air was scented mostly by the sea.

Then he poked about The Hill—street layout, getaway routes—before cruising past Jack Tremayne's house. A kilometre from the business district, it was a concrete and glass slab fronting King Edward Park and otherwise lacking anything to draw the eye. As if conscious of that, someone had stuck a palm tree and a fountain in the stretch of terraced lawn between the house and the street. There was a curving driveway lined with low shrubs. A double garage at the side of the house, open to show a black BMW SUV and a black Audi TT. His and hers, Wyatt thought.

He parked in the next side street and strolled around the block. Open street access to the front of the house, but a tall hedge dividing it from the houses on either side and at the rear. He crossed the road to explore the park. Headed back up the slope just as a white Caprice pulled away from the kerb and a silver Camry took its place. Continual vigilance was built into him, like strapping a watch onto his wrist every morning. He thought at once of surveillance, a changing of the guard. He strolled past the Camry, taking in short haircuts, collars and ties. One man even had a lanyard around his neck. Plainclothes police? Probity Commission?

He tingled, a faint synaptic snap deep inside. He wasn't a thrill-seeker—in fact he'd walk away from a job if it didn't look or feel safe. His main emotion was the wariness of long habit. But he tingled to think that other players were in this game. So long as they didn't see him. And so long as Tremayne knew they were there. It might spur him to run—and that's when Wyatt would strike.

He returned to his car, made another quick tour of the suburb, used a public men's room on the foreshore, then returned to The Hill and parked where he could watch both the house and the people watching it. He'd been in this kind of situation before, not knowing if he'd be tailing anyone, or for how long, but he was prepared to wait: emptied bladder and bowels, food, water, a bottle to piss in if the wait was prolonged. A full tank of petrol. A towelling hat, a baseball cap, two pairs of shades—aviators and wraparound—so he could vary his silhouette from time to time if watchful eyes were checking rear-view mirrors.

Three hours later the Audi reversed onto the street with a woman at the wheel. Wyatt's target was Tremayne. But he was said to be reclusive, and there'd been no other action, so Wyatt started his engine. Waited to see what the silver Camry would do before he pulled out to follow.

The Camry stayed put. Wyatt waited for half a minute more, aware there might be surveillance vehicles he hadn't spotted, but there was no further movement in the street. He put the car in gear and pulled out.

The Audi was easy to follow. But he remained alert for late-appearing surveillance vehicles behind or in front of it or keeping pace on the side streets. Nothing. The wife was of no interest to anyone but Wyatt just then. He trailed her for half an hour, always keeping at least two vehicles between his car and hers, staying as much as possible in her blind spot. If she ever drifted into the overtaking lane he remained where he was, or overtook some time later. He doubted she was aware of him, but thirty minutes is a long time to stick with someone. He varied the hat and glasses combination three times as he tracked her.

She took him to a resort motel outside Wyong. Wyatt slowed and sailed past as the Audi turned into the carpark, then he parked the Corolla at a nearby golf club. He changed his headgear again and hurried back on foot, lucky that a bus was pulling away from a stop outside the motel so his running along the footpath aroused no interest.

He missed the bus, pantomimed the reaction of a man

frustrated with timetables and hard-line bus drivers and glanced toward the motel lobby. Lynx Tremayne, a tall woman wearing a plain black skirt and a white top, hair in a bun, carrying a briefcase, was strolling in as if she had business there. But she cast a casual glance at a parked bronze Lexus as she entered.

The man who emerged from the Lexus a couple of minutes later was Jack Tremayne's lawyer.

13

LYNX TREMAYNE PROPPED HERSELF on one elbow and ran her gaze along Will DeLacey's naked body. She'd rearranged her features into what she imagined was post-coital softness—she'd been acting all her life, so she was pretty confident she had it right. Will DeLacey gazed back at her with what she supposed was love now that the lust was sated. She didn't really do love; but Will told her he loved her fairly frequently. Like all lawyers he was an accomplished liar, but she believed he was telling her the truth about that at least. Not that she cared, but it might come in useful down the track. And he was…okay. Too pale, body hair too dark, no hard planes. Good-looking once but losing it rapidly. The sex was fine, and she liked the sense of transgression. Boredom and restlessness, they had always bothered her.

'Things any better with Jack?' he said.

His voice was a nice bass rumble. She liked that about him.

'No,' she said, shaking her head, trailing her hair over his cock.

'Oh, God,' he said.

She did it again but absently, gazing out at the golf course. Their motel suite overlooked green slopes dotted with strange pastelly men and women chasing balls around and cheating on their scores.

Will coughed to recover and said, 'He'll be called before the commission soon, darling.'

Jesus, really? She was no one's darling. William DeLacey, flat on his back, was suddenly too close, too pungently damp and sticky, and Lynx wanted sharply to be alone. Resented his need for reassurance that she desired him physically and emotionally. That she'd make a life with him when Jack got hauled off to jail.

She nodded. 'He's getting antsy.'

William shrugged. 'He knows he's looking at jail time.'

Lynx Tremayne stroked him from throat to navel. She could see in his eyes that despite the turn in the conversation, he wanted her fingers to stray lower. He was entirely predictable, where Jack wasn't. Or rather, her husband could be predicted always to have some means of escape up his sleeve, no matter what kind of mess he'd got himself into.

Like his current mess, which was making him edgy, but with a submerged light in his eyes. 'You'll stick with me, right, babe?' he'd asked that very morning. Not seeking confirmation, exactly; more like a warning.

She didn't know how she'd survive if he was declared bankrupt, stripped of what remained of their joint assets and sent to jail. Certainly there was no spare cash around, or the authorities would have found it in one of their raids.

It had been like attracted to like when she met him. Like most escort services, hers catered to convention hacks—husbands and fathers who were variously shy, drunk, impotent, thankful, underappreciated and aggrieved. Jack Tremayne had been different. He hadn't pretended he was on a real date with her; and he'd made her laugh, which always counts for a lot. And it wasn't until the second or third time with him that he told her she was beautiful and sexy, and even then he said it offhandedly, like it was too obvious to bother saying. He was no movie star, but his looks had grown on her. Nothing was sacred to him, except money. And he had a slippery mind. So—they were evenly matched.

Except there was a good chance he was going to jail, and their reputations were in tatters and she'd lost most of her friends, and that was only the beginning.

William broke into her thoughts. 'I have a meeting with him tomorrow—tactics if we go to court, which silk to engage—but it's going to feel strange...'

Lynx leaned to tug on his chest hairs with her lips. 'Don't for God's sake say anything about me. He's pretty perceptive.'

'Shit yeah. It's like I can feel him probing around in my brain sometimes.'

Lynx laughed, a rich, natural chortle. 'Exactly.'

She noted with satisfaction the wince of jealousy on William's face. It suited her to keep him a little off-kilter. But, God his mind was working slowly today. The sex, she supposed. What she wanted was for him to start wondering why Jack wasn't more nervous. What Jack might have in mind. Where his *hidden* assets were, if he had any.

And if Jack had his own personal—solo—escape clause.

Other things being equal, she'd always choose Jack ahead of William. So long as Jack could stay out of jail and keep making money. But they were flat broke now, and even if he was only locked up for a short time, they'd be starting all over again. At her age? No thanks.

If only Will would start using his brain and stop thinking like a small-town solicitor. 'If Jack's charged and prosecuted, he'll need money.'

Will snorted. 'A lot of money.'

She coaxed up some tears. 'I feel so let down, you know?'

'Oh, babe.'

And he was clasping her to him, pressing her face into his shoulder. She badly wanted a shower and time to herself. But she still needed to get his thinking on track.

Pulling free, she added, 'He's ruined my good name. My friends won't talk to me. We look like losing the house. Going forward, life doesn't bear thinking about.'

Stung, William said, 'Lynx, I keep telling you—I'll look after you.'

'But what if I'm liable for his debts?' Dimpling a breast with her forefinger, she said, 'What if *I* go to jail?'

DeLacey pulled her down again. His breath gusted in her face: 'You won't. I'll make sure of it.'

Lynx Tremayne doubted that. Anyway, she needed him scared, not heroic. 'Will, you don't think there's a chance *you'll* go to jail, do you? Ever get too creative with the paperwork? Sign things you shouldn't have?'

A great run of denials streamed from his mouth—well, he *was* a lawyer—but she could see from the trace of panic in his eyes that he'd been fudging things all his life without affecting his sense of himself as a decent person. If there'd been a warning voice in the back of his head, he'd ignored it. Until now. She pressed her advantage.

'What I'd really like is if you could have another look at the paperwork. Hidden assets. Property we needn't let the authorities know about. And an indication of what Jack's up to.' She ground against him. 'You and I have the *love* to make a life together but think how much better it would be with the money to back it up.'

14

WYATT SLIPPED INTO THE carpark and placed a tracking device on the Audi, then another on the Lexus. He waited. He hadn't looked hard at William DeLacey yet, but he recognised him from the Tremayne research: news photographs of the solicitor protesting the heavy-handed tactics of the Probity Commission in seizing files related to the Tremayne-Roden group of companies. But if he was Lynx Tremayne's lover...

Ninety minutes later, Wyatt tracked DeLacey's Lexus back to Newcastle. It turned into the carpark at the side of a two-storey building near Lee Wharf and he drove past, parked near Throsby Wharf and walked back. Corris House, according to a discreet sign between a couple of low shrubs. Home to an accountant, a financial services firm and Anderson, Grieve and Mott, lawyers. Wyatt returned to the car and watched the building. A small but busy regional city business premises. Harbour views and a few well-heeled clients, judging by the car and foot traffic. For long periods there was no activity at all.

He waited, and he thought. In his line of work, inference was as necessary as direct observation. He had witnessed a tryst between the wife and the lawyer of a man reputedly about to flee Australia with a nest egg worth a million dollars. What did some random information and a few vague suppositions add up to in this case? Wyatt let his mind circle slowly outwards, making possible, probable and likely connections and seeing how they stacked up against each other. Maybe a picture would emerge. If not, he'd observe and think and learn some more.

By late afternoon he decided he'd learnt all he was going to by sitting there. He left the harbour and went to the municipal library wearing his birdwatcher rig. Head down to avoid CCTV, he logged on to a computer for thirty minutes. William DeLacey was forty-five, a Mount Isa miner's son. He studied law at Bond University and clerked with a supreme court judge. Poor and clever, thought Wyatt. But not ambitious? DeLacey had worked at two suburban Sydney firms, commercial law, before moving to a house in the Newcastle suburb of Tighes Hill with his wife, a primary school teacher who'd wanted to live closer to her ailing parents. One child, Down Syndrome. Joined Anderson, Grieve and Mott in 2015. Yet to be made partner. One mismanagement lawsuit, settled out of court. Appeared to have the backing of his firm, but the lawsuit, the Probity Commission raid and the headlines would take a toll, Wyatt thought.

Was he ripe for helping Tremayne escape? Or helping the wife move against her husband? Was he worried he'd go to jail alongside his client? Did he intend to leave his child and his mousy wife for Lynx Tremayne? Did they know about the money?

The wife and the lawyer were definitely players. But until he'd gathered more facts, there was little more that Wyatt could do.

He bought Thai takeaway and returned to his Airbnb cottage to unwind. It didn't work. He was in the middle of a job that didn't have shape yet. After eating, he stalked about the cottage, trying to fit the facts and suppositions together. All that did was reveal more gaps and widen existing ones.

Mid-evening, he switched on the TV. Four men with code readers, earpieces and balaclavas, another watching split-screen images on a laptop: a gang, he realised, executing a bank heist. He felt depressed. The story was inane, the gang dynamics ridiculous, the gadgetry mostly invented and the character roles unprofessional. But more than anything, Wyatt was reminded that the technical world was passing him by. He could barely outwit the alarm system in a suburban house these days.

He switched channels and watched an apparently mediaeval world in which humans of a modern sensibility spoke like seers. Their queen was named Calisi, which Wyatt had thought was a control virus for rabbits. He supposed adults wrote this kind of thing and perhaps even watched it, but it wasn't anything he needed to know about. He went to bed thinking about Jack Tremayne's money.

ON TUESDAY MORNING A message from Phoebe Kramer was waiting. Her father had been accused of orchestrating the assault of another inmate. His day-release privileges had been revoked. *And he says be careful, something's up, he was being monitored.*

Wyatt messaged back—*thanks*—and headed to Newcastle airport, where he hired a Hyundai and drove it to The Hill. Cruised past Tremayne's house. No black Audi, no black BMW, and no white Caprice or silver Camry. He returned mid-afternoon. Both cars were there—and Tremayne's BMW reversing from the driveway. Wyatt wasn't superstitious about luck or chance, but knew them as factors in any job. He accepted his good fortune and steered into a side street long enough to let a white Falcon pull out and follow the BMW before he tailed both cars down to the harbour. Tremayne parked at his lawyer's building. The white Falcon parked short of it. Wyatt drifted on past and into a spot vacated by a Kombi van. He adjusted his mirror and waited. An hour went by.

But he was curious about the Falcon. He got out, strolled along the footpath, just some guy out for a walk, perhaps intending to go as far as the lighthouse or Nobbys Beach. Two heads on board, a man and a woman, conservatively dressed, sunglasses.

Wyatt walked on. Federal police, he thought, Fraud Squad or Probity Commission investigators. At least three teams on rotation. Costly. Maybe they suspected Tremayne was about to run, or were interested in who he was meeting as they fine-tuned the charges against him.

He returned to his car and waited behind the wheel with the rear-view mirror angled to show the lawyer's driveway. Thirty minutes later Tremayne's car emerged. Wyatt watched for the Falcon to slip into traffic behind it before joining the tail. Tremayne drove a short distance and pulled over on Hannell Street. The Falcon continued past him until it was a dot in the distance. Wyatt hung back briefly. Accelerated again, past the BMW. A quick glance told him that Tremayne was just sitting there at the wheel, looking out.

Looking at the yacht club.

Wyatt pulled in a hundred metres beyond the BMW and watched it through his mirrors. No sign of other surveillance vehicles. What was Tremayne doing? He'd sold his yacht. Did he own another? Maybe the lawyer owned one and was keeping the money on it?

Tremayne pulled out eventually, Wyatt let three cars go by before following. Left into Greenway, left again and back to the man's house. A white Range Rover was in the driveway this time. Tremayne parked in the street.

Wyatt drove past the house and into a side street. He locked the car at the kerb, strolled around the block, then down across the park and back again. Eventually evening drew in; he returned to his car by way of the footpath fronting Tremayne's house. No sign of surveillance, no occupied cars, no vans with generic business stencils scrolled along the sides. That didn't mean the house wasn't being watched, though. Within a few seconds he'd spotted movement in the window of a first-floor flat at the corner of the next side street. No lights on, curtains drawn but for a slight gap, and, as he strolled to his car, a sense of a face peering out and vanishing again.

There was no covert way of placing tracking devices on the BMW or the Range Rover. He needed a distraction. Making a fast, crouched run in the murky shadows, he entered the carpark at the rear of the flats and rocked on the wheel arches of four cars until alarms blared in two of them. Then along the street, away from Tremayne's driveway, to a sprawling Federation house at the end. No lights, no vehicles. A brick through a window proved that the alarm had been set.

Finally, he trotted along parallel streets until he was at the other end of Tremayne's avenue, where he set off another car alarm.

People emerged from their houses. Wyatt joined them in milling about, first slipping on the heavy-rimmed glasses, knowing they made him look concerned and harmless. Two people here, three or four there, a larger clump near the flats. He joined an elderly woman who was standing near Tremayne's driveway entrance. Folded his arms, looked baffled, made small talk about the state of the world.

In the confusion, all eyes on the apparent seat of the drama further along the street, he fastened tracking devices to the Range Rover and Tremayne's BMW. The woman, alerted by movement in the corner of her eye, gave him a sharp glance.

He turned his movements into a patting of his pockets. 'Must've left my phone indoors.'

Reassured, she said, 'Someone's bound to have called the police by now.'

Wyatt waited a while longer then headed towards the people gathered at the flats. He sensed that she'd follow him, a solid, reassuring presence. She recognised some of her neighbours now, which further reassured her, and Wyatt was able to slip away.

WYATT DROVE DOWN TO the coast road and cruised for an hour. Tremayne's street was quiet when he returned, few lights showing, no one strolling or standing expectantly at windows. He parked a block from Tremayne's house and settled in to watch. Early evening his patience was rewarded when the Range Rover reversed out of Tremayne's driveway and headed down to Memorial Drive, a long strip of sandy beach and rolling surf on his left, lit by the moon.

Not enough traffic to merit using the tracking device. Keeping the Range Rover in view, Wyatt followed it to Merewether Beach, where it signalled right and climbed a short distance up to Frederick Street and a large Federation-era Shingle style house on a double block. It was an imposing two-storey place, pale grey with white trim. Sea views, thought Wyatt. Heritage quality. Worth a few million.

The Range Rover pulled in and parked near the front door. Wyatt parked further along the street and ran back, concealed by hedges, to the letter box. He was in luck; the mail hadn't been collected. He had about ten seconds.

A flyer from a handyman, real estate bumf and supermarket catalogues; and a Red Cross charity drive letter addressed to Mr Mark Impey.

15

'THE IMP'S IN LOVE with you, babe.'

'I know,' Lynx Tremayne said, with the cute rueful smile she was famed for.

'Can't blame him, of course,' Jack Tremayne said, the gallantry reflexive.

She crossed her legs and leaned her breasts forward just slightly as she waited for the inevitable flow of questions. They were in the sitting room, which looked like a corporate foyer with the chrome, leather and glass, and the Antique White walls. But the leather was imported, the Ken Done paintings were genuine and you could buy a car with what they'd spent on the rugs, so fuck you.

'Was he here long before I came home?'

She shrugged. 'A few minutes.'

Lynx Tremayne watched her husband's gaze take in the two wine glasses. 'Uh huh. What did you talk about?'

'The usual. Nervous clients.' She paused. 'I think the strain's getting to him. Maybe if you showed your face a bit more it would—'

'He looked like he'd been caught with his fingers in the jar when I walked in.'

She shrugged to downplay her part in it. Mark Impey had been panting after her for years, too frightened to do anything other than drop in on her a couple of times a week, just happened to be in the area. Finding excuses to stand close, let his hand brush hers or his shoulder her upper arm or breasts. Fifty-three, a little portly; clean and neat and damp and needy. You couldn't imagine him in jeans and a T-shirt—unless both were brand new and ironed. Contradictory, but not in any interesting way: smart enough to withdraw his investments as soon as he'd made a profit, dumb enough to believe Jack was a financial genius.

She wouldn't mind getting close to his money but sex with him would be like fucking a pork sausage, and he'd have no personality that she wouldn't supply.

'He probably didn't want you to think the wrong thing. He showed up thinking you might be home.'

It was tedious. Jack had always known Mark had the hots for her, and always known she wasn't interested, but he liked to needle her. It was what he did, and it had started not long after his economic downturn. If the topic wasn't Mark Impey, it was her Pilates classes, her book group, the money she spent keeping herself looking good, her past life as an escort. Except that wasn't the word he used.

'Where were *you*, by the way?' she said.

He shrugged and poured another slug of scotch into his glass. 'Called in on Will.'

'And?'

'The wheels of the law grind slowly.' He glanced at the ceiling, then back at her with the amused contempt he reserved for the

Fraud Squad and the Probity Commission and their bugging devices.

Understanding, she said, 'I think I left a hose running,' and he followed her out onto the back lawn. Tricky shapes all about, the moon streaming down on date palms and jacarandas. Unless the authorities were crouched in the bushes with parabolic microphones, they were safe. 'What did he say?'

'He's drawn up a shortlist of top barristers for us with the right kind of experience.'

As far as Lynx Tremayne was concerned, there was no longer any 'us'. And she doubted there ever had been from Jack's point of view—or only when it suited him. She gave him her sweetest smile and said, 'The right kind of experience. In financial mismanagement, falsification of records, tax evasion, trading while insolvent, misleading and deceptive conduct and defaulting on loans, you mean?'

'Fuck you.' He paused. 'I was followed again. I'm wondering if they're building up to something.'

He'd dragged her to the window yesterday, pointed to a white Caprice. 'Surveillance.' Since then she'd seen a silver Camry and a white Falcon. It was pretty blatant. And clumsy? Had the plods set off all those alarms this evening?

If so, she doubted it'd been the scarily precise man and woman who'd interrogated her not long after she'd returned from shopping that afternoon. 'I had visitors today.'

Jack narrowed his gaze, as if reading something into the admission; as if he suspected she'd originally decided to keep her mouth shut. 'Go on.'

'Probity Commission, they said.'

'What car?'

'The white Falcon.'

'Describe them.'

She shrugged. 'A man in a suit, a woman in a suit. Very buttoned down.'

'While Mark was here?'

She shook her head. 'Earlier.'

'And?'

'Same as last time. Same questions, different people asking.'

Her husband was sour and suspicious. He had a right to be. His business partner had taken a deal to testify against him; he thought she might, too.

'Details, Lynx, okay?'

'The same dance as before, Jack, *okay*? They took a step in one direction, I took a step in the other. They circled around me, I stood still, smiling politely.'

He was in her face now, a fleck of spit on her cheek. 'Fuck the similes or metaphors or whatever, just give me the gist, all right?'

She said, 'Keep it together.'

'Fuck that.' But he lowered his voice. 'What did they want?'

They'd wanted to know how involved she'd been in his companies, did she remember signing such and such a document, had she in fact seen evidence that her husband was signatory to a blind trust overseas. But to see Jack squirm, to see what he might let slip, she said, 'They think you're lying about your assets.'

He reacted as if he were completely at a loss, making a huge, open-armed gesture. 'What assets? You told them we're skint?'

'I said I didn't know what they were talking about.'

'The dumb wife act. Good on you.'

That got to Lynx a little. Face composed, voice neutral, she said, 'It's true, right, we're existing on our savings?'

Jack screwed a nasty look onto his face. 'Of course it's true, as they well know because they're monitoring our accounts.'

'Yes.' She paused. 'Well, I think you're right. They are building up to something.'

His expression was opaque. 'That's okay. I can hold them off for now.'

She didn't want a blasé Jack, she wanted a panicky one. 'The mortgage is due soon, sweetheart. Legal fees—which will start being astronomical when your case gets to court.'

'When *our* case gets to court.' He stood there brooding. 'Next time those pricks want to talk to you, call Will. You need to avoid self-incrimination. Let him do what he does best, okay?'

What Will DeLacey did best was flick her clit with his tongue. 'I know how to handle pen-pushers, Jack.'

'Just do as I say, Lynx, please,' her husband said, and he turned to re-enter the house.

She trailed him, eyes burning into him as the night deepened behind her.

16

BRAD SALTER, FLAT ON his back in the prison infirmary that Tuesday, a cop on either side of his bed. He tried for cocky.

'If all it takes to be the centre of attention is to fall over, I ought to try it more often.'

The older cop, who'd introduced himself as Detective Sergeant Greg Muecke, gazed at him wearily. 'Corridor CCTV has Sam Kramer and his goons at the door to your cell.'

'Kramer…Kramer…?' said Salter. 'Nope, drawing a blank.'

'Being hit on the head will do that to you,' said the second cop, a young smartarse named Henderson, seated on the other side of Salter's bed. This prick had never been on the end of a kicking that broke teeth and had you pissing blood.

Salter dropped the act. 'I don't know who you are or what you want, but I can't help you.'

Henderson guffawed at that. Leaned in and prodded Salter's bruised thigh. 'What did you do to get up Kramer's nose?'

Salter gasped, went white, and tried to shift away. It was a question he was rapidly tiring of. He'd been asked it by the boss of the prison, the doctor and even the odd screw sidling up to his bed with a sly you-can-trust-me manner.

'I fell over,' he said. 'Got tangled in my own feet.'

Muecke said, 'Fell over on the back of your head, your nose and mouth, your legs, arms, kidneys and coccyx.' He looked tired, and old with it. Sagging features, bristling eyebrows and yellowing teeth.

'It was a bad fall,' Salter said.

His mind was racing, putting things together. He was pretty certain that the older cop was the one who'd grilled Carl Ayliffe. That snippet of information had flashed around the inmate population before lights out. Then Carl had appeared at breakfast the next day with a bruised cheekbone and a shuffling walk— but apparently under Kramer's wing now. Wouldn't look at Salter, wouldn't talk. Stuck close to Kramer and his psycho goons.

Salter had known he'd be next and spent a tense few days until it happened. But it was curious that the cops were interested. Why? Carl couldn't have told them about Nick Lazar, or why he'd been asked to collect information on Kramer—he didn't know.

Muecke got right to it. 'You formed a friendship with an inmate called Carl Ayliffe, correct?'

Salter shrugged. 'Made a lot of friends. I'm a friendly guy.'

'Made a few enemies, too,' Henderson said, his round, unlined face a picture of disparagement.

Muecke flicked the younger cop a look, then swung back to Salter. 'Mr Ayliffe is a trusted prisoner.'

A pause. Salter didn't nibble.

'Day-release privileges.'

Another pause.

'Sam Kramer is likewise privileged.'

83

'But that's likely to change,' Henderson said.

Salter thought, *interesting*. He also thought he'd like to wipe the smirk off Henderson's face. 'So?'

'You are aware of Mr Kramer's reputation, I take it?' Muecke said.

'His reputation?'

'Fingers in many pies.'

'Yeah?'

'Perhaps you ripped him off? Underperformed? Or maybe you're working for one of his rivals?'

'Don't have a clue what you're on about,' Salter said, dropping his head back on the pillow, tired now, aching deep in his bones. Henderson's thigh-poking had set off a new, more acute pain, and the bed was narrow, the mattress cheap and soft.

'I put it to you that the beating you received at the hands of Mr Kramer was related to his extra-curricular activities,' Muecke said.

Salter went 'no comment', as he should have done right from the start.

'Was he dishing out a punishment, or was he after information? Both?'

Oh, most definitely a punishment. And a warning. And aimed at eliciting information. Salter was unconscious before he'd said anything. Had come to in the infirmary, sore all over, soaked in piss.

'Does he think you're a dog?'

'No comment.'

Salter wanted painkillers, but the infirmary staff were going about their business. Muecke and Henderson could be zapping him with cattle prods for all his carers cared.

'What's it going to do to your reputation in here when word gets out we've been to see you?'

Salter reflected that it wouldn't do a whole lot of good. 'No comment.'

'We can see to it that you're protected.'

'No comment.'

17

A COUPLE OF HOURS after the Bradley Salter interrogation, Muecke received a call.

'This is Natalie? You asked me to ring if there was any movement?'

Muecke concentrated fiercely, hunched in his ergonomic office chair. Then, making the connection, he relaxed and began to swing to and fro. 'Rowntree's.'

'I'm really really sorry but I lost your card and Mr Rowntree said not to say anything and I didn't know what to do.'

Muecke said, in the gentle, patient voice he'd sometimes used with his daughters over the years, 'Take a deep breath and tell me what happened.'

'That boat you were interested in.'

He stopped swinging. 'The *Santa Ana*? What about it?'

She sounded ashamed, then indignant. 'It left a few nights ago. They didn't pay for everything.'

'Had they finished the repairs?'

'No.'

I spooked them, thought Muecke. 'Natalie,' he said, 'I could tell you had doubts about those people. So did I. But I'd like to hear your version.'

'Well,' she began, and it poured out of her, how they treated her like she wasn't there, how she was expected to clean up bottles every morning, how she just knew the boys were sleeping with Mrs Reschke, who if you asked her was a bit old to be prancing around topless like that.

Muecke went still. 'Wait—she was sleeping with her sons?'

A snort. 'They're not her sons.'

Shaun Maxstead and Dustin Snell, who'd rolled up at Rowntree's one day, looking for work. They made Natalie nervous, something not right about them, but Mr Rowntree couldn't see it. He was pretty pissed off now, though, the way they'd shot through on him.

When he got off the phone, Muecke ran both names. Maxstead and Snell were marina rats from Cairns, originally. Named but not charged when a coral reef cruise operator was prosecuted for running ice and cocaine to shore from outlying cargo ships. Things must've got too hot for them, Muecke thought, so they headed south.

He checked his email. SA Police still hadn't sent photos of Dirk and Missy van Horen. He sent a reminder, and then a constable was knocking on his door: he was wanted upstairs.

THE ROBBERY AND SERIOUS Crimes inspector gave Muecke a bone-cracking handshake intended to demonstrate his sincerity, before telling him to sit. Sam Henderson was there, looking satisfied, squeezing out a meaningless smile as Muecke caught his eye.

Muecke turned back to the RSC inspector. 'Sir?'

'A heads-up,' the inspector said. Another fast-track graduate, ten years younger than Muecke, but balding. Flushed, as if he spent his lunchtimes celebrating successful raids.

'Okay,' said Muecke, wondering what fresh hell was coming his way.

'I've spoken to your boss. My officers were pleased to work alongside yours in your investigation into Samuel Kramer's suspected ongoing activities, and we appreciate your general input into possibly related matters, but, going forward, my department cannot justify continued time, effort or expenditure on what seems to be, frankly, a wild goose chase.'

He came to the end of this with a briskly indifferent smile. Then Henderson chipped in. 'But you might like to know, with pressure from us the prison will be revoking Kramer's day-release privileges, which will put a spanner in the works if he *is* up to anything.'

Meaning Henderson didn't think it very likely, the smug shit. 'Sir,' Muecke said, hating the tremor in his voice, 'you've just shut down my only chance of finding who he's working with.'

He looked past the inspector's shoulder at the dismal blurred buildings outside. It was like looking into another dimension. He shook himself inwardly to pay attention as the inspector droned on.

'But there are tried and tested channels, Detective Sergeant Muecke. Informants. Receivers of stolen goods. The family's phone and banking records. Meanwhile my squad needs to action inquiries and operations that lead to tangible results.'

'Like arrests,' Henderson said.

The inspector shot him an appraising scowl, then turned back to Muecke. 'Look at it this way: with Kramer restricted now, he's likely to make a mistake or rely overmuch on his people coming to him. Monitor his calls. Watch who visits. That's more likely to lead to a result than trying to locate one person of interest in a city of five million—one who might not exist or is quite innocent.'

He folded his arms. A warning note of authority on his big-boned face. 'Clear, sergeant?'

'Sir.'

'Speak to your inspector. I know if he's anything like me, he's snowed under with reports, leads and case files. New cases coming in all the time. There'll be plenty for you to do.'

Muecke said, 'Sir,' again, not meaning it, and left the room, heading for Property Crimes. His inspector was there, but his door was closed. He knows I was called to the Robbers, he thought, knows I'm disappointed and pissed off. Doesn't want to face me just now.

He swivelled in his chair and eyed the photographs arranged at the edge of his desk. His wife, Meg: absorbed in her arts degree these days, leaving him behind now that the kids were gone. His daughters, one at uni in Melbourne, one on a gap year in London. His dog, dead three months. The dog had loved him unreservedly. Wife and daughters continued to love him, he thought. If not unreservedly.

There were pitfalls in thinking too much. He snapped out of it by attending to emails, then slogged through the printed material scattered over his desk. A health and safety memo, a time-share brochure, a Police Credit Union leaflet. Still the Kramer case crept back in. Henderson's inspector was right: all Muecke had was rumours. Surveillance photos. A mystery man. *Shading*, not hard facts. His own boss was going to pull the plug, too, Muecke could feel his intention seeping under his door and spreading through the squad room. For a moment, he felt a pinch of panic.

He dealt with it. Took himself in hand and decided on a course of action. First, appear to go along with whatever shit had come, would come, his way. Second, keep tabs on Kramer's wife,

89

daughter and son. Third, show the Centennial Park image to a wider range of contacts. Fourth, have another crack at Bradley Salter. And Carl Ayliffe. What could he promise them, though? What clout did he have anymore?

He continued with the paperwork. When the surface gumf had been cleared away, Muecke saw that someone—probably his inspector—had dumped a handful of files on his desk. New and ongoing cases. Jesus, he was tired of life.

He flicked through them. Nothing new: a motor vehicle theft and rebirthing ring in Bankstown; an investigation into a Rural Fire Service probationer who'd been lighting fires near Cessnock; odometer tampering at used car dealerships in the Camden area; an aggravated break-and-enter at a shopping centre in the Hunter region.

No, a couple he didn't know. Strike Force Nimbus, involving Property Crimes and the Marine Area Command, looking into a suspicious fire that had destroyed three luxury cruisers at Morrisons Bay Marina. Strike Force Stratus, involving Property Crimes, the Fraud Squad and Newcastle City Local Area Command, investigating cases of investors lured into paying for non-existent houses, flats and blocks of land in and around Newcastle. Once of his colleagues, a Property Crimes senior sergeant named Brenner, had just returned from there.

Muecke hated arson cases. The smell, the messy forensics, the twisted wiring in the brain of your typical pyromaniac. But he'd spent some time working fraud cases and he quite enjoyed them. Maybe he could work the Newcastle case with Brenner?

He leafed through the material more thoroughly, and realised the case was bigger than it looked. An adjunct to a big Ponzi scheme investigation. Reports, statements, interview summaries, phone and email transcripts, banking records; photographs of the main players taken from social media, newspaper archives and

90

surveillance operations. Names were attached, with notes appended: dates, addresses, phone numbers, suspected crimes, links to the other players.

One surveillance photo showed an unidentified man, 'Do we know who this is?' scribbled on a yellow Post-it note attached to an envelope containing two photographs. Muecke felt a stir in his veins as he took in the long, hard limbs, the face inscrutable in one shot, showing a single look of scepticism and readiness in the second. Casually dressed, walking along a street in an area of Newcastle known as The Hill.

Sorry, can't tell you his name, thought Muecke. But oh, yes, I know who he is and what he does—kind of. And it's nice to know where he is right now.

HE KNOCKED ON THE senior sergeant's office door.

Kitty Brenner had her back to him and was writing on a small whiteboard. A list of daily actions, Muecke thought. She turned, a tall, sleek blonde of forty or so who had already edged past Muecke in the promotion stakes and would soon leave him far behind. Ambitious in a lean and hungry way. Not all that good at her job, according to canteen gossip.

'Greg. Can I help you with something?'

Muecke entered the room. He saw a flicker of irritation, a brief furrow between her pencilled brows: he should have waited for her to extend an invitation. But the annoyance was there and gone again and she capped the whiteboard marker, set it on top of a filing cabinet, and slipped with a graceful movement into the chair behind her desk. Gestured for him to sit.

'Strike Force Stratus,' he said.

'I'm just wrapping that up,' she said. 'No longer our concern.'

Damn. 'Can I ask why?'

She shrugged. 'Word from on high. Everything's been handed

over to the Probity Commission, part of a wider ongoing investigation.'

'Tremayne and Roden.'

Brenner aimed her gaunt cheekbones at him, dry hair swinging about her shoulders. 'Your interest?'

'What do you know about either of them?'

'Roden's in jail, Tremayne's next. Again, your interest?'

'Where did they put Roden?'

'Watervale,' Brenner said, self-assured but testy now, a still, tense figure on the other side of her desk.

Muecke hoped she wouldn't register the current tingling through him: *Watervale*.

She said, 'I'm waiting, Greg.'

'No interest in particular,' Muecke said. 'The boss put a few files on my desk, that's all, one of them being preliminary notes on Stratus.'

Brenner seemed irritated. Started to say something and thought better of it. She runs into inefficiencies every day, Muecke thought, and it drives her nuts.

'Ignore it,' she said. 'Like I said, it's in the past as far as we're concerned.'

18

Tuesday evening, Wyatt was back in his Airbnb cabin, running a Google search on Mark Benedict Impey. Impey had grown up in regional New South Wales; boarding school in Sydney; inherited an abattoir when his father died. A few years later he bought two more, then parlayed that into a chain of rural butcher shops and meat supplies to country supermarkets. Divorced, no children. Active in National Party politics; golf, charity functions. Internet images showed him at a ball, on a farm, cutting the ribbon at the opening of a supermarket. He was pink, slightly porcine. People probably underestimated him.

Impey met Jack Tremayne and Kyle Roden in 2015, invested heavily—shares and real estate—made a solid profit, then withdrew it all one year later. Apparently he was not as rapturously gullible as Tremayne's other investors. He went on to buy a cattle property, a yacht, the house in Merewether Beach. Remained friends with Tremayne and Roden and was on the record saying Tremayne was a financial genius, terrible what had happened to him, such a shame Mr Roden had proven to be a bad apple.

Jack Tremayne belonged to Impey's golf and yacht clubs, which probably counted for something in that social circle. Tremayne had made Impey a lot of money, which counted for more. The cool blonde beauty Tremayne was married to probably helped too. Wyatt found a society photograph, Tremayne beaming as he handed a cheque the size of a tabletop to a hospital CEO, Lynx Tremayne and Mark Impey off to one side, Impey looking not at the camera but at the wife. Wyatt thought his way into the man. Lynx Tremayne was unattainable; deep down Impey knew it but couldn't admit it. Meanwhile, remaining friends with Tremayne meant remaining close to the wife, and who knew what might eventuate?

Wyatt wondered: given that the authorities hadn't found Tremayne's nest egg, and it wasn't at the end of a paper or a digital trail, perhaps a trusted friend was holding onto it? Like me with Sam Kramer? He tried to picture it, Tremayne convincing someone—Impey, his lawyer—that he was the victim of impatient investors and a vindictive corporate watchdog. He'd done his best, selling up, clearing debts, but still the bastards were coming. So here's my last bit of cash, he'd tell this friend or colleague. I'll need it to live on, pay some bills, keep Lynx happy; eventually trade out of difficulties. It wouldn't be fair if government hacks got hold of the lot.

Or he'd hidden it, and only he knew where.

ON WEDNESDAY MORNING the white Caprice shadowed Tremayne again, and Wyatt shadowed the Caprice in a Kia he rented in an outer suburb of Newcastle. Tremayne took him to a gym, a coffee shop, the lawyer's office, lunch at an outside eatery on the waterfront.

Then a second team took over, a man and a woman in a white

Falcon. Tremayne went home. Mid-afternoon he played nine holes of golf, finishing with drinks in the clubhouse, where Wyatt took a table and watched the surveillance team, at another table, masquerading as a loving couple while the woman watched Tremayne over her partner's shoulder.

Tremayne sat alone at the bar. In the space of thirty minutes, he drained five beers. Passing club members said tight, well-mannered hellos, but didn't linger. The ostracism weighed on Tremayne. He would swing around and face the room, rake it belligerently, then turn back to the barman and order another glass.

He's bad luck, Wyatt thought. Tainted. If this whole exercise wasn't a waste of time—if Tremayne did have the money to run— he was the kind of man to delay for as long as possible, hoping his luck would turn. Today's itinerary, the golf, the drink in the clubhouse afterwards, wasn't cover for a bit of wheeling and dealing. It was a need to be loved.

So, a wasted surveillance, from the point of view of the man and the woman who'd tailed him here. But not wasted from Wyatt's point of view.

He watched and waited in that depressing room—poker machines, sticky floral carpet, shouts, too much noise and the stink of aftershave—and by early evening every table was full. As expected, he began to sense the resentment of recent arrivals who had nowhere to sit, a trio of women in particular. How selfish—a man alone at a table with empty chairs going begging. Their good manners held for a while, then turned. Suddenly they were sitting across from him, thumping down their glasses—'May we?'—and daring him to protest. Wyatt gestured graciously, they smirked. Then, one after the other, they took in his thin, remote smile and unreadable eyes. Felt the chill of his interest in them and fell silent. Unable to look at him or each other.

95

That's when Wyatt stood. He nodded, picked up his beer glass and began to weave through the tables as if looking for somewhere else to sit. Unsteady on his feet, a few drinks under his belt. And suddenly he was blocking the view of the agent watching Tremayne at the bar. She blinked. She refocused on this drunk waving his glass in the air and reaching for the empty chair at their table.

'Anyone sitting here?'

'We're busy,' she said.

Wyatt thumped into the chair, fixed the tabletop with fierce concentration and aimed the base of his glass at it. A wave of foam slopped onto the male agent's lap.

Shot to his feet. 'What the fuck?'

'Oh God, sorry,' Wyatt said, standing, tugging out a handkerchief and dabbing at the guy.

'Jesus Christ, just fuck off, okay?'

Wyatt screwed sozzled regret onto his face, leaned in, continued to dab. 'Mate, I'm really sorry.'

'Piss off,' the woman said.

Wyatt shoved the beer-damp handkerchief back in his pocket and tugged at his dishevelled clothing. 'Can I at least buy you guys a drink?'

'Piss off.'

He left. His face hadn't registered with them, only his behaviour. But he didn't linger.

He was down on the coast road before he retrieved the black wallet from inside the handkerchief and rifled through it.

It was doubtful that Tremayne's wider circle of friends were subject to wiretaps, bugs or surveillance. Costly, wasteful and unlikely to have been approved in the first place. But the lawyer was a different matter. Wyatt would need to get DeLacey away from the snoops.

96

Calling the office number for Anderson, Grieve and Mott, he was told that Mr DeLacey was currently with a client and would soon be leaving for the day. Did he have a specific matter in mind? Divorce, Wyatt said, and was told with great regret that Mr DeLacey handled commercial matters, but if he'd care to call the next day an appointment could be arranged with one of the other lawyers.

Letting the car screen him from view, he changed into a dark suit. White shirt, black shoes, blue tie; the heavy-rimmed glasses to soften the hard planes of his face. He drove to Honeysuckle Drive and parked in a side street half a block from Corris House; walked briskly back, swinging a briefcase. Late afternoon, the sun a molten ball a short time earlier but dimming now, the sky steel grey where it wasn't tinged red and purple. If surveillance had been placed on the building, Wyatt would pass as someone's client, maybe here to see his accountant. The last appointment of the day, entering a building where lights burned into the evening five days a week.

He found himself in a small foyer. No reception desk, just a greasy aspidistra in a silvery pot, a name board, a staircase, a lift and a service corridor leading to the back door. Listening for footsteps, voices, doors, Wyatt hurried down the corridor and out into the carpark at the rear, a space distorted by shapes and shadows—DeLacey's bronze Lexus, four crammed recycle bins, a small dumpster on wheels; ragged shrubs in narrow beds on three sides.

He stood in the darkest mass of shadows and waited, his eyes wide and unfocused. If he were to focus on one spot, followed by another, he risked missing the movement that might bring him down. Time passed. A rat twitched in a corner, a cat crept along a fence rail. Otherwise he was alone with his thoughts.

How to bullshit a lawyer? Maybe he didn't need to? It was

only necessary to unsettle DeLacey, after all. If he did have control of Tremayne's money, and was sufficiently unnerved, then he might consciously or unconsciously reveal that fact. Even, potentially, the location.

Wyatt waited. He'd identified his exit points. He had nothing to fear from the wildlife. He felt sharp. It was good to be working. And it was good to work alone. It might be quicker if he had a team to strongarm Tremayne and his friends, but Wyatt knew from bitter experience what could go wrong when others were involved. Useful expertise—safecracking, electronics, driving skills—always had to be measured against the possibility of impatience, greed, deceit, unreliability. The guy who boasted to impress his girlfriend afterwards; who turned out to be an addict or a stooge for another gang. Amateurs or idiots; shortcut takers and risk-takers. Other people, generally speaking, were a liability.

The thing to do about the great messiness of existence was read it, not be endangered by it. Read how a man like William DeLacey might react to a random life event—like, for example, a man stepping out of the shadows and showing him the ID of a Probity Commission agent.

'Mr DeLacey?'

The lawyer, tie loose and suit wrinkled after a day of meetings and paperwork, gave a jumpy squeak. 'Who the hell are you?'

Wyatt showed then pocketed the ID, confident that similar ID had been waved at DeLacey in recent weeks. 'A few questions.'

'I've answered all the questions I intend to answer. And why are you ambushing me like this? I'm on my way home—that all right with you?'

DeLacey aimed his key fob. The Lexus beeped and flashed. But he didn't move. Curious? The two men stood in the cone of yellow illumination cast by the light above the back door of Corris

House, the air scented by distant garbage, harbour water, vehicle exhausts.

'Won't take a moment, sir.'

DeLacey turned sourly to face the music. Thinning sandy hair, a small, moist, red mouth, a waxy, molten quality to his nose, cheeks and brow. Resigned now. 'Go for it.'

'Mr Tremayne has been paying you in a timely manner?'

'What? What the fuck are you on about?'

'He's sold some assets, we understand.'

'Yes, and he's doing the right thing with the proceeds.'

'Legal fees, court costs, that kind of thing.'

'Why don't you just get to the point? Think you can do that?'

'Aren't you afraid your client's going to run out of money soon?'

'Why do we have to do this here? I can insist on a formal interview, with legal representation, film and audio, you're aware of that? This is most unprofessional.'

The cat was back, stalking along the fence rail, a death-dealing flicker in the corner of Wyatt's gaze. 'You would notify us, wouldn't you, sir, if you thought your client was going to slip out of the country?'

'What? What are you on about?'

And the quality of his voice had changed. What does he know? 'You would inform us, wouldn't you, sir, if your client has put together a sum of cash and valuables with the intention of using it to finance, for example, a new life overseas?'

DeLacey opened and closed his mouth.

'Cat's got your tongue,' Wyatt said. 'I'll bid you good evening and leave you to your headaches.'

He returned to his car. A short time later—long enough to make a phone call—the Lexus appeared. Wyatt tracked it to the man's house. Saw him shut himself off from the world as the dark night stretched tight as a wire.

19

THURSDAY MORNING, LYNX TREMAYNE was distributing and turning tarot cards when her secret phone vibrated, close to her groin. There had been a time when she and Will took risks of the kind all adulterous lovers take. Spontaneous texts and calls; erasing the history immediately and hoping for the best. And given that Will was Jack's lawyer, calls to the house on The Hill, or even to Lynx herself, had been easily explained. Will was lawyer *and* friend.

Now, with the Probity Commission raids, Kyle Roden's trial and imprisonment, the media and an alphabet soup of federal and state agencies sniffing around, watching the house, tapping phones, monitoring bank accounts…Now she had a secret phone.

She touched it absently—small, slim, it barely broke the line of her pants—and gazed at the cards: what would it mean for the future if she were to call a halt to things now? Pausing to lay out the next card, she felt the unlucky sense of time being paused when it should be moving inexorably onwards. But William had texted her. They'd already had this week's motel fuck, so this was William in the grip of something other than lust.

Lynx glanced around the sitting room, the coldly gleaming surfaces. Jack was somewhere about. He tended to stay at home these days, besieged by creditors, the media and prowling investigators. Unable to feel him nearby, lurking in a doorway or a passageway, she finally fished out the phone and read William's text: *Need 2 c u urgent*

Lynx gazed at the cards uneasily, reading some high tide of panic behind the message. Enjoying the stiff, smooth sensation of the Celtic Cross in her right hand, she laid it out. Now for the result card—but she baulked. She didn't want to know.

Yet.

She texted: *where when*

The reply: *Cove asap*

The Stockton Cove Motel, one of their earliest fuck pads, a short ferry ride across the harbour from Queens Wharf. It meant getting in the car, driving, parking, getting on the ferry, getting off the ferry, walking at the other end. Lynx grabbed her jacket. She found her husband beside the swimming pool, staring at the chemical blue water. Unshaven, naked under a thick towelling robe. Not drunk, not even drinking, just staring.

'I'm off for a while.'

No reaction at first, the air around him—around the house— swollen by silence. Lynx thought of the tarot spread.

Then he turned his head to her, his features unreadable aside from a cloaked disdain in his eyes. 'Pilates? Shopping? Yoga? Boyfriend?'

'I feel cooped up, Jack.'

'Sure.'

He reached for a glass of orange juice, his pronounced knuckles flexing. Lynx saw him, not for the first time, as a man who would have no qualms about killing if circumstances demanded it. 'I'll be back after lunch.'

'Whatever.'

'Do you need anything?'

Like vodka. A joint. 'No,' he said, gesturing his dismissal.

GETTING OFF THE FERRY, Lynx took a moment to gaze at the harbour before making her way to the motel, a dismal line of small, paint-peeling, salt-damaged rooms on two levels. A curtain twitched in a ground floor window, a door opened, and William's head looked left, right and past her shoulder before jerking to beckon her into the miserable cave.

She glanced at the faded bedspread. It smelled in here. Like the timid hopes of the type of person who had to save up for a seaside holiday. She wouldn't be taking her clothes off today. William closed the curtains and the light went out of the sky. She saw smudges of tension and tiredness under his watery eyes, and the confused and despairing expression of a man who felt the ground shifting under him.

'What?' she demanded.

'Well, a kiss first,' William said.

She put a little oomph into it but only to steady him. Then, more gently, 'Something wrong?'

'I was bailed up last night. About to get in my car and this guy appears out of nowhere.' He stopped.

Was she supposed to guess what came next? 'Okay.'

'Probity Commission, Lynx.'

'So?'

'You don't get it. A Probity Commission guy having a go at me after dark, as I'm about to drive home?'

'Will, it's part and parcel. You're Jack's lawyer, of course they're going to try to rattle you.'

'It was an ambush,' he mumbled, his momentum stalled by her composure. He was simply forlorn now.

Lynx sat on the edge of the bed, hating the dipping of the mattress. She patted the bedclothes. 'Sit.'

He looked grateful for the offer of comfort. He lowered himself onto the bed and rubbed the tops of his thighs.

She stilled his hands. 'What did you say to him?'

'I didn't say anything. I'm not stupid.'

'Okay, what did *he* say?'

Lynx saw the knotty mess of confusion and panic in his eyes. She knew some of his history. Before moving to Newcastle he'd been charged with ninety counts of professional misconduct at his Sydney firm, the result of a Law Institute investigation uncovering discrepancies in his accounts. He'd admitted to mixing trust and non-trust monies; been reprimanded and banned from receiving trust monies for six months.

No jail time. They look after their own, she thought.

Then he'd been investigated for engineering fraudulent lawsuits to protect the assets of financially troubled clients from genuine creditors. As a result, he'd been sacked and eventually found his way to a second-tier firm here in Newcastle.

A man with a certain Teflon quality. But not a streetfighter. Easily spooked by someone stepping out of the shadows.

'William!' she snapped to wake him up. 'What did he say?'

She saw Will take charge of himself; hold a thread of terseness in his voice. 'He gave every indication that Jack's about to go down.'

'We all know that.'

'But they suspect he doesn't intend to hang around for it. They think he's put together a stash of money and he's going to run.'

Lynx was silent. She didn't feature in her husband's plans, then.

'Lynx? What do we do?'

'I need to think,' she said, shrugging into her jacket for the chilly ride back across the water. 'I'll call you.'

It was dark when she reached The Hill, the house promising a residual sense of comfort and familiarity despite her mix of anger, dread and panic. Despite the presence of her treacherous husband, who would leave her broke and alone and a laughing stock.

She went straight to the tarot array and played the next card. The Tower of Destruction. The tower struck by lightning and a man falling to his death.

20

MEANWHILE, AFTER HOURS of fruitless surveillance, Wyatt had changed into his suit and knocked on Mark Impey's door. Held up his Probity Commission identification. 'If I might have a word, sir?'

'I've already spoken to you people. Numerous times.'

'Just a few quick points of clarification, sir, and I'll be out of your hair.'

Impey showed him into the house. Wyatt murmured approvingly as they passed through a large hallway with a broad staircase and several wide doorways. Through one of these to a beautiful reception room with dark-stained timber joinery, an elaborate plaster ceiling, bay windows and an Art Nouveau fireplace. Books upright and aslant in a massive bookcase. He peered at them as he was ushered towards an armchair: biographies of sporting heroes and businessmen, a range of self-help manuals with titles like *The Pillars of Success*, *Heal Your Inner Self* and *How to Think Big*.

Noting the exit points, he took a small spiral pad and a pen from his pocket. 'Now that you've had time to digest our previous interviews with you, Mr Impey, is there anything further you wish to add?'

He saw Impey digest the implication that the commission had caught him out somehow, and swallow. 'Am I in trouble?'

'I don't know—are you?'

More nervous salivating. 'Do I need a lawyer?'

'I don't know—do you?'

Impey wore dark trousers and a white shirt. Not overweight but a faint bloat about him, a sense of flesh straining at fabrics. His face was sweat-shiny—partly nerves, Wyatt thought. Partly his system.

'I'll ask again: is there anything you wish to add?'

Impey tried to rally. 'Nope.'

'It didn't alarm you when Mr Roden went to jail?'

His manner lofty now, Impey said, 'I'd counted Kyle a friend, but ultimately he betrayed that friendship.'

'He cheated you? You lost money as a result of investment decisions made on your behalf by Tremayne and Roden?'

Impey couldn't believe what he was hearing. 'Do you people ever do your homework? I *made* money investing with Jack and Kyle. I didn't lose money.'

Wyatt made a note. 'You made money—then got out when the going was good.'

Impey tried to read his writing. 'If you're implying I got out because I was worried, then you're mistaken.'

'But you suspected your friends were running a Ponzi scheme.'

'That is a lie.'

'You didn't see the warning signs?'

'There were no warning signs. Signs of what? Market fluctuations? All part of the ebb and flow.'

'Dividends dried up.'

'It's not unusual for investors and advisors to hit a rough patch. Global market forces beyond their control. You wait these things out, you don't panic—that's what novice investors fail to understand.'

'You have faith that Mr Tremayne will recover?'

Impey heaved onto one buttock and fished out a handkerchief. Patted his brow and upper lip. 'I do.'

'It hasn't occurred to you that your friend could well go to jail?'

'Look, what's this about? I'm not a partner in Mr Tremayne's business, silent or otherwise. An ex-investor, that's all. Not a signatory to any document, not a guarantor, nothing. I was once an investor but having made a small profit I decided to invest elsewhere. There was nothing but a wish to diversify behind that decision. I didn't see warning signs, as you put it, and indeed I got out some time before the current fuss.'

'Fuss,' muttered Wyatt. 'And you remained friends with Mr Tremayne?'

'Is there anything wrong with that?'

'And his wife?'

Impey tensed minutely and swallowed again. Wyatt didn't know what that meant; perhaps something big. 'Meanwhile, Mr Impey, I understand that calls to the general Tremayne-Roden switchboard are diverted to your mobile phone.'

'People want to hear a reassuring voice. Staff have been laid off, Kyle's in prison, Jack's been getting hate mail and abusive phone calls...as well, there has to be some point of contact for worried investors.'

'You're a very good friend to Mr Tremayne, yes?'

Wyatt saw Impey hesitate, recover and cock his head. 'Is there a point to these questions?'

'A friend who might conceal from authorities the existence of certain funds that rightly should be returned to the liquidators of his companies.'

Wyatt watched Impey. If Tremayne's million-dollar stash existed, and if it was in this house, the man would flick his eyes to it—a room, an attic, a cupboard, a cellar. Instinct. He wouldn't be able to help himself.

But Impey screwed puzzlement onto his face. 'What funds? The poor man's affairs have been trussed up like a Christmas turkey by you people.'

'Do you believe Mr Tremayne when he says that millions of dollars of client investments are held in an offshore trust that only he can access?'

'I've seen the paperwork!' Impey said, looking unconvincing. He's seen paperwork, Wyatt thought. He isn't sure it was genuine, or what it proved.

'You do understand why we were obliged to seize Mr Tremayne's passport, don't you?'

'Ridiculous. Absolutely ridiculous.'

'Of course, he could still sneak out of the country if he put his mind to it. If he had a spare million to live on. Buy false ID and retire somewhere that has no extradition treaty with this country.'

Impey swiped his forehead again. 'Jack isn't a quitter. He'll have his day in court and be exonerated and the markets will rally.'

'He's in debt, Mr Impey. Nothing left to fund his defence.'

'It might interest you to know,' said Impey stiffly, 'that he's paid several of his debts in recent weeks.'

'Is that a fact?' Wyatt said flatly. Small debts, to forestall criticism?

'Jack Tremayne is a friend. Friends help each other out. He

made me a lot of money, so the least I could do was help him.'

Wyatt tingled. 'You've been giving him money. Has that been declared?'

'If you must know, I bought his boat from him. He wasn't in a position to keep running it, and my buying it did both of us a favour—it gave him an injection of funds and me a boat I knew was in good nick, saving me a lot of hassle.'

'An injection of funds,' Wyatt said.

Impey tried and failed to look relaxed about it.

21

ALL MARK IMPEY WANTED to do was wind down. He'd spent most of the morning and afternoon putting out fires for Jack, and now this—targeted by some guy from the Probity Commission. Some hatchet-faced thug you wouldn't want to meet on a dark street, and he'd invited him into his house.

First up today he'd visited a woman paralysed from the waist down after a truck knocked her off her bike. The fortnightly dividend from the $342,000 she'd invested with TR Futures was intended to provide for her daughter, who'd quit her job to be her carer, but the payments had stopped.

'Jack's hands are tied, Mrs Gann. The money's there—I've seen proof—but it's overseas and he can't access it while the Probity Commission has his passport.'

The daughter had fixed Impey with a look. All his life, women had done that. 'There is such a thing as an online transfer, Mr Impey.' She added sweetly, 'But perhaps Mr Tremayne is now so destitute that he no longer owns a computer?'

Women had been making him feel like this—dull and clumsy—all his life, too. He left with his tail between his legs and called on a dentist who'd expanded his practice on the strength of early high returns. 'What's going on? The dividends have dried up and I can't service the loan. Why won't Mr Tremayne take my calls? Should I be worried?'

'I'm sure it's fine, Dr Cochrane,' Impey said. 'It's possible Mr Tremayne was overseas when you were trying to contact him. As you know, he spends the European spring in Paris because of the ease of real-time trading on the US and European markets.'

'From his five-star hotel room, I suppose,' spat the dentist, 'while his investors go down the gurgler.'

Impey tried to dampen the flames. 'If you could be patient a while longer the money should start flowing again.'

'Look at me,' Cochrane said, gesturing at the belt cinched around his waistband. 'I've lost ten kilos in a couple of months. Jenny's had to go back to work, never mind that she's got cancer. And our friends have started to avoid us.'

'These things take time,' Impey said, anxious to leave the miserable wretch in his half-completed new surgery.

'We did so well at the start!'

'There you go,' Impey said with relief. 'Jack's the maestro. He made a lot of people a lot of money over the years. This is a market glitch, that's all, you have to expect those over the long term.'

A couple more creditor sob stories and Impey had been glad to call it a day. But a tiny voice had begun whispering from the deepest corner of his mind: Maybe Jack's businesses *were* falling in a heap. Too many creditors appearing with hard-luck stories. The authorities knocking on doors with search warrants. And Kyle Roden claiming in court that he and Jack had continued to invite and accept investments in TR Capital despite knowing the firm was facing insolvency.

'The prick's lying,' Jack had said after the trial, his arm around Impey. 'Am I responsible for fluctuations in the market? Is it my fault I've been betrayed by people close to me?' There'd been a *tone* in Jack's voice.

Impey said, 'I won't let you down.'

'Jesus, mate, no,' Jack said, appalled. 'You're one of the good ones.' And a couple of seconds later, he was sobbing. He was on the ropes. No cashflow—temporary, mind you—but he still needed to service his loans, had to pay the lawyers. He'd grabbed Impey's arm, his face wretched: Who'd look after Lynx if he ended up in jail?

'I will,' Impey said. Then added, 'I mean, I'll make sure she's okay.'

'I've decided to start selling off some extras,' Jack said. 'Paintings, jewellery, the boat.'

'The boat?'

Windward Passage, a beautiful ocean-going Alaska for which Tremayne had paid more than a million dollars. Impey had been on board many times: cocktail parties, touring through the Whitsundays...

'We've had some great times on it, haven't we? You, me and Lynx. But it's an extravagance, given the current situation. I've got no choice.'

Feeling a strange burning inside, Impey had said: 'I'll buy it off you.'

Jack was astounded. 'Mate! No. Surely not.'

'I've lusted after that boat.'

'Well, she is a beauty. But—no offence, mate—you're no sailor.'

That had done it for Mark Impey. 'I can learn,' he'd said, and the next day he began transferring $995,000 into various trading accounts, per Jack's instructions.

It felt satisfying, helping out friends in need. He hadn't been quite so quick to acknowledge his other feelings—the kudos that came with owning a boat in the small Newcastle business community; how he could keep Lynx—Jack and Lynx—close with the occasional cruise.

But now it was two months later and he'd yet to take *Windward Passage* for a spin. First there'd been a contaminated meat scare at one of his abattoirs, then he'd thought how foolish he'd look to Lynx—Lynx and Jack—if he took them out on the boat and didn't know how to sail it. And he'd had to help his mother sort out her investments.

His mother. She'd met Jack and been charmed by him, and two weeks ago had asked Impey to invest a hundred thousand dollars of her savings in Tremayne Growth Capital. He'd checked in with Jack.

'It's safe, right?'

Jack had looked him in the eye, a study in candour. 'I made *you* money, right?'

'Yes, you did.'

'A lot of money in a very short time, correct?'

'Yes.'

'A lot of people a lot of money.'

'True.'

'I made you a lot of money, Mark,' Jack said, and then a pause full of significance before he added: 'And yet for whatever reason—and I'm not quibbling or querying your judgment—you decided to withdraw your capital last year and invest in blue chips.' He'd held up his hands as if to soften the criticism. 'No offence, not everyone's got the balls for the cut and thrust of the marketplace. But if you *had* stuck with me, would you have got your panties in a twist about a temporary correction? No. You're too experienced for that, you know about market trends. A bit of loyalty, mate,

113

that's what's needed. I made a lot of people a lot of money, and this is how they pay me back?'

Impey had gone home afterwards wondering if Jack was trying to shame him into reinvesting. When really the bloke should have shown a bit of gratitude.

Then last week he'd come to Impey saying, 'They're circling me, mate. I can feel the bastards closing in. I'm telling the truth, but no one listens. A little bit of reassurance from an independent source such as yourself would go a long way…I need to get through this shit so I can go back to making money for people again.'

And so Impey had spent recent days quieting some of the rumbling. He'd visited investors, made phone calls, sent emails, he'd even gone on TV for Jack, stating that he'd seen, with his own eyes, bank transfers and receipts related to the so-called missing millions. It *was* tied up in a blind trust overseas; people shouldn't fret.

It was exhausting, if partly rewarding: he'd given $9,900 to two elderly, distressed creditors left in the lurch when their dividends had lapsed. Jack knew and was grateful. 'My own funds are tied up as you know, or I'd have paid them myself.'

But it was time to admit to himself that a warning voice had been sounding in his head even before the Probity Commission man's visit. He'd had trouble sleeping, he couldn't concentrate; today he'd felt like a fraud when trying to reassure investors. He didn't want to be seen as disloyal, and he certainly wasn't about to turn on Jack; but thank God he'd withdrawn his own investments that time. Otherwise he might be broke now. No house bought for three million and now worth five million. No yacht. No cattle property on the Clarence River. No half share in a resort at Mount Tambourine…

First thing in the morning he'd tell his mother not to invest in any of the Tremayne companies.

HE CROSSED TO HIS front window and watched the moon-streaked ocean, the running lights on a passing freighter out there in the darkness. When he'd first met Jack, back in 2015, Lynx had been there: gracious, stylish, aloof. She had class. And as the years had gone by and he saw more of her, her cool shell had seemed to melt. There was nothing between them; she was married. And yet there was, somehow, something between them.

Like the other evening. Impey could still feel the exquisite pain of Lynx Tremayne taking his bottom lip between hers in a brief, tugging hello kiss—then Jack had shown up and he'd had to stand there enduring their husband and wife kiss, their laughs and murmurs and in-jokes, thinking he should probably just go home and wondering if they'd share a laugh about him if he did.

Then the alarms had started up all along the street, and Jack went tense. 'What do you bet it's the feds, tripping over their own feet?'

Impey had left soon afterwards. And that look Lynx gave him as he left…*Sorry, Mark, come see me again soon.*

Impey pictured *Windward Passage* tossing gently at anchor. God, he'd sail off with Lynx Tremayne right there and then if he could. If she would. And sometimes, when she gave him that sleepy-eyed look, he almost thought she would. There was something of the vagabond about her, under the classy veneer. He could see her on deck or on an island, no knickers or bra, a filmy cotton sundress. Bare brown feet. An all-over tan. Hungry for him.

Lynx and her unfathomable secrets. His mate's wife. A guy he admired—kind of.

Who might be preparing to run—*with the money I gave him.*

It was a night of sounds and shadows, but Impey had second thoughts about pouring another scotch. He grabbed his car keys.

WYATT WATCHED.

Mark Impey had seemed jittery just now. Not a strong man. Easily manipulated. If he had Jack Tremayne's money for safekeeping, it would panic him to think the Probity Commission knew about it. Doubt, once introduced, works on a person. Wyatt imagined the voice in Impey's head: Jack's crooked, Jack's going to run.

Will he go to the money?

As if on cue, the garage door rose. The Range Rover backed out. Wyatt waited until Impey was a hundred metres down the street before activating the tracker and pulling out, headlights off. Impey turned, turned again. When the Range Rover was briefly out of sight, Wyatt switched on his lights. He followed Impey north-east on Memorial Drive and north on a series of smaller streets that took him to the other side of the spit of land, to Hunter Street and the marina. A tortuous route. But not the sudden spurts, turns and doubling back of a man shaking a tail, thought Wyatt: this was a man fretting on what he should do next.

The Range Rover pulled into the marina carpark. Impey got out and by the time Wyatt had parked and entered the area he'd vanished. A couple of hundred vessels, many docked, others stored. Pontoons. Fuel bowsers. Canoes and paddleboats for hire. Restaurants.

People were about—boat owners, diners, security staff. Wire fences and locked access to the moored yachts. Wyatt retreated. He returned to his car and watched the Range Rover. Impey appeared half an hour later, empty-handed, and Wyatt followed him back to Merewether Beach, thinking of his own next moves.

22

MARK IMPEY HADN'T FOUND anything on *Windward Passage* last night. He wasn't even sure what he was looking for. So many storage places on board, mostly nautical gear.

He needed to try something else, and by 9 a.m. Friday was on a flight to Sydney. There were private inquiry agents in Newcastle, but it wasn't impossible that word would get back to Jack. Or Lynx.

Reaching McQueen and McQueen in Glebe, he filled out the paperwork while a receptionist watched, and was eventually shown in to see Carmel McQueen. 'Which McQueen are you?' he joked.

If he thought that might break the ice, he was mistaken. 'The wife,' she said, a taut woman in her forties with short hair, clipped nails and the humourless air of a fitness fanatic. 'I handle financial, my husband handles personal deceit.'

This was fascinating to Impey. 'Personal, like a wife or a husband having an affair?'

'Bulk of our work. That and workplace dishonesty—fake credentials, pilfering. But your application'—she waved it at Impey—'says you want a financial rundown of a man named Tremayne.'

'Correct.'

'Hence you get me, not my husband.' She paused. 'Ex-Fraud Squad.'

'Good.'

She thrummed with energy and still hadn't smiled. 'I know who Jack Tremayne is.'

Impey said cautiously, 'Okay...'

'Not a problem,' she said, dismissing it. 'How deep?'

'Sorry?'

'By lunchtime today I can have everything that's on public record. Or I take a week and you'll know where he buys his socks and how much he had in his piggybank when he was six years old.'

Impey felt like he was being steered. But time was of the essence. 'What about if I pay you to spend *all* of today and get what's on public record and as much, er, *hidden* stuff as you can?'

Carmel McQueen considered. 'Come back at four.'

NEEDING TO BE CLOSE to the main players, able to track their movements, Wyatt had moved to a small boutique hotel, a converted warehouse, near the waterfront. You needed serious money to stay there, and if you had serious money you probably weren't a man who sneaked through windows and stole things. He was invisible for now.

He'd eaten breakfast at 6 a.m. and by eight he was tracking Mark Impey again. The airport. He watched Impey board a plane bound for Sydney. No luggage: a day trip, but there was no point in waiting around. He drove back to the city. He didn't feel frustrated, exactly—he always worked without emotion—but shadowing Tremayne and his wife and associates was work of a diffuse kind, necessary but unlikely to amount to much. Likewise bailing up DeLacey and Impey in the guise of a Probity Commission investigator: psychological manoeuvring. An inexact science in which moods and personality came into play.

He needed to search Impey's boat. Use his hands and his eyes and his brains to find Tremayne's running-away stash.

By mid-morning he was at the marina. It was risky here, a busy world of marine security, tourists, sailors; the yachts rolling at anchor, the ping of rigging against the clean, stalk-like masts. But he felt more focused, calmer and more competent than he had for days. He hated inactivity, waiting. It induced a lethargy that would surely bring him down one day.

This time Wyatt was an experienced outdoorsman with money. Expensive windproof jacket, trousers and sailor's jumper, a beanie on his head and a big Nikon with a long lens around his neck. Glasses again, to divert attention from his eyes. He'd noted the escape points—too many of them, if he counted the paths, the grassy areas and the harbour waters. No law nearby, that he could see.

'Beautiful day,' a voice said.

It wasn't, not especially. A chilly day, with a gusting wind. But Wyatt knew what the man meant: the good-to-be-alive quality of an autumn day with direct sunlight and a brisk wind. He turned and smiled and said, 'That it is.'

A man of retirement age with a veiny nose faced him. Overalls, a greasy beanie and a high-vis jacket, *Security* stamped on the chest. 'Help you?'

'I'm in the market for a cabin cruiser,' Wyatt said. 'Ocean-going, not a little sheltered-waters job.'

'Okay...'

'Like this.'

The camera was digital. Wyatt had taken photographs of Alaska 49, Conquest, Sea Ray and Riviera yachts from an online brokerage site and cropped the captions. He turned the little screen to the security guard, scrolled through.

'You didn't take these here.'

Wyatt shook his head. 'No, just got in this morning. I've been up and down the east coast, looking. Byron, Coffs, Noosa, Gold Coast...'

The guard cast a look over his marina. 'This is all your smaller stuff,' he said, gesturing at the rows of small, single-masted yachts. 'Your weekend shore huggers. Bigger stuff's over there.'

He pointed. Wyatt had already spotted the great, gleaming hulls and raked superstructures. There was no easy access to that area of the marina, however, with locked gates on the network of fixed and floating docks.

'Can't get in there by any chance?'

'Sorry, no. Anyway, none of them are for sale, far as I know.'

'It's just so I can take photos to show the wife.'

'You've got all you need there in your camera,' the guard said. 'Nothing new to see here.'

'No worries.' Wyatt didn't push it. He might be remembered for an hour or so; if he kicked up a fuss he'd be remembered for a lot longer than that. He strolled back towards the foreshore footpaths, and when he looked back a young Chinese couple was asking the guard to take their photograph with the tossing masts behind them.

GREG MUECKE, STILL IN Sydney, was at his desk rereading the Stratus file, noting the names and numbers of Fraud Squad, Probity Commission and Newcastle plainclothes investigators. He called the Newcastle police station first, asked for a detective

120

sergeant named Agostino, and was told that Agostino would call back via the Parramatta switchboard: 'For all we know, you're working for the *Telegraph*.'

A few minutes later, Agostino was on the line, a light young voice telling Muecke about Jack Tremayne's business partner: 'As far as we could tell, Roden was completely wiped out. Had to sell his house, Range Rover, Coffs Harbour beach shack, stocks and shares, liquidated everything. It all went on fines and legal bills.'

'Tremayne himself?'

'A different kettle of fish. We haven't found hidden assets of any kind, but that's not to say they don't exist.'

'How's he managing for money?'

'He's started selling assets. But it looks like he thinks the case against him'll fold—he's not trying too hard. Sold his yacht, but that's about it.'

'So he's not skint yet.'

'He cries poor, but he's slippery.'

'Will he stick around?'

'After he goes to prison, do you mean?'

'Will he stick around if he's charged?'

After a beat, Agostino said, 'Do you know something we don't?'

'Not really. A guy I've been interested in down here managed to show up in one of your surveillance photos.'

'Which photo? Got your copy there?'

They spent a minute matching the case-file number, photo number, date stamp and general description, and Agostino said, 'This guy. We only saw him once. Decided he was just some random pedestrian. What's his name? What's he done? Should we be worried?'

'Don't know his name, and I'm not even sure if he's done or about to do anything. It's just, we think he pulls the odd job for a man named Kramer, who it so happens is in jail with Roden.'

'Be interesting to know what they talk about, if anything,' Agostino said.

'Yes, it would,' Muecke said. 'Let me know if he shows up again?'

'Will do.'

Muecke knew he'd be going to Newcastle in the next day or so, but first he needed to fill another gap in his knowledge, so he called a contact at Watervale prison, then Kyle Roden's lawyer. 'You're a tick boxes kinda guy,' his wife used to say. And according to one of his annual performance reviews, 'a pedestrian determination' was the 'hallmark' of his 'approach to policing'. Admin were thinking of bringing in self-assessment; if they did that, Muecke was tempted to write, 'Still standing.'

Roden's lawyer, a man named Sleiman, was brusque on the phone, but grudgingly agreed to meet Muecke at Watervale later that morning. He listed what his client would and wouldn't say, and what Muecke could and couldn't ask.

'Yeah, yeah,' Muecke said.

Sleiman, a man of watery blue eyes and florid cheeks, was waiting at the gate. They were shown to the room where Muecke had interviewed Carl Ayliffe. The same hopeless odours, the same unplaceable sounds echoing. He shook Roden's hand and said, 'First things first—you're not facing fresh charges.'

'Good to know,' said Roden sceptically, clearly believing that even if that was true he'd be disadvantaged somehow. His appearance had changed in the few weeks he'd been in prison. He was no longer the plump, agreeable everyman depicted in the photographs Muecke had googled. Thinner, paler, he looked permanently aggrieved, drained of his old benevolence. He didn't trust Muecke. He edged his chair away from Sleiman's.

'So, what? New fines on top of the ones that wiped me out?

Good luck gouging more money out of me.'

Sleiman patted his forearm. 'Relax. Just listen to what Sergeant Muecke has to say.'

Roden folded his arms. 'Be my guest.'

Muecke said carefully, 'I understand that you have formed a friendship with an inmate named Samuel Kramer.'

Roden went very still. 'No comment.'

'Kyle,' Sleiman said.

'No. Fucking. Comment.'

Sleiman gave Muecke a look: you wasted a trip. Muecke ignored him, leaned over the table. 'I know all about prison grapevines, Mr Roden. You've nothing to fear concerning this little conference. As far as prison staff know, I've come here to question you about financial irregularities in the real estate business you were operating before you met Jack Tremayne.'

At the mention of Tremayne's name, Roden's eyes slid to the side. Muecke could read the thoughts: dismay to learn that the police knew he'd been talking to Kramer about Tremayne.

Now: what had he told Kramer? 'I imagine Mr Kramer showed a lot of interest in what you had to say about Jack Tremayne.'

Roden leaned toward Sleiman. An exchange of urgent whispers. The lawyer turned to Muecke. 'My client neither confirms nor denies talking to this Kramer fellow. If he *did* talk to him, he didn't know who he was, and the subject matter was unimportant anyway.'

Muecke had to laugh. 'Fucking lawyers. But at least we've got beyond "no comment", so that's nice. Tell me this, Mr Roden: I expect Jack Tremayne was the sort to put a lot of money away for a rainy day?'

'No comment.'

'Yeah, yeah. He's pretty smart, I understand. Quick on his

feet. Yeah, I can see him with a nice little nest egg.'

A kind of fury flickered in Roden's face, as if his own capabilities had been denigrated.

Muecke tightened the screw a little more. 'According to some of the newspaper reports, Mr Tremayne was dismayed to learn you'd operated a Ponzi scheme behind his back.'

'Fucking liar!'

'I think you're right, I think he's in it up to his neck. But there's a very good chance he'll avoid jail. He might not have his business; might lose all his friends. But he'll be out there, and you'll be in here.'

'If he doesn't go down it won't be because he's got good lawyers,' Roden said, steaming now. 'It'll be because he's got a big stash of money no one knows about.'

'To fund his defence.'

'Aren't you listening? He's going to do a runner.' Roden folded his arms and sat back. Then, as the triumph leaked away, Muecke saw his eyes fill with fear.

'Mr Roden,' he said quietly, 'did you tell Sam Kramer about Tremayne's stash?'

Roden's gaze flicked about the room.

'I'm satisfied that you did,' Muecke said. 'It needn't leave this room. If Mr Kramer presses you, simply act disgusted, it was a fishing expedition regarding financial irregularities in your old real estate firm.' He paused. 'I'm sure you know what form Mr Kramer's displeasure takes?'

Roden's head moved: barely a nod.

23

WHILE HE WAITED FOR Carmel McQueen to do her research, Mark Impey took a ferry to Taronga Park Zoo. He bought an ice-cream and wandered around feeling curiously liberated. He was allowed to do this. His own master. He was a man with means and leisure time and a vanilla Cornetto.

He should really be at work, though. Correspondence, phone calls, emails. Guilt. It was there in everything he did. A day at the zoo, digging into his friend's past, lusting after his friend's wife. Using his friend to make a profit, then pulling out while others less astute lost everything.

When he returned at 4 p.m., Carmel McQueen said, 'I see that you once invested with this man. I seriously hope you don't intend to again.'

She held up a hand. 'That's *opinion*, you understand. Don't mistake it for advice.' She tapped a thin file. 'There are no judgments in here, only matters of fact.'

'I understand, and you don't need to worry about me.'

She shot him a sceptical look, then shrugged. 'Some highlights. Mr Tremayne first came to official attention late in 1998, when he faced an ICAC inquiry into alleged property development corruption on the south coast.'

'What happened?'

'Nothing much. To him, at any rate. Other heads rolled. But you might call it symptomatic.'

'Okay.'

'After that he kept his head down for a few years, but he'd start a company, and when it began to fail, he'd strip it of cash and assets, then liquidate and start another just like it. It's called phoenixing.'

'I'm familiar with the term.'

McQueen straightened the edges of the report with her utilitarian fingertips. 'Now, his various Newcastle companies. Eighty million invested, in all.'

Impey shook his head. 'That can't be right. He told me ten.'

'Eighty. And at least two hundred investors.'

'He told me thirty.'

'He lied. He also doesn't have a financial services licence.' She cocked her head at Impey. 'You've gone on record as defending him.'

Impey winced. He supposed it was inevitable she'd find that out. 'I'll be blunt. I'd considered him a friend, and I made a profit investing with him in the early stages. But I've been hearing conflicting stories lately and I don't want to leave myself open to being sued.' He paused, thinking of the chilly Probity Commission investigator. 'Or audited or cross-examined or—'

'Wise man,' McQueen said briskly. 'Now, there is more in this file, and I suggest you go home and read it closely and think about it with a clear head. The clear head that persuaded you to withdraw your investments with Mr Tremayne eighteen months ago.'

It was almost praise, and he almost basked in it, but he didn't think she was all that impressed by him. Truth be known, he was a timid investor, always had been. Invest, watch it anxiously, pull out as soon as it made a modest profit. A cautious path to modest wealth. No one would splash his name around in the media.

'I can't thank you enough,' he said.

'You know what you have to do,' she said.

But he didn't. *What?* he almost wailed.

WYATT WAS AT A drone shop sandwiched between a stonemason and an antenna manufacturer in an industrial park south of the city.

'We can get you in the air for a hundred bucks,' the salesman said. His name was Drew; young, twitchy, as if his fingers needed a joystick. He indicated a wall of garish cardboard and cellophane boxes behind the cash register and a small craft, resembling a crouching spider, hanging by a cord from the ceiling.

Air-8, $99.95, according to a placard suspended beneath it.

'Flying time?' asked Wyatt. The Air-8 looked insubstantial to his eyes.

'Ten minutes.'

'I'm going to need longer than that, I think. Range?'

'A hundred metres.'

'And a longer range,' Wyatt said. 'Something with a camera, too.'

'This has a camera. Can I ask what you want it for?'

'I own some dense bushland,' Wyatt said, gesturing to the west. 'Sometimes when stock force their way through a hole in the fence, I have trouble finding them.'

He didn't say sheep or cattle, in case the kid had some kind

127

of farming background. 'So, a good range, a longish flying time, and a good camera,' he said.

Drew brooded on that. 'Can you go a thousand?'

Wyatt shrugged. His gadgetry budget was growing, but the rewards at the end would make up for it.

'What have you got?'

Drew took him across the shop floor, a space crammed with more hobby drones in bright packaging and revolving wire stands of brochures, manuals, spare engine parts, cameras, propellers and radio and Wi-Fi transmitters. A large pillar in the centre carried the Civil Aviation Safety Authority drone regulations. Wyatt glanced at it as he passed: no flying higher than 120 metres; no flying within thirty metres of another drone; operate only in daylight…

'This one here's a pretty decent quadcopter,' Drew said. 'Chinese made, photo and video capabilities, very light, very portable. You download an app to your phone and connect it to the controller for live view.'

'Flying time?'

'Half an hour.'

'Range?'

'Up to seven kilometres. Return-to-base function. Smooth video feed. Good resolution.' He paused. 'No good for stunts, though.'

Wyatt smiled thinly. 'Stunts don't interest me.' He thought about the choppy sea this morning, the pitching yachts at anchor. 'Operate okay in strong winds?'

'It's fitted with stabilisers,' Drew said.

Wyatt nodded, thinking it through. 'I'll take it.' He looked around the shop. They were alone. 'And thirty minutes of your time, out in the carpark.'

'Deal.' Drew's restless hands clenched. Selling drones was all well and good; flying them was better. 'Pay me and we can download the app and I'll put a sign on the door.'

And after the training session with Drew, Wyatt drove back to a strip of shops closer to the city. Boutique coffee joints, bistros, cargo bikes for hipsters—and I-Spy, which sold security systems, alarms, GPS trackers and spy cameras.

Wyatt came out half an hour later with a long-range, long-battery-life tracking device. It was small, sturdy and waterproof, with a powerful mounting magnet. It would work internationally and could be monitored by mobile phone. Wyatt was beginning to think he was watching the world.

By 5 p.m. he was back on the esplanade with only about forty-five minutes of daylight left. The air colder, the wind dropping. Fewer people about and he had a stretch of the foreshore to himself. The marina, three hundred metres away, was a forest of masts.

He launched the drone and navigated it towards the marina section where Mark Impey's boat was moored, watching the camera feed as grassy sections, then paths, docks, choppy surface water and tossing mast tops slipped by beneath the lens. But from above it was difficult to distinguish one craft from another. They were all just long, broad, well-kitted-out cabin cruisers. He needed to bring the drone down to a couple of metres above deck level and that meant all kinds of extra hazards. Power poles, mast cables. The risk of being seen.

'Cool.' A kid's voice.

A teenage boy, alone. Glasses, a school blazer, grey gabardine pants and a skew-whiff, tightly knotted tie; a backpack dragging down his right shoulder. Wyatt wondered how to play it. Was a kid going to report him? He was more likely to want to see him as a guy playing with a cool toy. But if Wyatt told him to get lost he'd remember the experience. And meanwhile, Wyatt needed to know which was Impey's boat. He gestured to the kid to come closer and check out the visual feed. 'One of these boats is mine, if only I could find it. The first time I've ever used one of these things,' he added, playing up the helpless middle age just a little.

'Oh, yeah. How come you're looking for your own boat?'

Wyatt made a rapid assessment. The kid looked geekish. Not with friends but alone. Curious, not suspicious. Possibly lonely. He watched the boy's eyes flick between the screen and the joystick controller; could almost see his mind working.

Wyatt said, 'You had any experience with one of these?'

'Sure.' Offhanded.

'Really?'

'Yeah. My dad's like a wedding photographer.'

'He films weddings with a drone?'

'I do that part of it, for the DVD. He takes still photos.'

'Lucky I met you,' Wyatt said. 'Mainly what I want a drone for is to spot fish from the air. Marlin and so on, deep-sea fishing. Right now I'm trying to work out how to get a shallow angle shot so I can spot which boat is mine.'

'Let me have a go,' the boy said, his hands as tense as Drew's.

'She's called *Windward Passage*,' Wyatt said. He passed over the controls and watched as the kid brought the drone down and made a pass along the dock.

Seconds later, the boy said, 'There it is.'

Wyatt took a look: one hull among several. He needed to know its precise position in relation to the others.

'Can you give it a bit of elevation? So I can check everything's secure up top?' He watched the live feed with the boy. 'Bit higher, bit higher...'

Great. Seven craft, and *Windward Passage* was the second from the south-eastern end of that branching arm of the dock area.

'No point going any higher. You won't see clearly in this light,' the boy said.

'That's okay, I've seen enough. I'll have another practice at home tomorrow.'

The boy returned the controller reluctantly. Time to head home. Homework. Dinner. More homework.

'You can fly it back if you like,' Wyatt said.

The boy almost snatched the controls from him.

24

IMPEY'S FLIGHT GOT IN at 6 p.m. and he drove straight to The Hill. If both cars were there he knew he might chicken out. He couldn't tackle Jack with Lynx in the room, and he couldn't enjoy quality time with Lynx with Jack in the room.

And it was wrong anyway. She was married. Maybe if Jack went to jail she'd be free, but what if she stood by him? Impey imagined she was unhappy, but maybe she thought he was a ridiculous clown and her husband was a god. He was still tying himself in knots as he cruised past the Tremayne house.

The BMW was there but not the Audi. Thank God. He pulled up to the kerb, got out, strode up the slope to the front door.

'I need to talk to you,' he said, when Jack opened the door.

A flicker on Jack's face, which the old Impey, super sensitive, interpreted as a dismissive eye-roll. But instead of rebuffing him, Jack stepped aside. 'Come in, then.'

Almost seven in the evening and Jack was unshaven. Tracksuit pants and a hoodie; bare feet with yellowing toenails. Had he even showered that day? He looked both ways along the street before shutting the door.

The new Impey found himself saying, 'Well might you check the street, Jack—I had an interesting visitor last night.'

'Well might I what?' said Tremayne absently. 'What are you on about?'

'A Probity Commission fellow wanted a word with me—about *you*.'

Tremayne gestured as he led the way through the house to the sitting room. Pizza slices in a box, a half-empty bottle of shiraz. He flopped onto a sofa. 'Sit down. What's this about the Probity Commission?'

'As I said, I had a visit.'

'Yeah, and?'

'And it was from a Probity Commission investigator!'

Tremayne shrugged. 'Do you have investments with me? No. Are you employed by me? No. Are you a signatory to anything involving my companies? No. Nothing for you to worry about.'

'But I've been vouching for you and now I think maybe it's time I stopped doing that. For my protection and yours.'

Tremayne shrugged again. 'Up to you.'

Really? Was that it? In the face of Jack's unconcern, Impey began to doubt his ground. 'I've learnt some disturbing things in the last few hours,' he said, hearing a contemptible little tremor in his voice.

'Oh? Like what?'

'You're supposed to have a licence.'

'Not if you're operating on the scale I'm operating on.'

'That's just it, they say you've got *dozens* of investors, *tens* of millions of dollars invested.'

'Who is "they"?'

Impey looked away. 'Just things I've heard.'

'I think I might have to ask you to leave, Mark.' Tremayne stood. 'It's unconscionable to me, to know you've been checking on me behind my back.'

Impey bit his lip. He always got things wrong somehow. 'It's just that I'm worried, Jack.'

Tremayne sat again and stretched his legs out. 'I understand, Mark. It's been a stressful time for you. I want you to know that I value our friendship above almost *any* of my friendships and relationships. You've stuck by me through thick and thin. Others deserted me, you didn't. I admit, I made some mistakes in recent years, judged the market poorly a couple of times, but dishonest? No. Never. It's not in me. Have I run away and left others to pick up the pieces? No. I'm still here, and I intend to face the music.'

Impey continued to gnaw at his lip. 'The Probity fellow said he thinks you'll run.'

Tremayne's jaw dropped. 'Run! How? And if I was going to run, wouldn't I have done it by now? Fuck you! Fuck the lot of you!'

The rage spat out suddenly—then vanished just as quickly. Tremayne shot Impey a look and said, calmly, 'It's not a nice feeling, being doubted by a man you'd considered a friend.'

'It's just…' Impey said, wanting badly to be reassured.

Jack Tremayne spoke with studied dignity. 'If you feel that you cannot continue vouching for me, I understand.' He stood, gestured towards the door.

Lynx's Audi was pulling in as Impey left. He gave her a hunted smile and a choked-down hello and scurried to his car. Felt a surge of guilt as he drove away. But before long he began to rebuke himself. What did he have to feel guilty about? He reached his home, parked the car in the driveway, went inside and sat for a while. He could feel strange forces moving around out there in the darkness: was he being watched, too?

He sat, and a strange clarity came over him. He prepared the house: left the Range Rover in the driveway, turned on a selection of lights and opened the curtains a crack. Then he called a taxi and slipped out the back way onto the next street. The taxi took him to a bistro near the waterfront, where he ate a bowl of pasta before heading across the road to the marina.

He hadn't looked properly last night. Too rattled by the Probity Commission investigator. Too dark, too late. But this time he turned on all the interior lights. He used a torch, too, to make a detailed examination of the storage bays. He found a large blue tarp, tins of paint, plywood sheets. Also, significant quantities of fuel, water and food—and a rifle. Had that stuff always been there? He didn't know. He'd simply paid Jack for the boat and left it moored in the marina.

Next, he went around and knocked on all the panels and shone the torch beam on the screwheads, looking for fresh scratches. Below decks he found a panel that might have been tampered with. He unscrewed it, pulled it away. Nothing, only three vertical drain pipes. The head, he thought, gauging where he was in relation to the main stateroom ensuite: toilet and shower. Wait. *Three* pipes? All three had joins. Two showed the red staining of plumber's glue solution; the third, larger than the other two, did not.

He wrapped his hands around it and twisted, and out it came. Inside was a nylon bag containing bearer bonds, a box crammed with diamond, ruby and emerald rings, a Rolex, many bundles of currency—euros, sterling and US and Australian dollars—a tiny pistol and a passport. Jack's face, but not Jack's name. Benjamin Meyn.

Impey replaced the pipe and the panel. He shouldered the nylon bag and left the *Windward Passage*, stopping off to talk to the security guard along the way.

135

'You'll let me know if anyone pays any particular attention to my boat?'

'Yes, Mr Impey.'

Impey kept a fully restored E-Type Jaguar in a storage unit thirty minutes south of Newcastle. He took an Uber down there, stowed the nylon bag and had the Uber take him back to a street two blocks from his house. He was trembling. He feared Jack Tremayne, and a part of him was full of doubt. What if the stash was to fund Jack's legal defence? He wouldn't want creditors or the authorities getting their hands on it.

And another voice in his head was saying, *Bullshit, Mark.* A fake passport? And clearly the Probity Commission thought Jack was going to run. If he wanted his bag of goodies back, he could just come and ask for it. But he'd better have a convincing explanation.

WYATT RETURNED IN THE dead hours of Friday night wearing a thin wetsuit and a waterproof pouch under loose blue trousers, a maroon jumper and a dark grey jacket. Dark colours for a night of moving shadows. Ordinary autumn-wear colours. Not black, a colour to stir suspicion in a passing policeman or security guard; but colours of concealment even so.

Slipping from one patch of darkness to another, he made his way to a small shed. He stripped and folded his outer clothing into a bin liner, which he stowed on top of cardboard boxes in a nearby dumpster before sliding into the water.

He swam slowly, barely disturbing the surface. A small boat, returning late from somewhere, hummed up Throsby Creek and under the Couper Street bridge, setting up a hard chop against the moored yachts, the small hulls pitching like frenzied animals for a minute or two.

He found *Windward Passage* and pulled himself aboard, keeping low. As expected, the below-decks area was sealed off by a locked door. Impey would have a key, but the important question was: did Tremayne still have one?

Wyatt took a lock pick from the pouch around his waist and broke in. He searched the staterooms first: one king size with ensuite, a queen and a room with two bunks. Then the galley, the second head and the storage areas, noting the powerful engines, long-range fuel tanks and well-stocked pantry.

He found a safe. It was a rich man's safe, from what he could tell: outer wall, a layer of insulation, an inner liner and a serious locking mechanism. Bolted to the hull in one of the storage areas. He itched to open it. But would Tremayne use it as a hiding place? Unlikely—it was Impey's boat now, Impey would want to use the safe. Anyway Wyatt didn't have the gear with him to crack a safe.

He returned to the galley and suddenly torchlight came bobbing along one arm of the marina, sweeping erratically: someone in a hurry.

Wyatt took the GPS tracker from the pouch, dropped to the floor, snaked his arm under the sink and smacked the device's magnetic base against a metal bracket. Movement and a footstep above his head.

'Anyone there?'

A male voice, and Wyatt guessed the man was looking at damp footprints on the deck by now. He crept to the door and, when it swung open and the torch was poking about, he jerked on a knobbly wrist, a uniformed arm.

The guard flew past him and sprawled across the floor, and Wyatt slipped back onto the deck and into the water.

25

Lynx Tremayne had thought long and hard, and by Saturday morning she knew what to do. She texted Will DeLacey: *dinosaur motel noon*

She found him waiting for her. They'd used the dinosaur motel once before. A tourist place north of Newcastle that overlooked a scruffy little dinosaur park, the pitifully small creatures cracked and faded from years of exposure to sunlight and small, disappointed fingers. And the room was a wash of pinks and greys, colours that Lynx hoped might have disappeared at the end of the eighties. Then, when William moved the bed on its castors so he could watch himself fucking her in the mirror, two crumpled tissues came to light. It was an effort for Lynx to find an erotic spark.

Not helped by William himself, who was particularly unsexy today. Thrusting and grimacing, straining for a release that didn't arrive, until he went soft inside her.

He jerked away as if he couldn't bear to touch her. Sat on the edge of the bed with his back to her. A damp, mottled, unappealing back above hairy buttocks. Then he was shaking, and at last a sob broke free.

Oh, for Christ's sake. Lynx scooted closer, not letting her breasts or stomach touch him, and draped an arm over his meaty shoulder. She stroked his neck and cheek. 'Something wrong?'

He let it all out then, heaving and shuddering. It was embarrassing to witness, frankly. Still.

'Sweetheart?' she said.

'Sorry,' he gasped. 'Sorry.' Turning to face her when, really, she'd rather have kept looking at his back than his pot belly and gluey dick.

Lynx kept her distance. She screwed concern onto her face. 'What is it?'

More tears. 'The partners have said they need to let me go.'

Well, of course they have. 'Oh, no,' said Lynx. 'That's so unfair.'

'And I've been served,' he said. 'Subpoenaed to appear before the Probity Commission next week.'

In the wash of weak autumn sunlight entering the room through the window, his face was devoid of confidence and authority.

'Was it the man who bailed you up outside your office the other evening?'

'Different one. Two of them.'

'When do you have to appear?'

'Next week. I'm ruined, Lynx.'

Lynx Tremayne looked stricken and it wasn't entirely an act. She sat up, reached for the bedclothes and tugged them to the tops of her breasts. They comforted her. They blotted out most of William, too. It's interesting how you can fall out of…love, lust, whatever…in an instant, she thought.

139

'Do you think they'll come after me as well?'

Will's gallantry had deserted him. He said dismissively, 'Hardly likely, is it? Me, I could lose everything.'

Your job, such as it is; your reputation, ditto; your mousy wife and retarded daughter. 'You're a good lawyer,' she soothed. 'You're smarter than a bunch of pen-pushers.'

'Lynx, I could go to jail!'

Get your shit together. And don't spit on me. Lynx patted him half-heartedly. In truth, she was spooked. Events were slipping from Jack's control—hers, Will's—quicker than she liked. What she needed to concentrate on now was her exit strategy.

She thought about the people who'd been watching her house. She'd believed they were only interested in Jack—but maybe they were also interested in Will. Interested enough to follow him? Also interested in her? She suppressed a sudden panicky giggle to think of two surveillance teams bumping into each other at this godforsaken shithole.

Would they use her infidelity to goad Jack somehow, rattle him, get him to confess? She'd never witnessed his dangerous side, but she knew it was there. He'd said once, soon after they got hitched, 'You won't be sleeping with anyone else. If you do, I'll kill him. Then you. Slowly.'

William was weeping again, on her shoulder and upper right breast. A gusting creep of wetness. She reflected that Jack liked to surround himself with weak people. William. Mark.

Me? Not me.

She thought of what she might do with Jack's running-away money—if it existed. Steal it for herself, let it go cold for a year, divorce Jack in the meantime and start again quietly somewhere new. Or steal it and run. Or steal it with William and run with William. Better still, steal it with William's help, then ditch him.

IT WAS PILLOW TALK of a kind she'd never engaged in before, but the money talk calmed them both, brought some focus.

'We do have to consider that it's all bullshit, there is no money,' she said, 'but the Probity Commission man raised the possibility, and if I know my husband, he will have something up his sleeve.'

For once, William didn't take a remark about Jack as a reflection on himself. 'Let's just act on the assumption there *is* a hidden stash.'

'Let's,' she agreed. 'I started looking as soon as you told me about the guy who bailed you up. But I can't find any paperwork indicating a house or a storage unit or anywhere else I can think of where he might hide it.'

'What about in someone else's name? Friends, family?'

'The Probity Commission's been all over us. Jack wouldn't be so dumb.'

Will looked deflated. Christ, she was going to have to spell it out for him. 'If only we could get Jack to break cover somehow...'

She could feel William musing on that, his body tense and expectant, and unpleasantly warm. She wanted to peel her hip and upper arm away from his, but he was sensitive about body language.

After a while he said, 'That might happen if he has to face court. He'll go for the money then.'

'But what if he keeps stonewalling? Time goes by and everyone drops their guard, and suddenly we all realise he's done a runner. We need something else to give him a fright. Something he can't bear to lose, something he'd willingly fork out for.'

A long few minutes passed and then William stuck his face in hers, his breath gusting. 'There's *you*,' he said.

'Sorry?'

'You're worth something to him.'

THEY SAT PROPPED UP on pillows for the next step. Lynx absently hauled the sheets up each time the bedding slipped. William, multi-tasking, plotted and looked at her nipples.

'You'll have to stay somewhere else for a couple of days,' he said. 'Somewhere no one would think to look for you.'

'Okay.'

'And leave your purse and phone behind. I'll get you an untraceable one, so I can let you know when I have the money.'

'You won't run off with it yourself, will you?'

She thought that was actually unlikely. However, as one thieving dirtbag dealing with another, it was a concern he'd expect.

'No,' he said stoutly. 'I want to be with you, Lynx.'

'What if he calls the police?'

'We tell him if he does that, you die. We tell him if he does that—or refuses to pay—then certain information about his financial dealings is released to the police.'

'Do you actually have information that could sink him?' Lynx asked, bending to take the flesh of William's upper arm between her lips. Too close for comfort to his armpit, but it couldn't be helped.

He gave a little shiver of pleasure. 'He must know there's material out there that could put him in jail. But is he really likely to go to the cops? He's been running rings around them for so long now, are they likely to believe him, or even care?'

Now that the plan was taking shape, Lynx could see the holes in it. A practical tone reasserted itself in her voice. 'Will, listen. What if he *does* contact the police?'

'We don't make it easy. We send him to a string of different locations. Meanwhile, I'll be watching. If I see any cops I'll call you and you can miraculously escape from your kidnappers.'

'Christ.'

'You need a good story. You think you were grabbed by people who lost money to him.'

But the key question, from Lynx's point of view, was what if Jack suspected her, or him, or both of them?

'He won't, if he's frightened enough. He'll want you back. He'll want to avoid any more bad press, too.'

'Will, realistically, how are you going to get him to run around Newcastle while you watch for cops? We give him a time limit, like thirty minutes, and watch what he does. If he doesn't leave the house, we call it off. If he runs straight to the police, we call it off. If he heads somewhere unexpected, that's where the money is.'

Will DeLacey gave the appearance of a man weighing opinions raised by a woman and finding, to his surprise, that they were worth considering. 'All right,' he said. 'Could work.'

26

IT WAS NEVER QUIET in Property Crimes and that Saturday was no different, especially with Kitty Brenner steaming along the corridor towards him. Reaching Muecke, she snarled, 'What's this about you flying up to Newcastle today? I told you, it's out of our hands and I don't need you freelancing on my watch.'

The senior sergeant had the stark look of an avenging angel. Muecke was sick of it all. He reached back for his almost-forgotten street-cop grittiness and put some gravel into his voice. '*Your* watch? Get the fuck out of my face, senior sergeant. A different case. None of your concern.'

For the merest instant, a period so fleeting it might have been imagined, he saw the cold gleam of her soul. She doesn't forgive or forget, he thought. He'd have to watch his back.

'To hell with separate case,' she said mildly. 'It's all connected.'

Muecke said, 'Talk to Sam Henderson in Robbery. We were watching a man here, and now he's popped up in Newcastle.'

'Don't give me that. You went out to Watervale and interviewed

Kyle Roden yesterday. He told you something that's got you tearing off to Newcastle.'

'With the boss's approval.'

She took a step back, regarding him a little too coolly for his peace of mind. She wore a jacket, a slim-line skirt, court shoes: interviews with heavy-duty people today, he thought. She might be so busy brown-nosing she wouldn't insist on flying up with him.

'What did Roden tell you?'

Muecke weighed it up. Brenner had spent a week in Newcastle with a pair of junior officers and might have uncovered something that would help him.

'I've got some free time before I need to drive to the airport. Buy you coffee?'

She came closer, stirring the air: shampoo, a hint of perfume. 'Tell me now.'

'Remember that collection of Kelly memorabilia?'

They'd all been briefed on the robbery. Brenner gestured irritably. 'What about it?'

'And those rare banknotes?' continued Muecke. 'I'm looking at one man for both—and several other robberies. I think he acts on information from others. I think he's in Newcastle to rob Jack Tremayne.'

'Tremayne's broke.'

Muecke shook his head. 'He's got a stash, according to Roden.'

Brenner's face briefly registered dismay and worry, then the look vanished, replaced by her usual sourness. 'That makes it a property crime, does it?'

'Kitty,' Muecke said, 'I know something about this guy, so they want me to fly up and brief them. I'll only be gone a day or two.' He paused: 'I won't be leading raids, I won't be covering myself in glory.'

She flushed, turned on her heel and marched away.

His phone pinged for an incoming email. SA Police, responding to his request for photographs of Dirk and Missy van Horen. Peering at the screen, he saw a tall, bearded man standing beside a little dumpling wife. Clearly *not* Bryce and Felicity Reschke.

MUECKE'S PLANE LANDED AT noon, but the briefing was not until 4 p.m. He went looking for the airport's security suite. Forty minutes later, by way of facial recognition software, he had isolated the man from Centennial Park entering the main terminal by one door and exiting by another. He wore jeans and a jacket and carried a small weekender suitcase. 'What day is this?'

'Tuesday.'

'Can you follow him a bit further?'

'Give me a moment.'

Muecke waited. The security technician, diffident and grey-faced, as if she spent all of her time indoors, began switching between other camera vantage points, tracking the man on her bank of screens.

'Car rental,' she said at last.

'Okay. Where did he come from? Did he fly in?'

More keys clacking, more cameras logged onto. 'That's weird. Long-term carpark,' she said.

Not weird, thought Muecke. The guy didn't want his car spotted in Newcastle. 'Is that the only day he was here at the airport?'

Another wait. 'In the past week? Yes.'

'What car did he arrive in? Or leave by?'

The answer was disappointing. The technician found the car—a Toyota Corolla—but the numberplates were smeared with mud. He washes it off as soon as he's out of the carpark, Muecke thought. He began to see a careful mind at work. Not that it was helpful to know that. A pattern suggested itself, however. The guy probably drove to Newcastle from an outside base and rented a car, as needed, from different locations around the city or in nearby towns. Might have used his own car on the first day but was careful not to repeat that.

'What car-hire firm?'

'Budget.'

'What kind of car?'

He waited. Soon she had a small white sedan driving away. 'Looks like a Hyundai. They're popular.'

All part of the pattern, Muecke thought. He walked through to the car-hire booths. One Budget staffer was on the phone, the other busy selling an insurance upgrade. Muecke waited, and when she'd handed over keys and paperwork and turned to him with an expectant smile, he fronted up to the desk with his ID and a printout from the surveillance files.

'On Tuesday of this week, ten in the morning, you rented a white Hyundai to this man. I need his name, address, credit card details, licence details, anything you can give me. It's in regard to a very serious crime.'

The staffer, young, glanced at her offsider. 'I'm not sure that I'm allowed…'

'Terrorism implications,' Muecke said, with an air of impatience barely suppressed.

She recoiled from the counter, looked at him in stupefaction. The other woman was still on the phone examining her nails, close up then at a distance, but aware of everything happening nearby. Putting the phone receiver to her breast, she said, 'It's okay, Sherry, it's not going to hurt.'

Sherry stared again at the photograph, as if she was looking at the face of a suicide bomber. She turned to her screen, tapped some keys.

'Here it is: Adam Palmer. He's from Brisbane.'

I bet, thought Muecke. He noted all the details from her screen. 'The payment went through?'

'Says here he paid in cash.'

'So you didn't process the card.'

'No.'

'Is that usual? Accepting cash?'

The other woman had hung up the phone. She wandered over, looked at the screen, then the photo. 'I remember him.'

Muecke waited. Most of his life was spent waiting. Finally, he prompted: 'And?'

'He said he'd bought his wife a bracelet for her birthday and reached his daily limit and could he pay by cash. If there were extras, then we'd charge the card.'

'He returned the car?'

'To our city branch.'

Got back here how? wondered Muecke. He could check taxis or Ubers, or airport bus CCTV. But what would that tell him?

'Undamaged? Tank full?'

She looked at the screen. 'Yes.'

'So you had no reason to test the validity of the card.'

'Like I said, he paid for everything in cash, fair and square.'

MUECKE WAS IN DOWNTOWN Newcastle by 2 p.m. He gave a lot of thought to his next stage and decided against approaching Tremayne or Tremayne's wife or Tremayne's lawyer—at least not without permission from the feds and the locals, who would not give him that permission.

It would be a long shot talking to them anyway. Would they have seen the guy he was after? Would they admit it if they had?

According to his research, one of the Tremayne-Roden companies was still trading. The office, on Ravenshaw Street, was blank-faced, as if in hiding. He stepped in off the footpath and found a small reception area in darkness, the desk unattended, a screensaver roiling away on a computer—maybe the receptionist walked off for good and switched off the lights behind her, thought Muecke.

There was a hallway entrance in the back wall, a hint of light spilling from an office somewhere along it; a male voice sounding heated. Tremayne?

Muecke knocked and called out. The voice stopped. Said, 'I have to go,' and a handset was clattered onto its base.

The man who appeared was plump, clean, worried-looking. Muecke knew the face from his research: Mark Impey, a friend of Tremayne and his wife.

'Sorry,' Impey was saying with a shallow, uncertain laugh, 'we're a bit short-staffed at the moment. In fact'—he mopped his face—'we're going out of business and I had some tidying up to do.'

Another laugh. A man who laughs too often, at nothing, Muecke thought. He showed his ID.

'Police?' A plump hand went to his collar. 'Actually, I should apologise if I gave you the impression I work here. I'm not an employee. I was helping out earlier in the week and I just came back to...to...'

'Perhaps you can help me with something,' Muecke said.

The man looked hunted. 'If I can.'

Muecke didn't know what the lines of influence and communication were in what was probably a small, tightly knit business community. He didn't want to scare Tremayne into running too soon. But Impey was on the periphery...

He took out the surveillance photograph. 'Have you seen this man around at all?'

Impey looked confused. 'I don't understand.'

'What don't you understand?'

'Don't you people talk to each other?'

'You know how it is,' Muecke said. Something was about to fall out.

'He works for the Probity Commission,' Impey said.

'Ah. You met him?'

'He came to my house. Quite rude, I thought. Quite unnecessary. Not very professional.'

'Did he ask questions? Tell you anything?'

Impey agonised. 'To be frank, he put the wind up me.'

'Did he give you a name?'

Impey winced. 'I forget.'

'Okay.'

Then Impey said primly, 'Actually things have gone a bit too far for my liking.'

'Right...'

'It's about Jack Tremayne. I've done all I can for him, I'm washing my hands of it.'

'Uh huh.'

'I only hope he does the right thing.'

This was a man you had to coax information out of. Muecke said, 'You think he might do the *wrong* thing?'

FOUR P.M., A BRIEFING room at the police station on Watt Street, Muecke tapping the Sydney surveillance photo and saying, 'This man passed himself off to Mark Impey as a Probity Commission agent. He gave Impey to understand that Jack Tremayne has a hidden stash and intends to do a runner.'

Agostino was at the briefing, looking put out that Muecke had been acting alone on his turf. 'You think your guy's after the stash?'

'I do.'

150

'How sure are you Tremayne's got a hidden stash?'

'Kyle Roden confirms it.'

'You spoke to him?'

'Yes, in Watervale.'

'Could be sour grapes.'

'Could be. Or it could be that Tremayne has a trick up his sleeve.'

'Why would your guy pretend to work for the Probes? Why alert Impey, who could be in on it?'

'I think to see what might shake loose. It's probable that no one knows where the money is except Tremayne. You got nothing when you raided his place, right? So maybe a friend's helping him. So—scare the friends and see what happens.'

'Be interesting to know who else he's taken a run at.'

A City of Newcastle inspector said, 'You don't think Impey's the friend? About to cave?'

'He's not someone you'd trust with a secret,' Muecke said.

A Probity Commission investigator was comparing the Sydney and Newcastle surveillance photos. 'Certainly looks like the same man.'

Muecke ignored him and so did the others. 'Tremayne could be getting ready to run, right now, today.'

'He isn't,' Agostino said.

'I guess you're watching him,' Muecke said, 'but he's slippery from all accounts.'

Agostino shrugged, as if to say his team was slipperier. A nice enough guy, thought Muecke, but young and ambitious. The arrogance was an immutable trait.

'You want this man?' the Newcastle inspector said, indicating the surveillance photographs. 'Not Tremayne?'

'Correct.'

'Because we don't have the resources to look for him.'

This could take all year, thought Muecke. He was supposed to fly back to Sydney by Monday. 'Perhaps if I could have access to your footage? Photos? Wiretaps?'

'Not wiretaps. And it all goes back weeks.'

'I'm game, just give me a desk and a monitor,' Muecke said, pivoting out of his chair. 'Maybe I can find where Tremayne's stashed his loot and wrap it all up for you.'

They had their doubts. They'd have preferred it if he just went home.

27

Nick Lazar was catching up on paperwork. He'd been hired to do a party starting at midnight, so he had time to spare. He'd just emailed the last invoice when a shadow appeared on the other side of his frosted-glass office door, a rippling shape beyond the discreet gold lettering. A tentative rap of knuckles, the door rattling, a little loose in the jamb.

Lazar called, 'Come,' expecting some fresh bullshit. There'd been a lot of that lately; summonses, debt collectors.

Joshua Kramer slipped in, flushed, probably high. Thin face sharp, smiling nervously.

'Nick.'

'Josh. You've got another gig?'

The kid was wearing jeans and a hoodie. He edged onto the visitor's chair as if seeing Lazar, being in Lazar's company, had caused a shift in gravity. 'I've put the band on the backburner for now,' he said.

Damn good thing, thought Lazar. He waited.

Kramer shifted on his buttocks and dug in his jeans. 'Got you that hundred I owed you.'

Which would pay for about ten seconds of Lazar's lawyer's time. 'Thanks, Josh.'

The kid jiggled his knee.

Lazar said, 'Did you get around to asking your old man for help?'

Kramer shook his head wildly. 'No. Nope. Not him. Nope.'

'That would be a no, then,' Lazar said with a smile. Sometime in the next few years the kid might reveal what was on his mind. Lazar tapped the keys on his calculator, made a note on a pad. Busy, busy.

And the kid said, 'You thought any more about, you know...'

Lazar was nervous suddenly. Walls have ears. He checked his watch: almost five-thirty. 'How about we go around the corner for a brew, Josh? I'm just about finished here.'

Out where the early-evening sky was a desolate mix of blackish greys, coldness seeping from sooty walls and a drizzling rain. It was a short walk to the pub, but pubs have ears, too. Lazar stopped beneath a shop awning, a dismal light within, a lone barber reading a newspaper in one of his chairs.

'Have I thought any more about what, Josh?' He seized the kid's forearm for emphasis. 'Quickly now.'

'About Wyatt,' Kramer said, accusatory neediness in his eyes. 'About the money.'

Lazar released him. He checked both ways along the footpath: they were alone. 'Not really my concern.'

'I thought, you know, with your contacts and everything.'

'Thought what, exactly?'

The kid shouted, 'I thought you'd help me, man.'

'I have helped you. Discount rates, and I've been carrying your hundred-dollar debt.'

Kramer's stoned eyes were damp holes of darkness. 'Not that kind of help.'

'Then what? Be clear.'

Kramer took a breath. 'Help ripping Wyatt off, okay? That clear enough for you?'

'Keep your voice down.'

'You were interested, I could see it in your face,' Kramer said, clutching his chest for warmth. He was shivering, underdressed for a cold, wet May evening.

Lazar tired of playing hard to get. 'Think about it, Josh. We don't know where the guy lives. We don't know when or where or even *if* he's going to be briefed by your father again.'

Josh Kramer stared miserably at his wet feet. A clump of people hurried by. A dog sidled up as if to share a secret and rested its flank against the kid's calf. Kramer gave it an ineffectual kick and almost fell over; the dog skittered away with a look of betrayal.

Lazar gazed at Kramer with deep distaste, but the kid didn't notice. Still looking down, he said, 'I can't think what else to do except draw him out somehow, like bump off my sister or something.'

The kid didn't mean it, clearly—he wasn't thinking. But Lazar was.

BRADLEY SALTER HAD BEEN back in his cell for two days with nothing but grudgingly doled-out paracetamol to take the edge off the pain. His bruises were coming up in technicolour but the swelling had receded, the noise in his ears was down to a dull roar, and his piss was no longer likely to attract vampires. He'd heard that Kramer's day-release privileges had been revoked and his goons sent to a different prison but didn't take much heart from the news. Kramer was already reaching out to some of the psychos in the joint and he still had some of the screws in his pocket.

And so Salter became like a freshie in fear for his life. He kept to the shadowy areas of corridors and rooms, close to the wall when he rounded corners and wide of open doorways. He was jostled and tripped. His food was spat in, his plate tipped to the floor. Two cell searches. Rec room chairs jerked away as he tried to sit. 'Maggot', 'dog' and 'rat' muttered in his ear. He stopped showering. When he got too rank he gave himself a whore's wash at a laundry sink. He tried keeping to his cell or the library. Keeping close to the screws when he walked the yard.

As for Kramer, the prick ignored him. Face blank, as if Salter didn't exist, whenever they encountered each other in a doorway or corridor. Which Salter read as the calm before the next storm. A pre-emptive strike was the only way to go, to which end he'd filched a toothbrush from the infirmary.

It weighed on him, the eternal vigilance. The fact that Kramer was likely to take a second run at him. What was the prick waiting for? Trying to wear him down? It seemed unlikely the guy had washed his hands of the matter. He'd want to know who, on the outside, was moving against him.

The waiting took another toll. Salter's hair was like straw, his skin like paper. He wasn't a men's cosmetics kind of guy, but he asked his lawyer to bring him a moisturiser and a decent shampoo the next time he visited. Nothing too poncy; he didn't want to smell like a bunch of flowers. Both were confiscated. Both were given back later, pretty much empty. What, they thought his lawyer was smuggling a gun in a bottle of Pantene?

All he could do was embrace his outcast status, along with his bruises and stitches. And ignore Nick Lazar; not bother to check the iPhone for messages. Lazar owed him.

Then he ran into Carl Ayliffe leaving the library just before dinner that Saturday. All alone, no Kramer or Kramer goons about. He slapped the kid's cheeks, left, right, and got up in his face.

'Rat me out, would you? Fucking little maggot.'

Ayliffe dropped to the floor, his face mucus-streaked and pitiable. 'Please, he made me.'

'Could've lied.'

'He was going to break my fingers.'

Salter kicked him in the head and stomped on his ankle. 'And you told the cops as well? You don't do that, you fucking miserable waste of space. Didn't anyone tell you that?'

Ayliffe rolled into a ball and wailed. A complicated feeling of disgust crept through Salter. A memory trace of worn lino and pitted chrome table legs. The underside of the table a mosaic, briefly distracting, of dead wads of chewed bubblegum…And then his father's right leg swinging, the work boot snapping in.

Jesus, he'd become his father. He was a cliché.

He reached down, hauled Ayliffe to his feet and told him to piss off.

Alone then, a sense of foreboding like a thickness in the air. A dread of pitfalls out there in the rooms, cells and corridors.

He retrieved the iPhone from its nest in the library and, while it booted, walked to where he could see along the corridor yet avoid the cameras. He was still alone. The phone lit up and he saw that Nick had texted several times, called twice. Salter sent him a text: *call*.

While waiting, he reached out and absently turned a book spine the right way up. Then, realising the book had been mis-shelved, moved it to the correct position. Quite a few of the books were out of place. Someone who doesn't know his alphabet, he thought. He checked the corridor again. Six forty-five. If he wanted dinner, he'd better get his skates on.

The phone buzzed thirty seconds later. He said, 'Yo,' and Lazar was screaming in his ear:

'Where the fuck have you been?'

'Fuck you.'

'What do you mean, fuck me? You go off the radar, I have no idea what's going on.'

So Salter told him what had been going on. Sam Kramer had been grounded, Sam Kramer had beaten the shit out of him. 'Out of my hands now, Nick. You'll have to track down the guy you're after some other way. Meanwhile, you owe me. Big time.'

There was a long pause. 'About that,' Lazar said.

'You bastard. I'm coming for you when I get out.'

'No, no, not that—how would you like to make a bit more money?'

Salter was on his guard. 'I'm listening.'

'You must really hate Kramer.'

Where was this going? 'Yeah, so?'

'Could you take him?'

This was interesting. The chance to monetise an existing goal. Sweet.

'How much?'

28

MARINA SECURITY WOULD BE tighter now: Wyatt couldn't risk another search of Impey's boat. Early Sunday morning saw him sprawled on a damp park bench opposite Jack Tremayne's house. He looked as if he might have spent the whole night huddled there in his torn op-shop parka and unravelling woollen jumper, a beanie over his brow and ears, drizzled in the water droplets from the last leaves on the deciduous trees all around him.

He could also see the surveillance team, and a distant glimpse of his own Toyota with the fake Hertz sticker parked along a side street. The watchers were in the white Caprice today. Surely Tremayne knew that car by now? Unless that was the whole point.

At 9 a.m. Tremayne emerged in bicycle shorts, a hoodie and a helmet, wheeling a mountain bike. He set off along the street, a slow, gliding roll past the Caprice, which eventually eased away from the kerb and trailed him.

Wyatt chewed on that. If Tremayne ran now, he'd be faster, more agile, than on foot or in a car. There'd be nothing Wyatt could do about it without drawing attention to himself. Perhaps nothing the authorities could do, either, but they stood more chance of grabbing Tremayne than he did. Manpower, communication— the ability to throw up a cordon. But Tremayne wasn't dressed for an escape attempt, wasn't carrying a change of clothes or a phone or a wallet. He was simply setting out for a bike ride.

Still, were bike rides a part of his routine? Wyatt hadn't been watching the man long enough to know.

Thirty minutes later, Lynx Tremayne appeared. Jeans, trainers and a blue puffa jacket. Head down, walking briskly with no pause to check the weather or decide whether to go left, right or across the park. This wasn't a simple morning walk: too purposeful. Instinct told Wyatt to tail her.

Waiting until she was a hundred metres away, heading towards Newcomen Street, he ran to his car, stripped off the parka and jumper to reveal a thin hiking merino, newly purchased, and set off after her. He drove slowly, keeping well back, the blue puffa jacket easy to spot. Down Newcomen to Christchurch Cathedral, where she climbed into a Honda Odyssey. Wyatt couldn't see the driver; his impression was that it was a man. He tailed the Honda along Church Street, then into Tyrrell, and eventually to King Street and west from the downtown area. A stop for petrol, then to a street in Tighes Hill.

William DeLacey lived in Tighes Hill.

But instead of pulling into his street, the car stopped at a small playground and Lynx Tremayne got out. She made for a bus shelter and sat. Wyatt saw no reason for her to do that. And she simply sat; didn't crane for an oncoming bus or check the timetable. Yet she was impatient.

Wyatt continued to follow the Honda, which soon turned into DeLacey's street and into the driveway of his house, nose up to the rear of the Lexus. Wyatt had only seen the house once, and at night; in daylight it looked appealing: a renovated weatherboard with pastel grey walls, a white picket fence and a silvery gumtree in the backyard. Nothing ostentatious. But it would be costly to buy and renovate here. A house for a family who couldn't yet afford The Hill.

Wyatt found a parking spot at the end of the street and watched in the mirror. DeLacey was bundling luggage into the Honda, kissing his wife and daughter goodbye. Wyatt thought it through: DeLacey had kindly offered to fill the Honda with petrol while his wife finished packing and getting their daughter ready for the trip. A trip where? To see her parents? A holiday? To get them out of the way, anyhow, so he could move his lover in for a while.

When the Honda was gone DeLacey made a call. Shortly after that, Lynx Tremayne came in at a fast walk and brushed past DeLacey, who'd looked set to give her a kiss. Then both of them were inside the grey house. Wyatt watched for an hour, until he heard an alert on his tracking mobile. Jack Tremayne's BMW was on the move.

It had amused Tremayne, taking the agents in the white Caprice for a long, slow ride with the occasional zigzagging sprint. Down to the Strzelecki Lookout and back up through the park, trees lapping on both sides of the track; down Ordnance Street, then rapidly up Watts—where he gave the police station the finger— and west along the foreshore. He'd had to slow here—people in high-vis jackets preparing for some public event. He stopped and walked the bike for a while. Learned there was a fun run starting after lunch.

He bought croissants and rode slowly home via the Bogey Hole. Put the croissants in the oven to warm; showered, shaved and rubbed some product through his hair. Wondered who he was trying to impress. Lynx? They were barely talking these days.

161

He brewed a strong coffee, yelled, 'Lynx, coffee's up,' and perched on a kitchen stool. Coffee, croissants with honey, a bunch of pissed-off Probity Commission or fraud squad or federal police agents out there in the street…Life was okay if you ignored the bullshit.

The house was too quiet. He crossed to a front window: Lynx's car was there. She hadn't been in the bedroom before or after his shower; she hadn't been laying out her stupid fucking tarot cards when he walked through the sitting room just now…

He checked every room and the front, side and rear yards; the garage. Her usual bag was on the chair beside the bed. Her purse and phone were on the dressing table. He shrugged.

I go for a bike ride, he thought, and she goes for a walk.

Insistent now, coming from the deepest chamber of his instincts, a single word: *Run*.

DeLacey's caginess, Lynx's disappearances, Impey's jumpiness. But he wasn't a man who ever backed down, and to run would be to back down. He was smarter than anyone life had ever thrown at him. For weeks, months, now he'd tied everyone up in knots. Bought time. If he was patient he could outwait the Probity Commission. They were notoriously timid and he'd probably get no more than a rap over the knuckles. He couldn't blame them. The Federal Government strips thirty-eight million dollars out of their budget and expects them to shake a big stick at corporate malfeasance?

Run, the voice said.

He sat on the sofa to think, and fell asleep. Late morning his phone woke him. He stared groggily at the screen. Blinked. Looked again. Maybe he *hadn't* woken—maybe he was still asleep, caught in a strangling dream of all the things he feared most.

A series of photographs had pinged in: Lynx bound to a chair with grey duct tape, a strip of tape across her mouth, her eyes full of fear. She was in a room in a house but there were no markers, only a plain, pale yellow wall with a brighter patch where a photo, a painting or a poster had once hung.

Then a photograph of an A4 sheet of paper carrying a list of demands and warnings in twenty-point type. A further photo, the note now a pile of ashes.

Tremayne found that he'd grasped the neck of his shirt with one hand as panic clawed at his throat.

Then, as if a switch had been flicked, he was standing apart from all that. Curious that he'd reacted so strongly—reacted at all, in fact. Had he panicked for himself, for Lynx, or for the pair of them? At the same time, in another part of his mind, he was planning his next steps.

He was methodical, once he started moving. He filled a bumbag with all the cash he could find, together with a mobile phone, a key, a crumplable cap and tightly rolled surf pants. Then he stripped to his underwear and pulled on shorts, a T-shirt and running shoes. Locked the house, gave a little twiddle of the fingers to the man and the woman in the Caprice—they waved back—got behind the wheel of his BMW and headed down to the carpark at the rear of Will DeLacey's law firm.

He locked the car—he'd be sorry to abandon it—and crossed the road. Walked west along the foreshore promenade. Other people were streaming in; hundreds there already, under a large banner reading *Cancer Council 10 km Fun Run*. He found a booth and registered. Looked about him. Some of the runners were bouncing on their toes already, itching to get going. He checked the time: noon. The run started at 1 p.m. He tried to say hello to a couple of people he knew. One, a hard-nosed stoic, looked right past him. The other, her face registering cold dismay, thin black eyebrows arching in consternation and surprise, gave him a choked 'Hi.'

163

A sullen-looking cloud cover. It pretty much summed things up.

YESTERDAY AGOSTINO HAD GIVEN Muecke an office the size of a broom cupboard. 'Go your hardest.'

At least it had a landline phone, a computer and a desk, so Muecke went his hardest and didn't get to his hotel until 9 p.m. He was back at the rickety desk by 8 a.m., ready for another shot at the files and surveillance tapes. He'd organised the material into 'yes', 'no' and 'maybe' piles, and by lunchtime Sunday had whittled everything down to a few bank records, call histories and photographs that seemed suggestive of...something.

Then at twelve-thirty he walked down to the canteen for a stale ham, cheese and tomato sandwich and heard some minor commotion in the corridor on his way back.

Agostino and a couple of other guys, heading somewhere in a hurry. 'What's up?'

The Newcastle detective skidded to a halt. He had the look of a man called in to work on his day off: comb tracks in his hair and last week's suit. 'Probably nothing, but Jack Tremayne just did something odd.'

'Yeah?'

'Put on running gear and signed up for a fun run along the foreshore.'

'Doesn't sound like the Tremayne we know and love.'

'Christ no; but there are hundreds of people there. Literally hundreds.'

'Ah. All hands on deck.'

'Pretty much.'

'I'll grab my jacket,' Muecke said.

Agostino was itching to get going. 'Meet you there, mate. There'll be a few of us.'

A few of you running alongside Tremayne and several hundred others in your Sunday best? Muecke allowed himself a tired smile as he went upstairs, shouldered his way into his jacket and made his way down to the esplanade.

The first runners were powering away from the start as he arrived at Throsby Wharf. He wanted to say, 'It's a *fun* run,' but was pretty certain it wouldn't go down well. He stood on the sidelines, trying to spot one of the local coppers. No sign of anyone he knew, and no sign of Tremayne. Did they seriously expect Tremayne to be running with the mob?

He waited. Thought about his wife and kids. They were the sort to take part in this run. Joiners. They had a public sense, a community sense—something he'd lost along the way. They embraced life; he'd seen too much of it. And he knew if he ran with this mob of grinning nutcases he'd look a fool, with his pale legs. *Sound* a fool, with his ex-smoker's lungs struggling for air. He wasn't envious, exactly—it was barely fourteen degrees Celsius here, with a nasty chop on the harbour. But he had surely lost something, he thought, some old sense of living a useful, busy life. Some kind of shared feeling with Meg and the kids.

He spotted Agostino. 'Any sign?'

'Nada.' Agostino was showing the strain, with the wind thrashing his hair about and his face working anxiously. 'Zip. Zilch.'

'You don't honestly think he's jogging, do you?'

'Well, yeah. He was seen registering, seen heading away from the starting line. My main worry is, someone's going to pick him up or he has a car stashed somewhere.'

Or he's swimming across the harbour, Muecke thought. Or sailing off into the sunset.

That last thought tugged at him. 'A sometimes-praiseworthy lateral thinker,' according to another of his performance reviews.

His mind took him to Jack Tremayne's sale of assets during the last couple of months. Including a cabin cruiser, bought by a business associate.

Muecke wandered over to the marina and badged a security guard, an elderly man with a veined nose and cap flaps pulled sensibly down over his ears. 'A man named Tremayne sold a boat a few weeks ago,' he said, without preamble. 'Do you know who bought it?'

'Funny you should say that.'

Muecke looked at him. 'Is that a fact.'

'He sold it to Mr Impey, and someone sneaked on board a couple of nights ago.'

Muecke felt that old tingle again, even as he cursed himself for not knowing who the buyer had been. 'The boat's here? You can show me?'

'Sure.'

'Let's go,' Muecke said, harder now, to get the old guy moving.

Stopped and went back when he saw resistance in the man. 'Please, I'd be very grateful.'

'I was *attacked*.'

'When you investigated?'

'Yes.'

'Was anything taken?'

'Didn't look to be. Mr Impey said it was all intact.'

'Let's have a look. Do you mind?'

The guard was slow to move off, reinforcing the fact that he was near retirement age, generally overlooked, and not impressed by a pushy bloke with a badge.

'This way,' he said.

Muecke strained to keep his voice mild, his steps unhurried. 'Tell me about Mr Tremayne.'

'Had a lot of money, lost a lot of money.'

166

'And as a person?'

'Total prick. Completely up himself.'

'Mr Impey?'

'He's all right, better than most. Knows fuck all about boats, though.'

They reached an area sealed off by a metal gate, except the gate had been left open, and the guard was saying, 'There goes Mr Impey's boat now. First time it's been out in weeks.'

A sleek white vessel backing out, a gliding dart unruffled by the chop in the water. 'It might be his boat, but it's not him,' Muecke said, fumbling for his phone.

'Fuck me, you're right,' the guard said. 'That's Mr Tremayne.'

WYATT TRACKED TREMAYNE'S BMW to the carpark behind DeLacey's law firm and let the Corolla idle as he watched him cross the road. Some kind of running event. Nothing felt right about that.

He steered off the street and into the law firm's driveway and parked next to the BMW. Then he stepped over a low hedge, around the rear of the adjacent building and out onto the road again. He darted across, joining the people thronging to run or cheer the runners, and watched Tremayne approach a registration table inside a flapping tent. People jostled Wyatt, the disturbing randomness of a crowd. He wished he'd brought a gun along. He breathed in, out, until he felt loose again, his face calm, unremarkable, his senses sharp.

By the time he slipped through the throng to a patch of grassland closer to the water's edge, he was ready to play a waiting game. Tremayne would emerge from the crowd eventually. And from where Wyatt was standing, he could see the section of the marina where Impey's boat was moored. The running event was Tremayne's diversion. Wyatt understood diversions, he'd used them before—most recently burning oil drums in a Shell depot on one side of a country town while he held up a payroll van on the other. And so he waited, and he thought. Almost like breathing.

There was an electric energy in the air suddenly. A siren blast, raised voices, a sense of rippling zeal as the first clump of runners sprinted away. Quite soon after that, Tremayne emerged, walking rapidly, heading for the marina. He'd pulled on pants and a cap and no longer looked like a runner. Wyatt held back: the elderly security guard he'd encountered on Friday was standing between him and the first line of moored yachts, watching the runners as if they were a wondrously strange phenomenon.

Beyond him, Tremayne was unlocking a metal gate. Wyatt was about twenty metres from *Windward Passage* and he didn't think he could go through the security guard. Too many people about, spectators urging on family and friends, tourists gawking, press photographers, a mounted policeman.

And now a man with the tired eyes and permanently mistrustful cast of a cop was talking to the guard. Wyatt took a step back, and another, and turned his back, and a hundred metres in the other direction was a small, fast-looking runabout bobbing in the water beside a set of stone steps. A kid with the clear, open grin of someone who'd never been told no stepped out of the cockpit and lifted an esky to waiting arms on the shore. Wyatt set out to ruin his day.

29

'I'M TELLING YOU, IT was Tremayne,' Muecke snarled. 'Why don't you listen?'

He pointed. 'That boat is about to reach the open seas and Jack Tremayne is steering it.'

Agostino seemed doubtful. 'He was jogging, the last we saw.' He paused. 'Anyway, he sold his boat.'

'And that's the boat he sold,' Muecke said. 'Why can't I get through to you? He would have kept a key. And obviously he knows how to sail the damn thing.'

Agostino turned to the security guard. 'What do *you* think?'

The man shrank, feeling attacked. 'It wasn't Mr Impey, I know that much.'

Muecke snapped out the words, driving his meaning home: 'And who is Impey? A close friend of Jack Tremayne's. The boat's new owner.'

Agostino said stiffly, 'I know who Impey is.'

He turned to the guard. 'Only one man aboard?'

'Far as I could tell.'

'Okay.' Agostino rolled his eyes. 'I'll give the water police a call.'

But the only available patrol boat was at the site of a jet ski accident some distance up the Hunter River. It would take time to return, and meanwhile Tremayne was a receding dot between the Nobbys and Stockton Beach heading for the broad Pacific. Tremayne could sail north, south, straight across to Norfolk Island, French Polynesia…Anywhere at all.

'The air wing?' Muecke said.

'Mate…' said Agostino, as if he'd suggested a direct call to the prime minister. 'Step at a time.'

Ten minutes later, the water police patrol boat came in fast, nose up in a bow wave. It throttled back, nose dipping as it swung around, and came in a deft, unfussy broadside to the dock. The boat was familiar to Muecke from cases he'd worked on Sydney Harbour: white, sixteen metres long, a crew of four but the capacity for more, with a high superstructure comprising the cabin, wheelhouse and masts. Speed, twenty-nine knots. Tremayne was in an equally fast boat with a long head start.

For a moment, Muecke thought they were going to tie up and stand around yacking, but a young water police constable beckoned them to step aboard. He took Muecke by the elbow.

'I can manage.'

'Just a precaution, sir.'

Then Agostino was aboard, too, and the patrol boat peeled away, curving around with a sharp tilt, heading for the gap between Stockton and the Nobbys. A fast streak across the harbour, and then they all became aware of a third boat.

'What the fuck's he doing?' Agostino said.

The young water cop sucked his teeth in approval. 'Nice boat. Cobalt Bowrider.'

'I don't care what kind it is,' snarled Agostino, 'I care what it's doing.'

So did Muecke, watching the other craft low and fast in the water, cutting across the bow of the patrol boat. He looked up at the water police skipper, who throttled back grimly and jerked the wheel as the intruder shot across. For a moment it was out of sight; then it howled back and closed in. When the two craft were far too close to each other, Muecke had just one thought: he wants to stop us getting to Tremayne before he does.

WYATT SAW THEIR ALARM, their immobilisation; saw them start to shout and gesture at him, gripping the rails as the deck pitched under their feet. Except, curiously, for the one who'd been talking to marina security. Plainclothes, older than the others, worn-looking. No fear in the thin, pale face; only the hard intensity of a hunter.

He knows me. Not my name or where I live. But he knows exactly why I'm here and what I've been doing.

He's hunting me.

Wyatt wrenched the wheel as he shot past again and came around hard. Steered head on towards the patrol boat, which turned slightly in anticipation, but slowly, too slowly, to avoid the collision. A long, glancing, fibreglass-ripping blow that shocked them all and left the patrol boat wallowing.

Wyatt peeled away, swung around and aimed at the rear section of the patrol boat. A mad scramble on board as the others watched helplessly and the skipper yanked on the wheel. Wyatt hit hard, the nose crumpling and rearing briefly and then both boats were dead in the water.

Wyatt's motor had stopped. He was holed, drifting. On the patrol boat they were getting to their feet and the detective in the sharp suit was yelling, pulling out his sidearm as the skipper was coaxing revs from his motor. A rough, coughing idle. Not fully disabled, but in no shape for an ocean pursuit. Wyatt's boat drifted further away, closer to the shore, listing now, and taking on more water all the time. He slipped over the side, watched by the older man. Wyatt imagined he saw a spark of something like humour or respect. Then it was gone, and the eyes were flat again and Wyatt was underwater.

Down into the murky darkness, where he swam for as long as his breath lasted, then to the surface to take another breath, and down again, and he thought he heard shouts from the patrol boat, answering shouts on the shoreline.

The marina, thought Wyatt. Lose myself among the hulls.

He came to the far western end. Hauled himself out of the water, paused and collapsed briefly, wanting to give in to the deep drowsiness of physical exhaustion. But people were looking twice at this drenched and squelching figure. He summoned up a flicker of energy and crossed Hannell Street to lose himself in the side streets. A few pedestrians eyed him, but he didn't seem to need their help—he looked off-putting if anything—so they left him alone. One dared to film him on his phone.

He reached his car eventually, sodden and chafed. He was surprised to see DeLacey's Lexus parked next to Tremayne's BMW. He didn't know what it meant and didn't have time to work it out. He opened the boot of his Toyota and tossed his damp, stinking clothes in before pulling on lightweight hiking pants, a heavy shirt, a windproof khaki jacket and a pair of black Dunlop Volleys. Finally, he shrugged himself into the straps of a small daypack containing his wallet, phones, and fake ID. Heard a voice around the driveway corner, closing in.

'We might get lucky and find a white Corolla here, too.'

Wyatt made a neat running leap onto the lid of the dumpster and rolled over the fence into the alley.

172

AFTER A FISHERMAN HAD towed the crippled patrol boat back to the marina, Muecke, seeing the water police officers settle in for an interminable recap for the shore police, had slipped away with Agostino. It would take the local plods ages to organise a sea-air search.

'I believe you now, mate, Agostino said.'

The younger man looked shaken. He looked angry, too. Good: Muecke could use that. He hurried across the road to William DeLacey's law office.

'You think the guy headed here?'

'Have to start somewhere,' Muecke said. 'Tremayne parked here, right? Maybe his wife's here, or his lawyer. Let's check the carpark first.'

'I don't know what that'll tell us.'

'I don't either. But let's see if Tremayne left anything in his car. Never know, we might get lucky and find a white Corolla here, too.'

Muecke heard it then, a thump and clatter, and ran to the corner of the building trailed by Agostino.

'Fuck me,' Agostino said. 'There *is* a Corolla.'

Muecke approached the little car feeling jittery. The boot was open, damp stains on the concrete around it, wet footwear and a wad of wet clothing inside it. He peered through the windows, then walked around the BMW, peering in. Pointed at the Lexus: 'Do you know this car?'

'Belongs to DeLacey, Tremayne's lawyer.'

Nothing in the Lexus, either. Muecke glanced around the space at the rear of the building. That thump he'd heard: the guy jumping up on the dumpster and over the fence.

He told Agostino exactly what he thought had happened and what he wanted Agostino to do. 'Saturate the area. Get his picture out. Keep an eye on stolen vehicle reports.'

'What are you going to be doing?'

'Hunting,' Muecke said.

In another man, it might have sounded self-important.

TOO SANE TO TRY a running leap, Muecke laboured onto the dumpster and landed with a thump in the alley behind the fence. Which way? He tried to read the man's impulses. He'll need cover: a crowd would be good, Muecke thought. But not the fun run. People ambling. Window shopping. People on a Sunday afternoon.

He buttonholed a couple as he trotted out onto the streets: where was the best shopping around here? The woman thought about it. Around here? Try King Street, the Marketown Shopping Centre.

Muecke was looking for a man above average height with dark hair—but he could be wearing a cap by now—and a sense of loose, coiled energy. He found one; but he wasn't certain. The man ahead of him was hatless, dark-haired; with a water-darkened collar, looked like. Muecke held back, watched, and understood: his quarry was using reflective surfaces to check for a tail. Shop windows, parked cars, probably even the sunglasses of oncoming pedestrians. Looking for anyone who lingered too long; someone not moving to the rhythm of the shopping throng.

And he knows my face.

Muecke ducked into a chemist shop and bought a towelling hat and sunglasses. He folded his tie into his trouser pocket and draped his suit coat over one arm, slipped back out onto the footpath.

The man had vanished. Muecke half-expected it. His little shopping diversion had been quick, but he was following a man who was super-aware and had probably seen him. A man who'd double back towards the confusion he'd recently caused rather than keep going as most people would do instinctively. Or maybe,

174

having flushed me out, he'll wait to see if I'm alone.

Muecke patted the inside pocket of his coat. His phone was missing. Fell out on the boat or in the alley, he thought. The guy's gone, or he's too far ahead, using the shops: in one door and out another. And I can't call for backup.

Meanwhile, though: how did the guy think he was going to get to Jack Tremayne?

CONFIDENT THAT HE'D SHAKEN off his tail, Wyatt caught a bus, hanging back until the doors were about to close before stepping aboard. He sat in the rear corner and looked out, concealed by the broad panel between the rear window and the first of the side windows. His gaze scanned restlessly, passed over suit pants and a white shirt, roamed on—and shot back to suit pants and white shirt. The plainclothes man had gone the hat and sunglasses route. Close but no cigar, Wyatt thought.

He got out three stops later near Railway Street, the last to alight from the bus, and caught a taxi to Westfield shopping centre in Kotara, then a train back the way he'd come, a taxi ride to Mater Hospital and an Uber out to the airport. It took most of the afternoon. He knew there'd be an alert out for him, but they'd be looking for a man taking a flight out of the city, not one who'd just arrived and needed a rental car.

Not the Budget booth twice in one week; Hertz this time. He offered a Visa pay card in the name of Sven Van der Horst. There was a thousand dollars in the account. He didn't want to do anything that would strike people as odd this time. Certainly no paying by cash. It had probably been a mistake, paying cash at the Budget counter earlier in the week, but some of the cards had been unused for a while: he didn't know if they'd been compromised. The Van der Horst ID was new, purchased last month.

This time he rented a white Subaru XV. Fast and tough, but

still a common enough vehicle on the roads of the country. And as he was walking to the Hertz parking bays, he felt a tingle in his spine. He turned his head, a casual movement, and registered a panicked flutter at the Budget counter. Two women, their faces studiously busy with paperwork. He'd been remembered. He wouldn't be holding on to the Subaru for long.

Wyatt set out on an indirect route to Anna Bay, where he intended to check in on Tremayne's movements using the GPS tracker and think through his next moves. He drove across to the town of Raymond Terrace, then east on Richardson Road. The adrenaline was in him, and that was useful but also dangerous. He switched to cruise control and set his speed to five below the limit.

Around past the airport again. Then to Williamtown where he headed east, and they found him, two patrol cars coming up fast in his rear-view mirror.

Wyatt accelerated until he was in a region of small shops and rear delivery lanes, the pursuit cars hard on his tail. He braked, shot into an alleyway and slowed halfway down it. He waited. The leading police car overshot the entrance, braked heavily, backed up, and came creeping up on Wyatt. He already had the Subaru in reverse. He took his foot off the brake and slammed down the accelerator. The Subaru shot back into the police car, crumpling the bonnet and with any luck crushing the radiator against the engine. Then into drive, and he planted his foot again. Made a hard right at the end, out onto a main road.

An evil scraping sound travelled with him. Some distortion of the rear panels, he thought. Tyre on wheel arch or alignment out of whack.

He swung around a bend and a divisional van was slantwise across the road, the young constables sensible enough to abandon it there and take refuge on the verge. Wyatt didn't ease off the

176

throttle. He aimed at the rear of the van where it was structurally weaker and there was a good chance of driving it forward. He rammed it at fifty k's, punched a gap and drove through.

But the Subaru was a mess, protesting from all of its organs. He was slowing and couldn't hold the car steady. He didn't have much time.

Doubling back along a parallel street, he found a plant nursery. Almost closing time, but several cars lingered and the carpark itself was a small garden, with red-gum sleepers stacked to make big planters for date palms and bamboo. Perfect screening for a few minutes. He steered off the road and into a shaded rear corner.

For a moment he was alone. Shoppers would be appearing soon, laden with plants and mulch. He could hear sirens in the distance. But he had a margin of safety.

Wyatt trotted across the road and into a side street. Modest country-town houses built for families. Footballs and cricket bats on front lawns, bins out for collection, a house that hadn't taken down its Christmas decorations. A dog sniffed incuriously at his ankles. Wyatt kept walking. He found a small brick house with a Holden Calais wagon in the driveway, gunmetal grey and tricked out with antennae and mag wheels. Not a family car. No kids' clutter about.

Wyatt darted back to a previous house, grabbed a pink tricycle left abandoned in a driveway and wheeled it to the brick house. He dumped it where the porch steps met the path that bisected the front lawn. It would be the first thing you saw when you opened the front door.

He gave a soft knuckle rap to the door, the knock of a shy child, and stepped to one side. The door opened. A man stepped out. 'Hello?'

Wyatt swarmed him, got him inside and explained what he needed.

30

TWENTY-FIVE GRAND to kill Sam Kramer.

In the pit of the night, Salter tried to put that into perspective. He'd be richer by twenty-five thousand dollars, of course. He'd have some kind of job with NightWatch Security when he got out, and Nick Lazar's eternal gratitude. And Kramer off his back. Not to mention revenge for being beaten up and pissed on.

Could he do it without being caught, was the question. He found himself checking blind corridors and empty rooms.

Another factor: yeah, he might enjoy killing Kramer, but who would get the *most* benefit—himself or Nick Lazar? Lazar's argument was if someone close to Wyatt was killed, it would affect him emotionally and lure him into the open. Salter thought this was horseshit, and meanwhile it was him, Salter, taking all the risks. If anything fucked up, he'd have another ten years added to his sentence.

As HE WAITED, HE worked on his weapon of choice. Or rather, necessity—you wouldn't attack someone with a toothbrush if you had a choice. After lights out he'd scrape the tip of the toothbrush back and forth on the coarse brick wall surface behind his sink. Spit on the tiny plastic shavings, rub his finger around until he got a gritty paste; mop it up with toilet paper and flush it away.

He thought about the survival techniques he'd learnt for himself the first time he went to jail (assault) five years ago. Unravel the mechanisms of power and respect, for a start. Someone holds a door open for you—why? It doesn't mean they're being a good citizen. Never hold the door open yourself. If you reach it first, you go through it first. If someone offers you a cigarette, you don't accept it: you ask yourself what they want in return.

Demand respect even in small ways. Never accept second best—patched-up prison clothing, for example, or half serves of grub. Acceptance means weakness. If someone blocks your path in the yard, you don't walk around him. If you do that he's got you: you're his. Take him on. Sure, you might get the shit kicked out of you, but you'll have earnt respect.

What it all boiled down to, the only sure survival technique: arm yourself. And so he worked on the toothbrush. Until finally he had a sharp, strong, stabbing instrument. Lethal, so long as it was inserted properly: straight in, not hitting bone. Otherwise it was just a length of easily snapped plastic.

He spent some research time in the library. Anatomy books.

KRAMER CAME FOR HIM late Sunday afternoon when most of the inmates were in the rec room watching the football. Kramer and two of his offsiders, interchangeable muscle with stubbled skulls and singlets. Salter got to his feet, hands loose at his sides. The toothbrush was in his sock, behind his right ankle. Couldn't bend to retrieve it: too obvious.

'Giving you another chance to come clean, Bradley,' Kramer said.

A psycho, but a cautious one, Salter thought. Mild-looking. But Salter recognised the gleam behind the glasses. A man who'd got few breaks in life and given none back.

Salter said nothing.

'Who's interested in me?' said Kramer. 'Who're you working for?'

'Fuck you,' Salter said, knowing in advance that he'd say it, just as Kramer had known he'd say it. Kramer gave a nod and his offsiders surged around him, filling the cell.

The instinctive part of Salter was all visceral fear but another side of him fully recognised that fear and told him to dump it: shake it off as if it would burn his skin. His body was a system of weapons, after all: windmilling arms, punching fists, legs snapping out. And voice box screaming, shrieks to curdle the blood, eyes white and spit flying as he launched himself at the closest Kramer goon.

But the space was small, he had to look in two directions at once—three; who knew what Kramer might do?—and now one of them was behind him, clamping his arms. He still had his legs and feet, and as the other man closed in, winding up to drive a fist into his guts, Salter kicked wildly, fury building with the memories of thirty years of slights and slurs, of all the people who'd held him back, held him down: his father, teachers, cops, officer-class arseholes like Nick Lazar. He didn't stop kicking. Shins, thighs, balls, stomping on toes.

'Fuck's sake,' one guy said, retreating.

Salter felt himself go down, his spine smacking hard against the floor, and they were piling on him, one pinning his legs, the other sitting on his chest. *Don't give up, never give up*, Salter said to himself, thrashing about.

'For fuck's sake,' the same guy said again, as if he'd never struck anything like it before.

Salter bucked them off and curled himself into a foetal position while they booted his kidneys and tried for his balls. And now he had the toothbrush.

He bucked and screamed as the two goons looked at each other and laughed, and looked at Kramer, who wasn't laughing but standing there in the cell doorway, unprotected.

Kramer saw something in Salter then, absolute focus under the apparent derailment, and began to turn. That suited Salter: Kramer's back was toward him when he got there and jabbed the sharpened plastic into Kramer's neck. The vulnerable area where the last vertebra meets the base of the skull. After that first quick thrust, he hammered it in with the flat of his palm, and Christ did it hurt. Then he jiggled the blade for good measure. Sever the spinal cord with any luck. With any luck, very little bleeding and instant death.

31

As soon as he'd cleared the harbour, Tremayne replied to the abduction text—*fuck you*—and powered north, hugging the coast. Past Anna Bay, past the Tomaree National Park, before turning into the Karuah River between Nelson Bay and Hawkes Nest. He felt himself begin to relax. He was getting away, the boat was as familiar under his fingers as his wife's body, and he liked the sensation of the wind, the rolling deck and the slap of the water under him. Here, semi-sheltered at the wheel, he was emerging from the domestic into the elemental. Transposed into a cleaner, edgier existence from the messy entanglements of the past months. His money troubles, Lynx, the government's nagging—for too long now he'd seen everything through the distorting lenses of those three things.

Five p.m. on a chilly Sunday in May. Less than an hour of useful daylight left. Not many tourists in the shoreline accommodation and not many other watercraft about. He glided further up the river until he found a suitable place to drop anchor, unseen from nearby houses and jetties. All the while the radio had crackled at low volume. Now he turned it up, listening intently, switching between the frequencies. His name was out, the name and description of his boat, and some confused chatter about an incident on Newcastle Harbour.

But he hadn't been sighted since, or not that the radio talk revealed.

He dropped into the storage compartment and hauled out a huge blue tarp, some plywood sheets, stencils and spraycans of paint, and worked feverishly in the dwindling light, renaming, renumbering, altering contours. She was called *Joi de Vivre* now, the decking was black, the superstructure reshaped and painted pale blue. It would merge with the sea and the sky if seen from a distance.

But they could still come for him; he needed the Sig Sauer. As he descended the stairs again, he found the fingers of his right hand curling in anticipation around a ghost pistol grip.

The gun was a micro-compact model: small, flat, comfortable and comforting to hold. Ready for use: he'd cleaned it a few weeks ago. Washed the cartridges and the emptied clip in dishwashing detergent, dried them, washed them again in bleach to finally rid them of prints and DNA, then applied a thin protective layer of gun oil before stowing the reassembled pistol in a freezer bag.

Working by torchlight, he removed the panel concealing the drainage pipes, put it to one side, reached in and turned the familiar third pipe. It came away too easily. It was too light.

It was empty.

He stood for a moment, unable to think. Then the answers came to him, along with a more intense flood of rage. He stomped on the pipe, cracking it, kicked the panel in, started splintering the fussy little storage compartments.

He roared up onto the deck. Stood, breathed in and out. A thread of stars was apparent through a dense cloud cover, giving no light of any comfort or intensity. There was an unnerving stillness here where he'd dropped anchor, and no hope of any kind. Only a darkness distilled from the sodden shoreline rocks and the leafless trees and his spent fury. It wasn't fair. None of it was fair.

TREMAYNE ROWED THE INFLATABLE canoe to a nearby beach, tied up and clambered to the top of a slope, where a track skirted the shoreline.

He walked two kilometres in the tricky light until he came to a house set well back from the road rather than proudly commanding a view over the bay. Not a holiday house, a battler's house, with an old F100 pickup in the carport and nets, poles and floats piled in the tray.

Tremayne rapped on the front door. A man of late middle age appeared, sun-cooked and knocked about by life, but not so that he was cautious of strangers. He gave Tremayne a smile, crooked and missing teeth showing through the whiskers. 'Help you?'

'I need your car.'

The fisherman was bewildered. 'Sorry?'

'Give me the keys. Now.'

'Hang on, bud. I—'

Tremayne drove his fist into the man's stomach, doubling him over, then kicked his legs out from under him and stomped for a while. 'It wasn't a discussion, okay?'

The old man was still. Unconscious, dead, one or the other. Tremayne found the Ford's keys in a bowl on the hall table. And glimpsed, at the end of the hallway, a sitting room and a grey curly head of hair aimed at a flickering TV.

Maybe I'm on the news, Tremayne thought, heading into the house.

He stepped around the knees of the old woman seated there. She looked up at him dazedly. 'Is it time for tea, dear?'

Senile.

Tremayne turned and left. Behind him she was saying, 'Have you done your homework?'

Tremayne grunted: homework. Yes I've done my fucking homework.

HE TOOK THE ROAD down through Anna Bay, then via Williamtown to Industrial Drive. The road was relatively quiet—Sunday night, families tucked up together, work day tomorrow. The Ford was old, eighty per cent rust and no power steering: Tremayne couldn't conceive of lives lived like that.

His mind rested briefly on the old fisherman. He'd killed twice before, a long time ago; hadn't really needed to since then. He'd tried briefly to examine his motives, thinking that was the sane thing to do, before deciding he had neither the time nor the inclination for self-analysis. He'd been pleased to note, however, that he'd been calm and professional about the killings, with none of the nervy messiness of a criminal.

He'd been interested in a girl at the time and had watched her for a while on campus—he was studying economics, she architecture—and spotted her crying one day. He asked around: an aggravated burglary had left her mother with permanent brain damage.

He followed the story in the news. The burglar, a junkie, was caught, tried and acquitted: the prosecution case was weak. But Tremayne, watching the jury, noticed several jurors glaring at another. Standing at a urinal later, he heard the guy had spent the whole trial doing Sudoku and ignoring proceedings.

He shot the juror first, using a rabbit shooter's .22 rifle he'd stolen from a Land Rover. Six months later, he shot the burglar with a .32 pistol he'd bought on the street. By then he'd lost interest in the girl—had never even spoken to her. The killings had been enjoyable, but not intensely so. He'd restored some kind of order in the world. He hadn't shot anyone with the little Sig Sauer yet.

As expected, there were lights on in Mark Impey's house and cop cars in the driveway. Tremayne could wait. If you waited, things happened.

Sure enough, by late evening Impey was alone. Tremayne slipped through the shadows to the side of the house and around to the back door, which was unlocked. Impey was sitting at the kitchen table with a bottle of scotch.

'Mark,' Tremayne said gravely.

Impey jerked violently, his glass scooting across the table and onto the floor. Every surface was spotless; Tremayne wondered if the guy ever cooked, ever had people over, ever left dishes in the sink.

'Christ, Jack, the police are looking for you.'

Tremayne screwed up his face, conjuring real tears through sheer will. 'It's Lynx,' he gasped.

'Pardon?'

Tremayne seized Impey's well-fed forearm. '*Someone's grabbed her.*'

'What?'

'Someone's grabbed her, and I need to get her back.'

Impey was alarmed. 'What? What do you mean?'

'*Look,*' shrieked Tremayne, fumbling with his mobile phone, scrolling, shoving it at Impey. 'See? I don't want her to die.'

Impey gaped wonderingly: the events of the afternoon, the madman in his kitchen. 'Who? I mean, why?'

'Someone who lost money—must be. That's something I regret deeply, I'll regret it to my dying day, but please, Mark,

186

I don't want her to die, I need to pay these people.'

Tremayne saw it then, the flash of guilt. *You stole my stuff, you prick.* He pressed on. 'I had backup money all saved up for legal costs and now I've got nothing. Nothing!'

'I thought—'

'Please, Mark, I'm begging you—I'm not angry, I don't blame you, but please tell me you didn't hand everything over to the police.'

Impey shook his head as if to say, or course not, he wouldn't do a thing like that to his friend. 'It's somewhere safe.'

'Please, is it here? You need to fetch it before they kill her.'

Impey was torn, beset by doubts and the desire to be loved, thanked and recognised. 'It's just that I—'

'I'm sorry if you thought I was pulling the wool over your eyes, but I knew if those bureaucrats got their hands on my money, I wouldn't be able to mount a decent defence. And there'd be nothing for Lynx if I had to go to jail,' Tremayne said, breaking again, hyperventilating and sobbing.

'Jack, all you had to do was trust me. I would've—'

'Mark! Mate, please, pay attention, there's no time for this. Midnight, I think they said.' He snatched back his phone and scrolled through with clumsy fingers. 'I'm pretty sure they said midnight.'

Impey still wasn't there. 'Jack, there was a gun with—'

'Protection! You saw that hate mail.'

Impey was chewing the inside of his mouth now. 'Was that you on Friday night? On the boat?'

'What?'

'Friday night. Someone snooping.'

Tremayne wondered if he'd sidestepped into a parallel universe. 'On the boat?'

'Yes.'

'Wasn't me. Please, Mark, no more of this, I need to pay these people.'

'Perhaps you should go to the police.'

'No police, or they'll kill her. Her phone goes to voicemail and no one's answering the landline. We need to get the bag straight away. You said it was somewhere safe?'

'U-Store. It's about half an hour away. So that wasn't you, Friday?'

Lynx, thought Tremayne. Or that sweaty turd DeLacey. This was taking too long, so he took a carving knife from a wooden block on one of the benches, bent down and stabbed Impey in the meaty part of his calf. No bone damage—he could still walk, even drive.

It also got him to focus. *'Why did you do that?'*

'Mark, I need you to pay attention.'

U-Store was in a desolate stretch of warehouses and industrial estates south of the city.

'You didn't have to stab me,' Impey kept saying, hands white-knuckled on the steering wheel, speed well under the limit, as if he was afraid the Range Rover might suddenly dart away from him. He zoned out once or twice, stopping too long at roundabouts and staring vacantly ahead, so that Tremayne would have to dig him in the ribs to get him going again.

'It's okay, everything's okay, soon it will all be over and I'll be out of your hair.'

'But Lynx…'

'Just drive, okay?'

'Is she really kidnapped?'

'Good question.'

Silence, nervy driving. Then Impey said, 'My sock's wet. My shoe's full of blood.'

'Soon be there,' soothed Tremayne.

'I was your *friend*, Jack.'

'Yes, Mark. You were.' Said with a flat finality that shut the other man up.

They reached a steel gate and Impey waved a card at the sensor. The gate slid open, he drove in. 'I feel faint. It's really starting to hurt. I'm losing too much blood.'

'Soon, Mark, very soon.'

Impey drove to a unit in the far corner.

'Out of curiosity, did you rent this place specially, or have you always had it?'

'Had it for years,' Impey said, slurring a little. Drops of perspiration stood out on his face. He entered a passcode and a roller door rattled upwards. Tremayne wasn't interested in the code. There was no reason to come back here.

They stepped inside and there was a quite beautiful old sportscar in British racing green.

'E-Type,' whistled Tremayne.

Impey looked bashful through the pain and sense of grievance. 'Spent years restoring it.'

Tremayne had already lost interest. 'Where's the bag?'

'Over here.'

Impey edged along the flank of the car to a couple of filing cabinets next to an ugly dresser. Tremayne kept close, ready to stab again, anticipating the various tactics Impey might have in mind. He tensed to see the man pull open the top drawer of the filing cabinet and haul out the nylon bag.

'Give it here,' Tremayne said.

He backed out with the bag and tipped everything onto the bonnet of the Jaguar. Impey flinched. 'You'll *scratch* it.'

'Yeah?' said Tremayne. Okay: everything was there.

He refilled the bag, keeping back the little Sig Sauer, and shot

Impey in the centre of his whiny wet forehead. Impey dropped in a nerveless heap and Tremayne locked the roller door on him.

He climbed behind the wheel of the Range Rover and crept out of the storage facility, thinking of the *Joi de Vivre* in one direction and Lynx and DeLacey in the other. The hours it would take him to attend to both matters.

But it wasn't really a tough call. *You thought you'd rip me off?* he'd say. *You thought you could sleep around and I wouldn't know?*

32

Voice uninflected, questions concise and clear, Wyatt ascertained that the Calais' owner was named Drew and that he was alone for the evening because his wife, Elly, was working a late afternoon shift at the hospital.

Drew was short and skinny, a small man who'd surrounded himself with big things: the car in the driveway, the TV screen—even his wife. Elly was a tall, plump, smiling presence beside him in the many wedding photographs crammed onto the sitting room wall. 'Please don't hurt me,' he said.

'I have no interest in hurting you,' Wyatt said. 'I want your car.'

Drew was confused, hearing no menace or malice in the words, but seeing a terrifying, unreadable flatness in Wyatt's face. An expression that might flip at any moment. 'Whatever you want.'

'Where do you keep tape and string? Thin rope?'

'Bottom kitchen drawer,' gasped Drew.

'Thank you, Drew. Come with me, please.'

Wyatt selected a roll of broad grey duct tape and they returned to the sitting room. Drew settled himself on one of the chairs unprotestingly, then screwed up his face in an awful realisation. 'Please don't hurt my wife.'

Wyatt needed Drew's cooperation, not his panic or bravado. 'Drew, I'll be long gone by the time she gets home.' He was careful to keep using the guy's name.

He started strapping Drew in: torso to the back of the chair, arms to his torso and upper thighs, feet to the legs of the chair, talking all the while, a reassuring patter to keep Drew calm and tight, giving him a sense of his place in an unfolding plan...

'I'll simply drive away, and you won't see me again...'

'I'll do my best not to cause any damage...'

'If Elly gets home at eight, you won't be tied up for very long at all...'

'You'll have a real story to tell...'

Drew nodded, beginning to relax. He was a man who fed on small talk. Wyatt, meanwhile, was running out of things to say. He had no practice with chatter: he could rarely think of things to say or reasons to say them.

'Elly's first shift since she broke her arm,' Drew was saying as Wyatt taped his mouth shut.

Wyatt wasn't interested in Elly's broken arm, but he did know that people had an inbuilt need to unload, to explain. A way to put the universe in order, perhaps. He stepped away from Drew and said, 'I also need some of your clothing. Then I'll be gone.'

Drew's shirts and trousers wouldn't fit, but Wyatt was able to squirm into a grey hooded top and a pale blue waterproof jacket belonging to Elly. He also spotted a yellow hard hat on a hook beside the laundry door.

A LONG DRIVE THROUGH the night. He'd expected roadblocks but all he saw was a lone police car and two officers set up for random breath testing. They formed a kind of actual and psychological border post: I'll be safe on the other side, he thought.

He stopped, lowered the window and blew into the tube as they eyed him incuriously, perhaps reassured by the hard hat on the seat beside him. Then they were waving him through with a gesture of torchlight. He accelerated unfussily away.

According to the GPS tracker he'd mounted on Impey's boat, Tremayne had sailed into the Karuah River north of Anna Bay and dropped anchor upstream late that afternoon. No movement since.

He drove on. When he finally reached a track above the river he switched off his headlights and steered the last two hundred metres by weak starlight, keeping his engine revs down, letting the car roll him along without needing to touch the accelerator. Soon he was immediately above the boat, tugging on the handbrake so there'd be no brake-light flare. He switched off, disabled the interior light and quietly slipped out of the car. He pressed the door closed with the merest click behind him.

He peered down into the water and discerned, among the conflicting mess of shadows, the hull of Impey's boat. His eyes adjusted. It had had a makeover.

He clambered down to a small crescent of sand and saw a small inflatable not far above the tide line. He waited, eyeing the boat. No lights, but too early for bedtime. Tremayne wasn't aboard.

A FEW MINUTES LATER, Wyatt was eyeing the splintered wood, the cracked and empty drainage pipe. Tremayne's been robbed, he thought, or there's been a struggle and he's fled. Some other means of transport, like a prearranged car. Wyatt could appreciate the kind of mind that planned a switch from a boat to a road vehicle, but how had it got here? Who would help Tremayne? Impey?

And why would Tremayne risk showing his face on land again? He'd gone to the bother of stocking up for a long voyage and disguising the boat. But why the apparent struggle in the storage bay of the boat? Or was it a tantrum?

All this week, Wyatt had had the sense of the wheels turning behind Tremayne's intentions: a controlling intelligence. Now he was thinking that something had gone wrong, someone had got to the money first. Or he was misreading everything and this was the final unspooling of a plan he couldn't work out.

He took the inflatable back to shore and returned to Newcastle by 8 p.m. Drew's wife would be home soon, and the first thing they'd do was call the police to report the theft of their car.

Parking at the rear of a BP service station, Wyatt bought black electrical tape and scissored it into thin strips and altered the letters and numbers on the Calais' registration plates. He drove to Merewether Beach, parked half a block away from Impey's house and climbed into the back seat. Watched for half an hour. No traffic, no pedestrians. He got out, approached the house and rapped on the front door.

No answer. Garage door closed. There was a faint spill of light from the rear of the house so he walked around to the backyard and through the side door into the garage. Empty. He tried the back door, which turned out to be unlocked. Into the kitchen: a light burning and blood glistening on the floor, a smear and several drops. He checked the other rooms then. No more blood and the house was empty.

Wyatt returned to Drew's car and checked his phone for activity on the various tracking devices. The boat hadn't moved. Nor had Lynx Tremayne's Audi. William DeLacey's Lexus had returned to his Tighes Hill house during the afternoon.

But Mark Impey's Range Rover was on the move.

Wyatt rolled out of there, one side street after another, passing a rusted-up Ford pickup at one point. It was an anachronism in a world of glossy money and cars.

Wyatt followed the route laid out by the tracker on Impey's car. First to a storage facility south of the city where there was no way of getting in without sounding alarms and creating a record of entry. Then to William DeLacey's house in Tighes Hill. Wyatt saw no sense to any of the movements unless everyone was involved. When he reached DeLacey's house he was twenty minutes behind whoever was driving Impey's car, which was on the move again. There were lights on in the house, the Lexus in the driveway.

Wyatt stepped onto the front porch and found the door open a crack. He paused a moment, wishing he had a weapon. There was a scent in the air, faint but recognisable: a gun had been fired. With one knuckle, he pushed the door wider and looked down along the hallway, which ran from the front door to an open-plan kitchen at the rear. Lights on, a chair on its back.

Wyatt crouched and shuffled sideways, making himself as small a target as possible, then, partly concealed by the doorjamb, called, 'Anyone home?'

Silence. No one belting up the hallway at him, risking a quick look or snapping off a shot. He unfolded to his full height and crept into the house.

Lynx Tremayne was in a sitting-room armchair. She'd been shot in both eyes. The lawyer was on the floor near the back door. Tried to run, thought Wyatt. Turned at the last moment and was gut shot. Not dead, struggling for a lifeline when he heard and saw Wyatt.

'Help me.'

There is no help. You're gone, thought Wyatt. 'Tremayne did this?'

DeLacey grimaced in pain. 'He wouldn't pay!' he said, astounded, outraged. He gagged and coughed up a mouthful of blood.

'Wouldn't pay what?'

'Ransom,' said DeLacey weakly.

These are some pretty awful people, Wyatt thought.

He took the Lexus.

ACCORDING TO THE TRACKING app the Range Rover had returned to Merewether Beach. It was still there when Wyatt arrived, parked in the driveway, so he checked the house. Still empty, the kitchen light on, the back door unlocked.

On his way out, Wyatt took the side street where he'd seen the F100. It was gone, leaving only a spoor of leaked oil.

He headed across to the foreshore and left the city, taking Nelson Bay Road east, and back up to the river where Tremayne had stashed the boat. Everything was outstripping him. He rode in the darkness with a still face, expressionless: a man alone with his thoughts. But events had got away from him.

He monitored his phone as he drove. As expected, the boat began to move eventually, out into ocean waters. Then north. Wyatt drove on.

But what was the point of that?

He braked. Pulled over onto the verge of a desolate stretch of the road and thought for a while. Start again? Keep tracking Tremayne's boat? He could do that, but not by car. Wait for the man to stop somewhere on the other side of the world? Time, thought Wyatt. Time and money. Maybe pull another job, if Sam Kramer could find a way to pass some intel to his daughter.

Wyatt checked his email drafts.

A message from Phoebe Kramer. Her father had been shanked in prison. No date set for the funeral. Josh erratic and secretive.

196

33

Wyatt emailed a reply: *On way.*

He U-turned and began the drive south to Sydney, a steady advance down a slow inland route to avoid the police. This hinterland was edgily desolate at night: small towns, farmhouses and emptiness. His headlights shaped the unwinding bitumen, nocturnal contours he couldn't make sense of. The eyes of occasional creatures glinting as they assessed him.

Too warm in the car. He cracked open his side window for a flow of night-chilled air to keep him awake and the rush of sounds that would prove he was moving. He was unsettled. His operating assumption, always, was that his plans were the best he could formulate, likely to lead to the best outcomes; but at the same time he was prepared for the worst to happen, so that he'd never be caught off guard. This time around he'd planned on finding Tremayne's running-away stash, the caveat being that it might not exist, or he might be too late.

So the fact that he hadn't been quick enough was not a

surprise. But he hadn't anticipated this feeling of letdown. Wyatt was not given to self-analysis; had never needed to be. But now he tried to measure what Sam Kramer's death meant to him. Clearly, he'd lost a source of reliable intelligence; putting a job together would be that much harder now. That was significant to Wyatt.

In addition, he'd made promises to Sam, and to Sam's family, to safeguard Kramer's twenty per cent. He'd honour these promises—not out of sentiment but because he'd promised. And if possible he'd find and kill the killer. Fix the imbalance caused by the killing.

Finally, he tried to reconfigure the recent and more distant past and work out what Sam Kramer the person meant to him. He'd used the word 'friend' in his thoughts, but only because no other label suggested itself. Sam had always done the right thing by Wyatt, so Wyatt had always done the right thing by him. Sam had never cheated on the thieves, hold-up men, safecrackers and drivers he worked with. He'd been a careful planner, a wise head, a logical thinker. He had contacts at all levels of Sydney society and knew both how to use them and how to look after them.

He'd given Wyatt a grounding long ago, starting with banks and payroll vans, and had been a reliable associate ever since. If he had human failings, Wyatt was interested only to the extent that they affected his ability to get the job done.

Associate…Friend…Suddenly Phoebe Kramer was in Wyatt's head. He'd made it a rule never to think 'if only'; never to dwell anywhere but the present. But now he found himself making an empathetic leap: Phoebe Kramer bereft. Grieving.

He didn't think she needed him. Wanting was a different matter. But he'd barely allowed himself to think about her as other than Sam's daughter until now.

And the family would need Sam's money. All of it—for the funeral if nothing else. A murder in prison meant an investigation, forensics, autopsy…The funeral wouldn't be any time soon. He wondered if he should have stuck with Tremayne. Dismissed the thought.

Wyatt considered all these things as he drove through the night, sifting through the array of facts, memories and suppositions. He valued his clear, sceptical mind, his sense of precision. But the sheer weight of events—Tremayne, the Newcastle murders, the death of Sam Kramer—was threatening to disrupt all that. He needed symmetry. He could not be a man at the mercy of doubts, scruples and uncertainty; a man who hesitated or fudged and got nowhere.

That would be fatal.

Meanwhile people he couldn't identify were after him. They could, he thought, be waiting for him.

HE DECIDED TO MAKE contact with the family first, unobserved, then find somewhere to stay. By first light Monday he was watching their house, an untended Californian bungalow on a quiet broad street in Mosman.

The aspect bothered him. Too many trees beside and behind him, in the foreground of the house, on an uphill slope beyond the backyard. Even more in the surrounding yards. He stood fused with a shadow bank that was losing out against the dawning sun. He watched with eyes wide and unfocused to gain a general impression, then homed in on the specifics. One tree or car or neighbouring house at a time.

There was plenty of movement in the suburb, as it happened, all of it benign. A woman setting out on her morning run, meeting and running with another woman half a block down. A man in a dressing gown fetching the morning newspaper. A taxi collecting a man in a suit. A woman piling two tracksuited schoolboys and their gym bags into an SUV.

199

Soon Wyatt would be spotted: an oddity on that street.

He stepped deeper into the shadows, intending to wait until there was movement at the bungalow and a chance to communicate with one of Sam Kramer's loved ones.

Before long, though, the street was too busy for him to risk it. He found a café and over breakfast made another Airbnb booking—a granny flat behind a house in nearby Middle Head—and arranged to rent a mountain bike.

As the day progressed, he made two passes through Mosman on the bike, three hours apart, and three passes by taxi and Uber. By mid-afternoon the street was streaming with a different kind of traffic: friends and family visiting the Kramers' house to pay their respects. At one point Josh Kramer drove away in his little red Mazda MX5. Then, late afternoon, the cop from Newcastle was there.

34

MUECKE HAD FLOWN BACK to Sydney at first light on Monday. Sunday afternoon and evening had proved frustrating, full of dead ends and his own sense of being an unwanted irritant in Newcastle. Again he'd been reminded that police work was never systematic: it was messy, subject to lucky breaks, deals and Chinese whispers, with missed opportunities, cock-ups, tainted evidence and loss of heart thrown into the mix. And waiting. Endless waiting.

Feeling haggard, the Property Crimes sergeant drove his venerable Commodore home from the airport. He was due at work by 8 a.m. but didn't feel the need to rush. Another shower, a fresh suit, a few minutes of Meg's company; the way she made coffee how he liked it.

He parked outside his Newtown house, a rundown terrace. The first students of the day—diligent Chinese and Indian kids— were heading off to early lectures. He locked the car and let himself in the front door. Home had always exerted a certain dark gravity on him, and he knew at once that he was alone. The mental image of Meg and her bustling and coffee-making was from his early married life. He could tell she hadn't been gone long, but these days she always had things to do away from the house. Her new life, the kids too old to live at home anymore, Muecke morose and preoccupied. Her breakfast dishes were draining on the sink and she'd left a note on the table: *Excursion, back tonight xxx* and a smiley face.

He remembered: a field excursion to convict ruins for her Australian history special subject. The kisses were automatic, of course; historical themselves, in a way. Still, they were kisses.

Muecke put the coffee on, thinking of the debacle in Newcastle yesterday. Tremayne's ruse and escape; the interference of the man Muecke thought of as Sam Kramer's associate; the murders. And Kramer shanked in prison, down here in western Sydney. Muecke had gone back to his hotel last night with a sense of the local CIB, the Fraud Squad and the Probity Commission scuffling about in the dirt, their investigations slightly clownish. If they couldn't grasp the contours of the case, what chance did he have?

He shrugged his weary shoulders into a fresh shirt and pulled on the grey suit, dry-cleaned last week. His place was here in Sydney. His case was here in Sydney. Kramer was deceased. That might have nothing or everything to do with the events in Newcastle, but it was all dead ends up there now. Any kind of forward movement would be down here. The man he was tracking would show here eventually, maybe glimpsed among the gravestones when Kramer was planted in the ground.

But *would* a man like that show himself? Muecke thought of other wanted men he'd known over the years, their propensity for bad thinking. Twice in his long career he'd served a summons on some break-and-enter hero living in an expensive harbour-view unit, only to recognise, and arrest, a friend of the guy—sitting right there on the couch with his belongings in the spare bedroom.

202

Crooks graduate to other crooks, especially if they live in fancy places, Muecke thought. They aren't smart enough to lie low. Muecke was hoping for some bad thinking in this case. Not really expecting it, though.

He made a number of phone calls and by 11 a.m. was in the Watervale Prison infirmary, interviewing Brad Salter, who was not alone.

'Thought I should have my lawyer present this time,' he smirked.

The lawyer shot out her hand; young, sharply dressed and with the attack eyes of a pit bull. 'Sarah Ogilvy.'

'Quick off the mark,' Muecke observed.

They both smiled.

Muecke said, 'It's my intention to interview Bradley in relation to the death of Samuel Kramer.'

Ogilvy said, 'My client, *Mr Salter*, has already answered questions in relation to this matter. He was attacked by three men. He defended himself. If not for the subsequent actions of corrections officers, he might have died.'

'Yeah,' Salter said. Ogilvy touched his forearm.

Muecke gazed at Salter. Broken nose, one eye blackened, old cuts reopened. 'Can you provide me with any further information in regard to the death of Mr Kramer?'

'My client has said all that he intends to say regarding this matter.'

'I put it to Mr Salter that the death of Mr Kramer was planned and orchestrated. Do you have anything to say in regard to that, Mr Salter?'

Police work was all about fishing and watching. Muecke, his eyes probing Salter's face, spotted a brief flare of guilt.

'I don't doubt that you were attacked,' Muecke went on.

'Nice to be believed,' Salter said, lifting a hand to his face.

'And were obliged to defend yourself.'

Ogilvy interjected. 'So how, DS Muecke, could the whole mess be construed as planned and orchestrated? And correct me if I'm wrong, you're Property Crimes, not Homicide.'

Muecke ignored her. 'I put it to you, Mr Salter, that the attack was a stroke of luck in that you already had a weapon at your disposal and had fully intended to use it on Mr Kramer at some future date, perhaps not in so public or risky a manner.'

'You are referring to the *shank*?' said Ogilvy, as if the word tasted bad. 'It is my client's assertion that the shank was never in his possession, except in the final moments of the attack, but was brought to the scene by one of his assailants, who intended to kill him with it. Fortunately, my client wrested it away from him in the struggle and, in a moment of life and death, Mr Kramer sadly lost his life. It could easily have been my client, or one of the others.'

As if pitching to a judge and jury. Muecke wondered what her pillow talk was like. He cocked his head curiously at Salter. 'I expect you're watching your back more than usual now?'

Salter's eyes flickered: he knows he's a target, thought Muecke. He continued to probe but Ogilvy continued to intervene, and Salter's face went dead above the resolute line of his lips.

Muecke tried another tack. 'I was interested to see who's visited you since your incarceration—and who hasn't. Mainly hasn't. You're not on many people's Christmas card list.'

'I fail to see...' said Ogilvy.

'One visitor, in fact: fellow name of Nicholas Lazar,' Muecke said. 'I did some digging. Served in Afghanistan with you.'

'So?'

'Sniper. You were *also* a sniper, isn't that right?'

'I don't know the relevance,' Ogilvy said, 'and I don't know how you unearthed that kind of information.'

'Lazar's business is failing,' Muecke said. 'NightWatch Security. A nice ring to it, but it isn't bringing in the bacon.'

'So?'

'So, he's forced to hustle for work. Bouncer at the odd pub gig, for example.'

'So?' said Salter again.

Ogilvy was silent, interested now to see where Muecke was going.

'So, one of the bands he provides security for is fronted by a guy called Joshua Kramer, who by a curious coincidence is the late Sam Kramer's son.'

'This interview is over. I am advising my client not to answer any more of your questions.'

'Who knows what kind of subterranean forces are at work, Brad. Better keep your mouth shut and your head down.'

A PUB LUNCH IN PARRAMATTA—the comfort of a plain old mixed grill in a plain old corner pub—then to the police station, where he wrote up his notes on the weekend in Newcastle and the interview with Salter.

Mid-afternoon, Kitty Brenner called him to her office. The door was ajar. Sam Henderson sat in one of her two stiff-backed visitor's chairs.

'You called?'

She indicated the second chair with the chewed end of a Bic pen. 'Sit.'

Muecke sat. He didn't know what to expect, but the senior sergeant's face radiated anger and Henderson was smirking. Muecke glanced about the office but found no clues. Just a potted plant and the usual office paraphernalia. Otherwise it was a spacious room filled with a wintry light—literally and figuratively.

'Greg, did you precipitate events in Newcastle?'

Muecke reminded himself that Brenner was superior to him in rank—but not that superior. 'What are you on about?'

'Word has filtered through.'

That's all she was giving him? And word from who? Agostino, probably. 'Filtered.'

'The investigation was under control, ticking over nicely, and then you arrived.'

Why wasn't the inspector making these charges? Or professional standards command? 'I had information germane to a number of parallel investigations up there. I passed on my information. That's all.'

'Bullshit,' Henderson said. 'You went around asking questions and poking your nose in. You asked to see CCTV footage, photos, surveillance reports. You interviewed witnesses. You ran around giving advice and orders...'

Henderson was a sneak and not very good at hiding it. Brenner, on the other hand, was showing Muecke a compact, unyielding face, with barely a glint of animation.

'You saw Bradley Salter this morning,' she said.

For a dinosaur cop like Muecke, modern policing was murky and paralysing. The mix of new-broom hotshots and old, lingering collusions meant that nothing got done, or certainly didn't get done well, or quickly. Ambitions were soured, energy lost, the will to arrest the bad guys sapped.

'All part of my investigation into Sam Kramer. Salter killed Kramer. Given his, shall we say, animus against Kramer, it was worth talking to him. Just because Kramer's dead, we don't have to close the books on some pretty big Property Crimes cases. Or is that your style, washing your hands of further investigation whenever you hit a snag?'

'You take that back.'

Muecke shook his head and stood. 'I've got work to do.'

'Really?' Henderson said, as Muecke left. 'Would that be through proper channels?'

LATE MONDAY AFTERNOON, Muecke drove to Mosman and knocked on Cindy Kramer's door. Turned to view the cars crowding both sides of the street while he waited.

Turned again when the door opened. 'Hello, Phoebe.'

'Mr Muecke,' said Sam Kramer's daughter, a pretty woman, her face tight with grief.

'Just came to pay my respects and offer my condolences.'

She thought about that; decided she believed him and stood aside for him to enter the house. Small, crammed rooms; a life that had been put on hold with the imprisonment of the main breadwinner. Put on hold forever now.

'I warn you, we have guests. Not all of them are going to appreciate your being here.'

She led him into a large, open-plan living area at the rear of the house—the only sign that money had been spent on the place since it was first built. A broad glass wall overlooked decking, mouldy canvas chairs, a stretch of overgrown garden and a back fence with a treed slope beyond it. In the room itself, a huddle of men, women and children, awkward in their best clothes.

Muecke recognised some of Kramer's associates from investigations over the years. One or two he'd arrested. There was no overt hostility; he'd been fair with them. But still, he was a cop.

Muecke suddenly didn't know what he was doing there. He spotted Cindy in her wheelchair, crossed the room, knelt beside her.

'Sorry for your loss, Cindy.'

She looked grandmotherly from a distance, round, greying and bespectacled. Closer to, with light glinting on her glasses,

207

there was a clipped hardness about her. 'A useless, overused expression.' She paused. 'But thank you.'

She continued to watch him. 'Sam had respect for you.'

She watched him try to deal with that. At one point, when he almost overbalanced on his haunches and grabbed the wheelchair to steady himself, she placed a hand on his forearm. Her gaze, penetrating, left him sharply etched; exposed. She said, 'He's dead, Sergeant Muecke, put it to rest.'

'I can't, Cindy. The ripples are still there.'

'You're wasting your time,' she went on. 'The fellow you're after won't show up, if that's what you're hoping.'

And there it was, out in the open. 'He might. What's his name, by the way?'

'Now, now,' Cindy said, with a little shake of her finger.

Muecke started to rise, but she wasn't finished. Giving him a look of entreaty and doubt, she leaned in and murmured, 'Josh has bought a gun.'

Muecke jerked back. 'You want me to...?'

'Yes. Please—before he hurts someone. Or you lot shoot him.'

Muecke left then, feeling a sense of restrained energy in the deepening twilight, feeling that every visitor to the street was an innocent blunderer and only he, Phoebe and Cindy maintained some kind of sustaining secret life. And the nameless man.

Joshua Kramer, Nick Lazar, Brad Salter, he thought. Where did the lines of influence lie?

35

IT WAS FIVE DAYS of movement and marking time. Wyatt switched to a different Airbnb for two nights, then rented a campervan. He checked both his safe deposit boxes: his money was intact, so was Sam Kramer's twenty per cent. Finally, he acquired two weapons on the street: a grooved stabbing knife with an angled tip, which he wore in a soft scabbard taped to the top of his spine, the hilt just behind the back of his shirt collar, and a little .22 Colt Cobra. The rest was an intermittent watch on the Kramer house.

Email drops from Phoebe Kramer kept him updated. Her father's autopsy had been completed. The homicide investigation was ongoing but the body would probably be released for burial by the weekend. As per her mother's wishes the casket, closed, would be available for viewing by friends and family at the house on the day before and the morning of the funeral, but Phoebe wasn't so sure about it.

Wyatt found these disclosures oddly intimate, a glimpse into an everyday life. He supposed, now he thought about it, that he expected to die alone and unregarded, and for a moment he was filled with regret.

But mostly he was scouting around the Kramers' suburb, street and house, watching over the family with one eye and keeping the other open for the law. He was also waiting for an opportunity to make actual, not electronic, contact. Phoebe Kramer's emails were firm on that subject. Don't come to pay respects. Don't come to the funeral. Don't come to the wake.

Too risky.

Wyatt knew that, but he felt, unusually, circumscribed; adrift. What did Phoebe Kramer mean to him—and why was he even asking the question? Did she mean something because her father had meant something? What had Sam meant? Nothing, really; or not much. A sliver of mutual respect; the rest was all business. Wyatt couldn't map the faultline between his thoughts and his feelings but he knew it must have been there all this time, lurking in the years of silence and denial. He badly needed action: clear, unambiguous. His hands in synch with his brain.

Friday was an evening of scrappy cloud cover, the moon showing through a frayed gap; chilly shadows contending with streetlights and the window-glow in every house. A hearse arrived at seven o'clock and Wyatt watched through the back window of a rented Ford SUV as the driver and his offsider wheeled the casket into the house. They did not emerge. The hearse sat in the driveway, nose pointed at the street.

A short time later, Phoebe stepped out. She powered down the street wearing a dress and a short-waisted jacket, her arms wrapped around herself for warmth. Her body, head down and visibly trembling, spoke of fury.

Wyatt stepped out and said softly, 'Phoebe.'

She jerked, stopped, whirled around. Stepped warily towards him. 'Are you crazy?'

210

'Something wrong?'

'Just a bit of tension with Mum. Where to display the coffin. And the hearse guys are being sleazy. Dad did business with them over the years and that's made them...presumptuous.' That was as far as she took it. Unblinking, severe, she said, 'I'm going back inside. You should leave. I want to see you, but only when it's safe.' She touched his wrist and strode swiftly back to the house.

Wyatt watched her go, and felt the bullet catch him above the hipbone, spin him around and put him on the ground.

Sniper? he wondered. Suppressed? Then the pain caught up.

He flopped onto his back in a wave of nausea. Tried to rise. He was some distance from his SUV. No good cover to crawl to; he didn't know where the shooter was anyway. He got to his knees, then to his feet, clasping the wound, feeling blood well between his fingers. And then a van swept in from the top of the street and the driver got out and rolled back the sliding door to the rear compartment and came barrelling at Wyatt. Disable me, then grab me, thought Wyatt. Simple, quick. The realisation seemed to wake him. Combined with the pain and shock to kickstart his old familiar singlemindedness.

Survive. Fight.

'Let me help you, buddy,' the van guy was saying. Getting a kick out of it. He was tall, a bag of bones, with a wiry competence, erect carriage and dead eyes. Wyatt knew the type: ex-military. Working with the sniper on the hill. Why would ex-army guys want him? A pointless thought just then, and Wyatt dismissed it. He groaned and sank, one hand on the ground to take his weight, the other up to ward off trouble. A move simply choreographed, one the attacker expected and understood. He found it amusing. He reached for Wyatt, and Wyatt continued the swing of his warding-off hand to the back of his neck.

He drove the blade into the other man's stomach, flexed his

211

wrist and split him open. A certain satisfaction uncurled within him. Not to have killed but to have acted.

But he was losing blood. All of his energy draining suddenly away.

Then Phoebe Kramer was there, swift and deft, a play of emotions on her face, saying, '*Quick*,' as she hauled him to his feet.

Wyatt heard two more shots, somewhere up on a nearby slope. He didn't know what it meant. Before he could put his mind to it he'd blacked out.

NICK LAZAR'S SNIPING RIFLE was a Steyr-Mannlicher SSG, .30 calibre, with a Redfield variable power scope for low light conditions. Ammunition to stop a man, not kill or shred him. He'd go for the fleshy part of the waist, he decided.

He'd fitted the barrel with a sound suppressor. You wanted a silenced shot, here in suburbia. Given that he was capable of grouping his shots inside a ten-centimetre circle at five hundred metres with a suppressor fitted, he was confident about this hundred-metre shot.

He wore a camouflage jacket and trousers, a khaki balaclava and lightweight boots. Not a surface on him could reflect a glint of light—not the toes of his boots, any part of his clothing, his face and hands. He'd hung the rifle and scope with camouflage strips. It was all overkill, but it gave him a nostalgic kick; took him back to the stony slopes of Afghanistan.

For months now he'd felt simultaneously rootless and pinned down. Drifting from one small, unlikely-to-be-renewed job contract to the next, all the while hamstrung by rules, regulations and bureaucratic bullshit. People suing him. Cops sniffing around.

But this—the gear, the rifle, his little sniper's nest on a hill slope overlooking a target area—brought back the sense of competence he'd had in his army days. Having a job to do and knowing he was the man to do it.

Marty Welsh felt the same, although he wouldn't be shooting anyone. His job was to grab Wyatt, bundle him into the back of a stolen van and make a fast run out to Lazar's storage locker in the western suburbs. Thirty seconds—shouldn't take longer than that to pick the guy up. No limit to how long they could take getting him to talk.

Soon after settling in on the hill, Lazar saw a Ford SUV pull up against the kerb on the other side of the road from the Kramer house and half a block down. Police? Only one occupant, a man. He sat there for a while then climbed into the rear, looking out.

Lazar adjusted the scope. Wyatt was a shadow in the back window. Great head shot. But a head shot was a kill shot. Wait to see if he got out.

Lazar murmured into his radio: 'The white SUV.'

'Copy,' Welsh said.

'Be ready in case he gets out.'

'Got it.'

Lazar watched Wyatt briefly before casting the scope over the other cars in the street, the houses, trees and garden shrubbery. Careful not to eye any one aspect for too long or the image would fix on his retina and destroy his sense of field and perspective. He kept his breathing slow and shallow. When he was finally ready to pull the trigger he'd breathe out; relax. A breath in would make him tight: spoil the shot.

If he was forced to take a second shot, he'd slip sideways to another location.

A hearse arrived and two men manhandled a coffin inside the Kramer home. The hearse remained. Some kind of protocol, Lazar guessed.

Then a woman left the house, stomping along angrily, and,

hallelujah, Wyatt climbed out of the SUV.

Lazar played the scope over Wyatt, then the woman. A looker, but not in any conventional way. A crooked smile and then a stern frown and she looked vibrant and intense, there in closeup. Saying something to Wyatt.

Lazar waited, indecisive for the first time. He had a clear shot at Wyatt, but the woman was a complication. Then she turned around and headed back to the house and when she reached her front door, he took the shot.

He watched it unfold. Wyatt clutched his side and fell. Welsh tore down the street in the van and piled out. Advanced on Wyatt, who tried to ward him off. The woman came running back. Welsh fell to his knees, cradling his stomach. The woman tugged Wyatt back up the street towards her house, and now Lazar had no clear shot and he was fazed, suddenly.

Moving from a panicked base, all of his old caution flying out the window. He began to pack away the rifle. Had got as far as stowing the telescopic sight when a man came heaving up the slope, panting for breath, saying something, and all Lazar registered was '…under arrest…hands…' and the pistol pointed at him.

Fuck that for a joke.

Lazar spun away neatly and merged with the dying light as he swung the Steyr around from this new location and the cop, expecting it, was swinging his firearm too.

AFTER HIS VISIT TO the Kramer house earlier in the week, Muecke had returned to the station, fired up his computer and made a number of phone calls. He'd already mined Facebook: Josh's singer-songwriter ambitions, his pizza 'empire', his band and all the gigs they'd played. Photos of Josh with his workers, waitresses, bartenders, pole dancers, bouncers and security staff. NightWatch Security, of course. Nick Lazar's outfit.

How involved was this kid? Muecke continued to dig around in the files on Tuesday, and made the arrest on Wednesday. Josh Kramer in his car, heading out of Mosman along a quiet side street. The charge: possession of an unregistered Czech-made pistol, tucked under the driver's seat.

'Why the gun, Mr Kramer?'

The kid shrank. 'No comment.'

'This thing looks like it'd blow up in your face.'

'No comment,' Kramer said, eyeing his little Mazda sportscar nervously as uniformed officers searched it none too respectfully while kids rode by on their way to school. Then he shrank further when one of the uniforms backed out waving a couple of freezer bags. 'Ice, boss. Some pills.'

'Personal use,' Kramer said.

'I bet,' said Muecke.

He'd tried to question the kid on the way to the police station. 'Do you think you'll be next, after your dad?'

'No comment.'

'Not frightened of Nick Lazar?'

'No comment.'

'I imagine we can make an arrangement for you to attend your father's funeral,' Muecke said, 'but right now I'm pretty sure you'll be remanded.'

'No comment.'

'Assuming you *want* to attend your old man's funeral. No love lost, as I understand it. He reckoned you were a loser.'

'No comment.' But a catch in the kid's voice.

That afternoon Muecke asked for three surveillance teams on the Kramer house, rotating every eight hours. Denied. 'Perhaps you haven't noticed, sergeant,' his inspector said, 'but Sam Kramer's dead. Soon to be buried. There's nothing to be gained by watching his house.'

And so Muecke had begun to keep watch himself. Barely saw his wife, forgot what his house looked like. Began to feel deranged from the lack of sleep. He learned nothing, saw nothing.

To break the monotony, he paid a call on Phoebe and Cindy, ostensibly to reassure them that Josh was all right.

'Can you just keep him there for a few days?' Phoebe said.

'Will do. When's the funeral?'

Sam's casket was being delivered to the house Friday evening, she told him. Friends and family would visit then and on Saturday morning; interment Saturday afternoon. 'I expect your lot'll turn out in force,' Phoebe said, tired and sour.

'I expect so.'

Muecke left them there in the cocoon of their grief and drove home to hug Meg. She wasn't there; late seminar.

Now, Friday evening, Muecke was in Mosman again, watching from inside the wooden framework of a house extension three doors down from the Kramers'. The owner was away. No twitchy dogs, no neighbours peering at him from behind their curtains. He yawned through the hours and fell asleep and missed the first stage of the drama. All he knew was a door had slammed, and quick, crisp footsteps were sounding and a man said softly, 'Phoebe.'

Muecke took out his service pistol: Phoebe Kramer was right there on the street, standing close to the man he'd been hunting. He hesitated. He was alone, no one knew he was here, what if the man was armed? And his weapon felt alien in his hand. He'd scarcely pulled a gun in all the years he'd been a policeman. He waited, and it was partly nerves and partly the fact that Phoebe was in the way. He didn't know when to act, or how to act. Not just yet.

Then Phoebe was returning to her house and the man was alone and Muecke heard a soft *whump* from somewhere above the street. The man said, 'Oh,' and stumbled and fell, clutching at his waist where blood was oozing. He wasn't fully down, it hadn't been a kill shot. Which means the kill shot is still to come, Muecke thought. Save a life or catch a killer? He found himself stumbling across a yard strewn with planks, offcuts and tattered plastic sheeting, over a fence and uphill to where he'd heard the muffled shot, labouring as he reached the top, regretting the years behind a desk, behind the wheel, switching channels with a remote.

Chest heaving, he began a sweep of the summit with his Glock; saw a leafy mass move, taking form as a man with a rifle. They fired simultaneously, Muecke's pistol snapping, the sniper's rifle sounding harsh at this range, barely softened by the suppressor.

Then silence.

Muecke's ears were ringing. But something else was happening to him. His body refusing to respond. Going loose. Flopping to the ground, his strings cut. Intense pain blooming in his left calf: trouser leg sodden with blood. The bullet went through, he thought—but nicked bone?

The sniper was also hit, bending over as if punched, one hand across his stomach. Muecke saw him move the hand, gape at the blood, clamp himself again. A look of resolve forming. He growled, lifted the rifle one-handed, the muzzle waving about as if lining up on an insect. He fired. The shot went high, stripping leaves. Meanwhile the pain was hitting Muecke, the uselessness of his brain and his legs, his return fire just as wild. He kept pulling the trigger, emptying the magazine, all of his shooting-range instructions gone from his brain.

When it was over he was deaf, and the sniper was down. Blades were whirring, stabbing, in his leg. He was about to slide into shock, he knew that much. He managed to call 000 before the world grew darker and then very dark.

In the days of surgery and reconstruction, Meg was there every day. A little remote and distracted, he thought. But also loving, as

217

if her emotions were elastic, somehow. Able to accommodate anything from a cancelled lecture to a bullet-riddled husband. He was grateful to have her; she was grateful he hadn't died. Both were grateful he hadn't lost the use of his leg.

His inspector came by, wanting to know what he'd thought he was doing, acting alone, running his own investigation. And, given the seriousness of his wound, had he perhaps considered retiring? There'd be an internal inquiry, obviously. He might consider talking to the police association and possibly even a lawyer.

That was on the one hand. On the other, a *Sydney Morning Herald* photographer sneaked a shot of him propped up on hospital pillows, scribbling in his police notebook. Words like 'heroic' were bandied about.

He followed the news on an iPad. The hunt for Tremayne was 'ongoing' and police were 'hopeful'. And one day an email arrived from SA Police: *Sorry, we sent you a photo of Albert van Horen and his wife by mistake: the attached are Dirk and Missy.*

'Ha!' muttered Muecke, taking in the happy couple saluting the camera from across a bistro table. 'The artists now known as Bryce and Felicity Reschke.'

'Talking to yourself again, Dad.' Amy, the London daughter, tanned from a holiday in Spain.

HE WAS MORE SURPRISED by his final set of visitors.

Phoebe Kramer wheeled Cindy into his room, saying, 'Don't get up.'

Roses rested across Cindy's lap. 'And you spent money on me, too,' Muecke said.

Phoebe twinkled at him. 'You know us—we hired someone to hit the giftshop.'

Muecke laughed, twisting to get comfortable. Got right to the point. 'You spirited him away in the hearse, right?'

'I see that being shot up hasn't tipped you out of cop mode, DS Muecke,' Phoebe said.

'Call me Greg. Did he make it?'

'Make what?'

'Are we going to do this? Your friend, the one you ran to when he was shot—is he okay?'

She looked baffled. 'I know that *you* were shot, and you shot someone else, but I'm not sure who else was shot.'

'Yeah, yeah, yeah,' Muecke muttered. 'How was the funeral?'

'Fine.' Phoebe seemed to draw a sombre veil down over her face for a moment. 'Mum, we should go, Sergeant Muecke needs his rest.'

'No, wait. Let's just not play the game for a little while,' Muecke said. 'Stay. You do me good.'

The three stared at each other, tourists in a border country of mutual regard between criminal and cop. It was tricky, but not dangerous. Muecke knew he'd sleep soundly tonight, pain notwithstanding. The Kramer women would sleep, grief notwithstanding. But Muecke wouldn't rest in his daylight hours and the women would know that. He'd come at them and they'd block him, and one day there'd be a breakthrough. Or not.

36

IT WAS PAIN THAT brought Wyatt back from the dead. His spine was bouncing on an unforgiving surface.

Realising he was in the bed of a moving vehicle, little curtained windows all around, he lifted himself onto his elbows, the pain shooting through him as his torso flexed, and looked towards the front. He was in the hearse.

'You're awake.'

Wyatt turned his head. The driver's offsider was perched in there with him. 'Don't tell me you're taking me to the crematorium.'

'Humour. A good sign,' the hearse guy said.

He introduced himself as Steve Britt. A squat, broad man with a square, overheated face, yellowing teeth and white hair springing from his skull and face. Wyatt flopped back again, exhausted.

Then he moved his hand to his hip, explored with his fingers, and raised himself to look. A cotton towel had been taped over the wound. Bulky; already full of blood. 'I'm making a mess of your lovely hearse.'

'We've never carried a live one before,' acknowledged Britt cheerfully. 'But we have had the odd fluid leak over the years.'

'Probably need to work on your embalming skills,' Wyatt said. 'Where are you taking me?'

'To see a guy who'll patch you up.'

Wyatt closed his eyes, trying to anticipate the pitching of the hearse as it rolled along bumpy streets and swept around corners. It was impossible. Everything hurt. He thought about the hearse, about the man who'd patch him up. Some struck-off doctor? It all spoke to Sam Kramer's network, he thought. An expert for every emergency.

THE NEXT TIME HE WOKE he was in a bed in the back room of a suburban house. A flame of autumn orange on the other side of the window—a pair of liquidambars losing their leaves. Otherwise, skeletal fruit trees and a wooden fence. No tennis court, swimming pool, dog kennel, clothesline, discarded toys or wheelbarrow. Nothing to reveal anything about his location or his hosts.

But the room itself had plenty to tell him. A hospital-grade bed, a white gown on a hook on the back of the closed door, a blinking monitor, an IV stand, boxes of compression stockings, syringes and surgical gloves on the shelves of a wall cabinet. The beige and white colours of a hospital ward. The odours of treatment and sterilisation.

He checked himself: he'd been freshly bandaged. Meaning the wound had probably been cleaned, sterilised, stitched up. And they'd have pumped him full of antibiotics.

There was a TV set on the wall, some breakfast show—what day was it?—the sound muted. He hunted around for the remote and switched it off. Keep things simple. He needed continued concealment, restored health and some understanding of the recent past. Forget Tremayne: no mystery there, just a man operating according to some monstrous logic of his own. Forget Phoebe Kramer: he needed to excise her. Focus on who had shot him and why.

He thought about the role of random factors. This job had been riddled with them. No plan, however well conceived and executed, will survive intersection with someone else's compulsions.

The door opened. A man entered the room, unhooked the gown and worked his way into it, regarding Wyatt without curiosity. About sixty, tall, clean and ascetic looking. He didn't speak; just took Wyatt's temperature and blood pressure, shone a light in each eye, checked his tongue, his pulse. Wyatt sensed a mind registering and analysing. The eyes were alert and bright, holding neither sympathy nor judgment.

He feels nothing about me, Wyatt thought. He's a man who notes, understands and accepts with no need to empathise. Wyatt appreciated it. If he was a doctor treating a gunshot patient with a question mark hanging over him, he'd take the same approach.

'You'll live,' the doctor said eventually. 'The bullet went straight through. No organ damage. Shouldn't get infected. You'll have massive bruising and feel tender for a while. You'll have two small scars when it heals.' Pause. 'Two more. You've been in the wars before.'

The voice was low and even with no wasted words. Again, Wyatt approved. 'How long?' he croaked.

'Until you can leave? Three, four days.'

'Do you have a name?'

The doctor, about to leave the room, stopped; almost curious. 'Do you?'

Then he smiled thinly, settled the gown on the hook and left the room. He didn't strike Wyatt as a man deregistered for some shameful puerility, like drugs or touching up women. It would have involved money, he thought. Medicare fraud.

WHEN HE OPENED HIS eyes again, Phoebe Kramer was there, intensely attractive, and he hadn't excised her after all. And he was vulnerable and self-conscious.

She saw all of this. 'It's only temporary,' she said. Smiling a little; but her face was clouded too.

'You got me here,' Wyatt said. 'Thank you.'

A think-nothing-of-it wave of the hand, then she began a systematic examination of him. His eyes and face, his shape under the bedding. 'Let me see.'

She lifted up the sheet and eyed the dressing over the wound. 'Much pain?'

'Some.'

Her eyes strayed to his bare hipbone and stomach, then to his arms and hands, the veins and corded muscles. Her interest was exquisite and finely honed.

'I'm at a disadvantage.'

'Hah.' She flashed him her crooked smile, showing her chipped tooth. 'If you think I'm getting my gear off too, you're mistaken.' She took in the bed. 'Besides, no room. You'll have to wait.'

So, that was an unspoken matter out of the way.

She pulled up a chair and sat beside the bed. 'We're in Pymble, in case you were wondering.'

'And the doctor?'

'One of Dad's…associates.'

She began to probe then, a subtle, observant interrogator. That last job, the events in Newcastle, the dead men in her street. Wyatt told her everything and speculated wherever there were holes in the narrative.

'Tremayne's gone to some tropical island, you think?'

He nodded. 'Or somewhere without an extradition treaty.'

'You'll just blithely follow the GPS signal.'

'Unless the police have my phone.'

'I have it,' she said.

WYATT DRIFTED INTO SLEEP and when he woke she was there with the watchful eyes and sustaining silence of a parent at bedtime. Except she was no parent, he told himself. And he was no child.

'Sorry I drifted off. I guess the doctor's pumped me full of sedatives.'

'Lucky you,' she said, then was silent, as if taking refuge in some private reserve where she couldn't be reached.

She roused herself. 'I have to be getting back.'

'You weren't followed?'

'That is a very real risk, Wyatt, but I've been here for a few hours and no one has come knocking. I'm not sure what our status is, now Dad's dead. Greg Muecke was sniffing around—the cop who arrested him. But he's out of action for a while.'

Suddenly it occurred to Wyatt: 'What day is it?'

'Monday.'

'You had the funeral?'

'Saturday.'

He said urgently, 'I left a rented SUV in the street.'

'All taken care of. I drove it away in all the confusion and returned it, wiped clean.'

'My clothes...'

'Burnt.'

He flopped back. 'I'll need my phone.'

'I'll bring it next time.'

HE DIDN'T SEE HER for two days. Barely saw the doctor, but a woman he guessed was the man's wife brought him his meals and fussed a little and changed his dressing.

'Margot Perkovic,' she said, when he asked her name.

224

'The doctor's your husband?'

She smiled, neither confirming nor denying, which pretty much summed up the way people operated if they belonged to Sam Kramer's tribe.

She brought him a radio and an iPad, and he followed the news trails. The hunt for Tremayne was intense; he was wanted for three murders, now that Mark Impey's body had been found. He was believed to be sailing towards the Marshall Islands in Impey's boat, but had also been sighted in New Zealand, Port Lincoln and Singapore. The men killed in Mosman had served together in Afghanistan and were understood to have suffered some kind of PTSD breakdown.

Then Phoebe returned, and he heard about her mother and her brother.

'I'll be her carer for as long as it takes. I'll care for Josh, too, within limits. Silly prick.'

'Don't let him bring you all down.'

She flared up: 'It's family, okay?'

Wyatt sank back. Her hand snaked into his in apology, a cool presence. He said, 'I'm getting out in a day or two. I'll work out a way to get you your father's money.'

She said, 'That would be handy.'

She added, 'But keep enough for your trip.'

And she said: 'See you when you get back.'

37

NAVIGATING WITH THE AID of a laptop, Tremayne steered a course up the New South Wales and Queensland coasts, through the Whitsunday Islands and up into the Timor Sea. Snap squalls, wind bullets hurtling out to sea, fast tidal currents and numerous coral reefs, all tackled alone. He sailed nervily through two storms, masses of dark energy roiling towards him. He thought about seeking anchorage in the worst of it, but knew it was safer to stay at sea, exhausted as he was. In those early days he was tempted to sail at night to put himself far ahead of search parties, far ahead of his crimes. He couldn't do that while the coastal waters concealed coral formations.

Then he was through Torres Strait and heading west in the Arafura Sea. Up into the islands of Indonesia, into calmer, safer conditions. He saw an assortment of sea craft as he sailed along, from canoes to massive oil tankers—but no patrol boats. He had long-range fuel tanks and all the supplies he'd need for an extended voyage, which was just as well. By now an Interpol alert would have been flashed to all the island nations of the Pacific, South-East Asia and the Indian Ocean. Instead of putting into port he'd drop anchor in shallow waters, leave the navigation lights burning, and motor on again the next day.

THE PIRATES BOARDED the *Joi de Vivre* near the Horsburgh Lighthouse in the Strait of Malacca. He didn't know he was not alone until a hand smelling of raw fish clapped over his face in the dead of night and he reared up in his bed in the main cabin. Four men—Malay, Indonesian, Singaporean; he couldn't tell and it didn't matter. They carried long knives and said nothing.

They were fast: one man stayed with the tip of his blade pressed against Tremayne's stomach while the other three stripped the boat: laptop, phones, radios; fishing, GPS and navigation gear. They found the safe, forced him to open it. Took the thousand dollars he'd stored there. And his Ben Meyn passport.

They also took the rifle, stowing it in a sack along with everything else, but didn't pay any attention to the panel over the false drainage pipe, even though it was cracked from his tantrum.

Then they were gone, up onto the deck and slipping over the side. Hearing a snarling motor, he ran to the rail. A speedboat streaking away into the darkness. Not a thing he could do about it.

Badly rattled, he just wanted to get going. But there were hours yet until dawn. What did he have left to his name? The boat, at least; the dinghy in davits on the stern, emergency life rings, lifejackets, hull protectors. His fuel, food and water. His almost-million in cash and bonds. The pistol.

And his life. Tremayne was a man who rallied, and he tried to rally now.

But he was reluctant to continue sailing west and north-west. The waters here felt unfriendly to him now. He knew there'd been

Chinese investors who lost money in his schemes and as the hours passed, he imagined them putting the word out to their friends and family in all of the Chinese communities between Australia and Europe. A stupid notion, he knew that, but he couldn't shake it off. His sense of luck running out grew stronger.

At dawn, Tremayne turned around. He steered north-east into the South China Sea, then through the Sulu and Celebes seas and east into the Pacific.

SOME DISTANCE NORTH-WEST of Kiribati, nothing around, dead calm, the boat uttered a sharp, brain-scraping, almost human wail that tossed him off his feet. When it stopped, everything was shaking unnervingly. He looked back at his wake: he'd just sailed over a shipping container. He didn't know if he'd been holed. He did know that the blades on both propellers were fucked—either bent or sheared off.

He checked his nautical charts. Kiribati was close, but there'd be officials, tourists. East of his position was a chain of islands marked uninhabited. One, Pentecost Atoll, twelve square kilometres in size, boasted an airstrip built during the Second World War. Also two shallow lagoons, coconut palms and plentiful fish and birdlife. Drop anchor there, lick his wounds, think— maybe even find a way to mend the propellers.

Tremayne limped along for two days, seas a moderate swell, winds twenty knots, the *Joi de Vivre* setting up a mad shudder if he tried for speed until, in drenching rain late on a Friday in June, he sailed through a gap in a ring of coral and dropped anchor in a sheltered lagoon. He was 350 nautical miles north of the equator. Thin, bearded, all of the recent past scorched out of him. Looking, he thought, as he caught a glimpse of himself in a wheelhouse gauge, like a lightly salted corpse.

WHEN THE RAIN CLEARED, he was astonished to find he had company—a tattered yacht moored at the other end of the lagoon. A two-master named the *Santa Ana*. Torn rigging and a patched hull, showing the wear of sun, wind, rain, coral and either carelessness or bad luck. Maybe both.

Then movement. Two men emerged from below and climbed down into a dinghy roped to the stern. Young, nimble; both bearded, blond, grimy and shirtless. One carried a rifle. Tremayne hurried below, pocketed his pistol and returned to the wheelhouse. The men must have seen him, but they didn't come for him. They rowed out to the mid-point of the lagoon and, to his bewilderment, started firing the rifle calmly into the water.

SHAUN MAXSTEAD AND DUSTIN SNELL were shooting fish for dinner. You had to be selective because most of the seafood in this godforsaken place was poisonous. The newcomer had aroused their curiosity, but only in an academic way. They'd been given no assistance to get off the atoll by any of the other visitors in all the time they'd been stranded here. They didn't expect it this time around.

The first boat to call in had been a big catamaran owned by a holidaying Asia Bank executive. She spent a day photographing the red-footed boobies, the unbelievably stupid swarming birds that overran the atoll, then sailed on again. She'd had two sons and three crew members with her—hard, suspicious, competent types—so Maxstead and Snell didn't dare try anything. Then a geomorphologist from Perth dropped anchor outside the lagoon, sailing a huge yacht full of grad students studying coral features of the earth's surface. Too many to tackle, and they kept to themselves. The third boat to visit was a powerful cabin cruiser with US Pacific Remote Island Area marine biologists on board. Some of the crew members wore handguns. Maxstead and Snell were advised to sail on, they were polluting the lagoon.

'Yep, no problem,' said Maxstead. Paused. 'Can't lend us some fuel, by any chance? We can swap you some fresh fish.'

A curt shake of the head, and no curiosity. 'Against regulations.'

'Some tinned food? We're sick of fish and stuff.'

'Regulations. Hang tight, someone'll be along sooner or later.'

Maxstead almost came clean then: we're out of fuel, out of food, our pump's broken, our sails are ripped to shit, and we're scared this fucking endless rain is going to reveal where we buried the van Horens.

He didn't say it. But for a brief crazy moment he thought he had. He and Dusty didn't speak much anymore, just grunted and had pretty much the same impulses, so he was dying to have a proper conversation with someone sane. Thoughts, fears. Maybe even a few hopes, if he could think of any. The isolation, the sun and the rain, the blood on the deck of the *Santa Ana*—he thought it probable he was living a bad dream.

So here was another visiting boat, and what were the chances anything useful would come of it? A nice enough looking cabin cruiser, but something was wrong with it. A bit of noise and vibration as it came through the inlet. One guy on deck at the moment. For all Maxstead knew, ten guys below, armed to the teeth.

He stood, aimed the .22 down into the water, his slim, hard body accommodating the motions of the dinghy. Dusty, helping him spot, pointed suddenly. 'There.'

'Got it.'

A perfect shot. Dusty scooped out the dead fish. You had to be quick or the sharks swarmed.

Fish tonight. Fish every fucking night. And they were down to their last couple of cartridges. Otherwise it was seabird eggs or coconut. Maxstead dreamed of a Big Mac or a meat-lovers almost every day.

'He'll have food, fuel,' Dusty said, eyeing the cabin cruiser. Still only one head on board.

'Uh huh. But will he come to the party?'

MAXSTEAD AND SNELL HAD grown up in Cairns with the sea in their blood—but not, Snell liked to joke, with their blood in the sea. Their parents—both sets specialised in remote parenting—paid for them to have Little Tacker sailing lessons in an Optimist dinghy, graduating to larger craft over the years. As soon as Year 12 was over, they both got marina and fishing boat jobs, with some charter work thrown in. From there to crewing on Whitsunday Islands cruise yachts. Girls, horny middle-aged women with their heavy tipping, cocaine, resort bars. Then one boss went broke, and another boss got busted for running cocaine and ice, which he'd been doing with Maxstead and Snell's enthusiastic cooperation. They escaped charges but suspicion stuck to them and they hightailed it south to Sydney, where they begged for work at every marina they could find, finally hiring on at Rowntree Marine in Sans Souci.

Then one day Dirk and Missy van Horen sailed in, wanting repairs. Except they were going by the name Reschke at that point. Dirk was an out of shape fifty-five. Fat, soft, a heavy drinker with a long line in bullshit. The boys loathed him. So did Missy, who was about fifteen years younger than her husband, a well-stacked bottle blonde. She liked to do both boys at once; Dirk, it turned out, liked to watch.

The van Horens intended to sail around the world. They'd come from Tumby Bay in South Australia and got as far as Sans Souci before bad weather struck and they realised the *Santa Ana* wasn't as seaworthy as she needed to be, and could Mr Rowntree carry out the repairs?

Except that the van Horens were as cheap as old Rowntree,

who paid bugger-all wages. They cut corners on the repairs and cheaped out on the equipment—but did offer Maxstead and Snell lodging on the yacht, all meals, a bed for the night and a head job whenever they wanted, as a result of which fucking Rowntree started docking their pay.

Maxstead and Snell were on the verge of quitting when the cops started sniffing around, which also freaked out Dirk and Missy. The four of them sailed off into the sunset with the refit still half-done.

Dirk had been cagey enough at Rowntree's yard—which wouldn't have been anyone's first choice as a place to refit a yacht—and on the open seas was even cagier, avoiding other boats, avoiding harbours popular with yachting types. Sailed right by Port Vila, for example, even though they hadn't stocked enough food.

Missy, complaining out of earshot of her husband, told the boys: 'It's not actually legally our boat. Probably not ours.'

That's when they learned the van Horens' real names, and how come they were flying under the radar. We're with a wanted couple on a stolen boat, they told each other. You had to laugh.

And it was liberating in a way. They didn't have to take any of Dirk's shit, and meanwhile they were getting to see the world. They sailed deeper into the Pacific…and the tearing winds, rain squalls, high seas and poor workmanship mounted up.

A fortnight later they found themselves limping into a lagoon on Pentecost Atoll, the *Santa Ana* barely seaworthy and taking on water. Almost no fuel left; broken pump; torn rigging; a gash in the fibreglass hull; most of the decent food gone.

Days passed, and no one came, and Dirk started to talk to himself and paddle about the lagoon, slashing at sharks with a machete. When Missy begged him to radio for help, he smashed the radio and tossed all the phones into the lagoon. He stopped bathing and started to accuse the others of plotting against him; then one day he came at Snell with the machete in one hand and a bottle of brandy in the other.

Maxstead was pissed off about that: he'd been told all the booze was gone. He went below and fetched the .22 rifle and came back on deck to find Snell pinned against the main mast with Dirk swinging the machete at him. So Maxstead shot Dirk in the head. Then, unable to get Missy to stop screaming, he shot her as well.

Two less mouths to feed—not that anything else got solved.

FOR A COUPLE OF DAYS it was a kind of standoff between Tremayne and the young men, who he assumed were the only other inhabitants of the atoll. They would appear intermittently, paddling, disappearing into the stands of coconut palms. They seemed to clamber like monkeys, tanned, thin, half-naked, half-wild. They frightened him; his wariness was unremitting. And the atoll was no tropical paradise. The rain pelted down every day, and when it stopped the contrast, the sudden quiet, was terrifying. He was a knot of trepidation in a landscape of silence and resignation.

He had a pistol, though. Was there a way to replace his propellers with theirs? Then what—take them with him?

He had a pistol.

But there was only one of him and two of them. No way he could hold a gun on both of them twenty-four seven.

After lunch on the third day there was a gentle bump on the starboard side and they were there: on board. Hard, simian, teeth gleaming through their beards, the light of recklessness in their eyes. Tremayne was a crook, he knew that. He was dishonest. But his universe was orderly: he had a place in (or outside) the law. These kids were literally feral.

He stood back, fear jumping in him. 'What do you want?'

'What do we want?' one of them said. He was scrawny when you had a closer look, with the offended air of a beggar who'd expected you to drop five bucks, not five cents, in his greasy cap.

Tremayne tried for a smile. 'Let's start again. What can I do for you boys?'

'Got any food?'

Tremayne's mind hunted. Food? Stacks of food. Tins, packets, frozen. 'Sure.'

'We'll swap you,' the second boy said. He lifted a rotting cane basket—probably things rotted very quickly here—and said, 'Fresh fish.'

'Fish, excellent,' Tremayne said. He pictured a fried fillet, his teeth chomping on a .22 bullet. 'What would you like in return?'

'Fruit. Got any fruit?' the first boy said.

'And, like, steak,' said the second. 'Got any steak? Potatoes?'

'And beer. Beer would be good.'

Tremayne felt like a stern parent. 'Beer's probably not a good—'

'Party. We could have you over for a dinner party.'

'Yeah. We'll cook, you row on over this evening. We'll do fish in coconut milk, then tomorrow night you cook for us.'

Tremayne found himself saying, 'Okay.' It would give him time to think.

'Here. Put these in your freezer. We've got more.'

The basket of fish. 'Thank you.'

'Bring beer, mate. We're gasping.'

38

ACCORDING TO THE GPS tracking app on Wyatt's phone, Tremayne's boat had stopped at Pentecost Atoll, a speck in the Pacific Ocean north of the equator and south-west of Hawaii. That was a week ago. He could wait to see if it sailed on to some place easier to reach. Or he could act now.

Physically, he wasn't ready to act—his flesh was still healing, and to reach the atoll would mean hours in cramped seating. Mentally? That was another matter. Too much could go wrong if he waited. Tremayne sinks in a storm, runs into pirates, is arrested by local police. And I go mad with the waiting, he thought.

He checked the internet. The quickest route was via Honolulu, then island-hopping by boat or plane. But that would mean going through US customs and immigration scrutiny. He didn't want to try that on a fake ID.

And so he flew to Vanuatu first, then island-hopped using a series of progressively smaller and dodgier aircraft. He didn't set foot out of the airport at Port Vila. He'd been there years earlier, on the hunt, but was incurious about how the place might have changed since. And he'd sailed home on a yacht back then. He wouldn't be tracking Tremayne by yacht, though. Time, distance, his injury. Too much to go wrong.

After landing on Tarawa, in Kiribati, he spent half a day talking to charter pilots. Why the hell did he want to fly out to Pentecost Atoll?

'Nothing there but rain and sharks and fucking birds all over the airstrip,' one pilot told him.

'The strip's a mess anyway,' another said. 'Covered in cracks and uprooted coconut trees.'

But they were landing-strip pilots, airport pilots. They gave him the name of a man who flew seaplanes around the islands: tourists, anthropologists, environmentalists, a bit of import and export. 'Mick's rough as guts. But he does know what he's doing.'

WYATT FOUND MICK FLEMING in a bamboo and coconut-frond bar on the waterfront. A New Zealander, about sixty, wearing shorts and a T-shirt. A weathered face of lopsided charm and cheerful vigour. Wyatt looked more closely: a face of scars and pockmarks.

Fleming, noticing the scrutiny, grinned: 'Pretty, aren't I? Overshot a runway when I was a stupid kid.'

He toasted the memory with a beer glass held in a big blunt hand. A steady hand, steady eyes. Not drunk, or not yet; and maybe he wasn't a drinker.

'Pentecost Atoll,' Wyatt said.

Mick rubbed thumb and forefinger down his bony nose a few times as he gathered his thoughts. 'It's a fair old hike.'

Wyatt waited.

'Thousand bucks?'

'Okay.'

236

Mick laughed, shook his head. 'Should've asked for more, right?'

'It might be my last thousand.'

'In which case,' Mick said, 'you want to go to that shithole pretty badly.'

Wyatt smiled. Let it fade into his hard face, and Fleming seemed to see him clearly for the first time. He showed a moment of hesitation. 'Ask why you want to fly there? I could put you on to a fishing charter guy.'

Wyatt had known to expect the question. And that his answer would depend on who was asking: their level of curiosity or acceptance. How closely they skirted around the edges of the law and responsibility. Whether they were thieves themselves.

Mick Fleming seemed shrewd, curious and more or less honest. He might act where a straighter or more timid pilot would fear to tread, but he didn't strike Wyatt as a man who habitually broke the law.

He took out the Probity Commission ID. 'Time is the crucial factor. A man of interest to us dropped anchor there a week ago. I need to serve a warrant on him and seize certain documents.'

Mick gave him a brooding scrutiny. 'You know he's there for sure?'

'GPS tracker says so.'

That reassured Mick. 'No place to hide, huh? Is he dangerous?'

Three bodies in his wake? I'd say so, thought Wyatt. 'If there's any doubt, I'll call for reinforcements.'

Mick Fleming smiled into his beer. 'Out in the middle of the drink.' He looked at Wyatt again. 'It's just that I've got an old .303 rifle.'

'Good.'

'Huh,' said Mick, as if putting that one word together with the shut-down face he'd seen on Wyatt a minute earlier.

FLEMING AIR CONSISTED OF Mick and a ten-seater Otter. They took off the next morning in calm, cloudless conditions, with no separation between the sky and the ocean that Wyatt could see. It was just a hazy blue.

'It can be deceptive,' Fleming agreed. 'Even for an experienced pilot. Your mind tells you one thing, the instruments another.'

'So, always trust your instruments.'

Fleming grinned. '*Generally* trust your instruments.'

Wyatt dozed. He struggled to find a comfortable position. And Mick said, 'What kind of cop are you?'

'Not a cop in the usual sense.'

'You've been hurt.'

Wyatt nodded, offered nothing.

'Like I said, I've got a .303 you can borrow.'

He didn't say where he'd stowed it. 'I'll keep that in mind,' Wyatt said.

Time passed, and they seemed not to move through the sky, except that the combination of blue and green in the water below changed from hour to hour, and there were tankers and rocky outcrops fringed with coral where the water whitened.

Eventually Fleming said, 'Here we go,' and he was sideslipping in the air, bringing the Otter around and down, into a shallow landing approach. 'I clock two boats, mate,' he said.

Wyatt had seen them: one at either end of a lagoon. A yacht with a narrow hull and masts, and the squatter shape of Tremayne's *Alaska*.

'Which one are you interested in?'

'The cabin cruiser,' Wyatt said, 'not the yacht.'

'Think they're in it together?'

'Anything's possible,' Wyatt said, believing it just now.

'I can't put down in the lagoon.'

'Understood.'

238

'I'll get as close as I can. You can take the inflatable.'

That suited Wyatt. He didn't want a witness to whatever might happen next. And he didn't want Fleming to get hurt.

Then they were planing along the surface of the water, the nose dipped, and Fleming coasted towards the coral reef at the entrance to the lagoon. 'This is it for me.'

'Thanks.'

Fleming fished under his seat. 'Take the blunderbuss.'

A Lee-Enfield .303 with a bolt action and a ten-cartridge clip. Dating from one of the world wars, Wyatt thought, turning it over in his hands. Heavy, the stock chipped and worn, the barrel showing signs of rust.

'Works like a charm,' Fleming said, watching Wyatt. 'Looks like you know your way around a rifle.'

'Army,' Wyatt said. He removed, checked and replaced the clip.

They manoeuvred a little inflatable into the water and Wyatt paddled around the curve of the coral and through a gap into the more sheltered lagoon. The water was clear. Full of fish with clean sand below. He looked back: the Otter rose and fell gently in the open sea. Fleming stood on a float, watching. Waved lazily when he saw Wyatt turn.

Wyatt resumed paddling. He was in a cocoon of silence. Nothing moved except for the minute lapping of the water and the motions of his arms. No wind. The two boats were utterly still. But he sensed eyes on him. The birds for all he knew, in among the coconut palms. No human that he could see, anyway.

He drew closer to a dinghy roped to the stern of Tremayne's boat and tied up. Blood: on the seat of the dinghy and on the steps leading onto the deck. Slinging the rifle across his shoulders, he climbed aboard. More blood, a trail leading across the deck. Wyatt followed it to the wheelhouse, which looked like it had been stripped of equipment. The blood trail took him below decks then, and he found Tremayne on the floor of the main sitting area, his torso saturated in blood.

Wyatt stood and watched and listened for signs of life, signs that other people were on board. Hearing nothing, he crossed the carpet, knelt, and touched his fingertips to Tremayne's neck. A thready beat. The man was barely alive.

Then Tremayne moved, grinding the barrel tip of a small pistol under Wyatt's ribcage. Wyatt stiffened, but that was all Tremayne had to offer. His arm went slack, flopped, the pistol tumbling from his nerveless grasp. Wyatt snapped it up, slipped it into a pocket.

Meanwhile Tremayne was struggling to speak, his breathing shallow and panting, the rise and fall of his chest barely discernible. Wyatt leaned in to listen.

'I went...dinner...shot me.'

'Who did?'

'Kids...Got one of them in the chest...'

Wyatt went back on deck and stared across at the tattered yacht. A hint of movement, as if someone was watching from a porthole.

He went below. The storage bay had been tidied, the drainage pipes concealed again since the last time he'd been here. But the panel was cracked, leaving a gap at the top, so he levered it off with the barrel of the rifle. The broad-diameter pipe came away easily, a black nylon bag nestled inside it. He tumbled the contents onto the floor: large denomination euros, pounds sterling and US and Australian dollars; rings, necklaces, a Rolex; bearer bonds. He repacked it all, shouldered the bag and returned to the main deck. Tremayne not forgotten, simply irrelevant.

A throaty rattle out on the ocean. Mick Fleming had fired up the Otter.

Wyatt ran across to the rail to look. The seaplane turned lazily away from where it had been floating but made no attempt to take off. It paused, moved further away, paused again.

Then, through a gap in the rocks, sand and coconut palms, Wyatt saw why: Mick Fleming was playing catch-me-if-you-can with a man in a dinghy. The survivor from the yacht? As Wyatt watched, the rower paddled madly, stood brandishing a small rifle, sat and paddled again. Mick gave the Otter some revs, moved away again.

Wyatt climbed down into the inflatable and paddled hard, the motions pulling at his twin bullet wounds. He felt faint and nauseous. When he was back through the lagoon entry, heading for the Otter, he saw that the drama was on hold. The Otter rested some distance from the gunman, propeller spinning lazily, the gunman sat slumped, dinghy drifting in a weak current.

Wyatt paddled again, drawing nearer. Reaching hailing distance, he called, 'Throw the rifle away.'

A face racked with distress stared back at him. Young, no more than twenty-five, with a wispy beard, salt-encrusted hair and sunburn. He caught the flat, hard look of Wyatt and broke, slumping. He looked at his hands on the oars. 'It's empty anyway.'

'Are you alone?'

'Am now.'

They both bobbed in the water a while and the Otter burbled, watching. 'There's food on the other boat.'

'I know, that's all we wanted, something decent to eat.'

Time passed, and the kid said, 'Is he dead?'

'If not,' Wyatt said, 'he soon will be.'

'He's got a gun.'

'Not anymore,' Wyatt said, and he started paddling again. Like Tremayne, the kid was irrelevant.

Mick Fleming in his Otter watched Wyatt's advance across the stretch of sea. He did nothing: simply floated there, in the middle of nowhere, a continuing sign of life in the presence of death.

Nothing was said, the inflatable and the rifle were stowed, and they took off. They were halfway to Kiribati when Fleming said, 'He could have taken a shot.'

'Empty.'

Another long silence, Fleming showing a reserve that Wyatt could appreciate. Then: 'I'll get the coastguard onto it.'

'And tell them...'

'I was scoping places for, ah, future charter destinations. Put down there; saw that something was wrong.'

'Thank you.'

A long time later, Tarawa lay beneath them. Mick took the Otter around in a slow, shallow curving approach and touched down on the sea. Motored in, tied up. Shook Wyatt's hand and said, 'You were never here.'

Which was, and wasn't, the story of Wyatt's life.